The Banks Sisters 3

The Banks Sisters 3

Nikki Turner

www.urbanbooks.net

Urban Books, LLC
300 Farmingdale Road, NY-Route 109
Farmingdale, NY 11735

The Banks Sisters 3 Copyright © 2017 Nikki Turner

ISBN 13: 978-1-62286-633-5
ISBN 10: 1-62286-633-9

First Mass Market Printing February 2018
First Trade Paperback Printing February 2017
Printed in the United States of America

10 9 8 7 6 5 4 3 2 1

This is a work of fiction. Any references or similarities to actual events, real people, living or dead, or to real locales are intended to give the novel a sense of reality. Any similarity in other names, characters, places, and incidents is entirely coincidental.

Distributed by Kensington Publishing Corp.
Submit Orders to:
Customer Service
400 Hahn Road
Westminster, MD 21157-4627
Phone: 1-800-733-3000
Fax: 1-800-659-2436

Chapter 1

Everything Exotic

"It's the fuel strainer, and I'd bet my cash on that." Rydah, dressed in an oversized blue Dickies work jumper, threw five one hundred-dollar bills on the hood of the Mascrati with confidence. Her hair was done, somewhat, in two messy braids.

Jack, a newbie at Everything Exotic Repair, said, "You're wrong, sweet thing. I'm positive that it's the fuel pump. I know these cars like the back of my hand," he bragged. Jack was a self-proclaimed genius when it came to fixing cars, and he never wasted an opportunity to prove it.

"Just put your cash where your mouth is," Rydah said, calling Jack out on his cockiness. Laughter erupted throughout the shop, and the fellas gathered around.

Jack, pride and ego on the line, dug into the back pocket of his dungarees, fishing out his wallet.

Rydah quickly peeped that the wallet remained closed as tight as fish pussy. "Man, put up or shut up," she said, both chumping and finessing Jack all at the same time. "My money is already on the hood. Alone."

Jack pushed air into his chest. In true male chauvinist form, he said, "I ain't never let no broad talk me down off of nothing." He pried the closed wallet open, peeled out a handful of bills, and tossed it on the hood, matching Rydah's wager. "It's your loss. I was only trying to save you some money, sweet thing."

The other mechanics shook their heads. They had seen it far too many times.

Rydah released an audible chuckle of her own. "Next time, save your breath. You'll live longer." Rydah felt bad for Jack. He had no clue as to what he'd gotten himself into. "You got a lot to learn," she said, "about cars and women."

The line in the sand had been drawn and crossed. There was only one thing left to do—Rydah called for Mickey to settle the bet.

She cupped her hands around her mouth and yelled "Ayeeoo, Michelob!" calling her co-worker Mickey by his moniker.

Mickey was six foot three and thin as a whip, with big hands and feet. And as usual, one of those huge hands of his was strangling the neck of a brown Michelob bottle.

"You're not suppose to have that on the work floor," said Jack out of the side of his mouth.

"No shit!" Mickey gave Jack a quick once over. "You got a lot to learn," said Mickey.

"I keep trying to tell him that," Rydah added. "But he's one of them dudes that knows so much that he don't know shit. Dumb like that."

Jack paid Rydah the same attention that he would've paid to a stain in his drawers—none. After all, she was a woman playing shop in a man's place. What did she know? Instead, Jack stood there, gazing at the beer bottle in Mickey's hand, giving a look that said "unacceptable in the workplace."

Mickey felt the side-stare.

"It's a psychological thing," he said by way of explanation. "It's filled with water. The feel of the bottle manipulates my mind into thinking that I'm having a cold one. It's part of my AA recovery. I haven't had a real drink in more than ten years."

Jack nodded his head. "I didn't know AA allowed you to even be around that type of stuff."

Mickey informed Jack that it was his personal alcohol treatment program. "I invented for myself," he said.

"And it's one that you shouldn't bother to try to figure out," Rydah said, "Just let it go. It works for him, and been working for him for a decade now. And that's all that matters." This time it was Rydah who nodded, but at Jack. "Like I said, you've got a lot to learn around here."

Jack continued to ignore her. Rydah noticed the shade but didn't let it faze her. She knew that the best way to get a man's attention was through his wallet.

"Mickey, we need you to look at this car to settle this bet for us, fair and square."

Mickey caught a glimpse of the pile of cash on the hood of the Maserati. He took the Michelob water bottle to his mouth, took a sip, and shook his head. Then he smiled at Jack. "Man, you let her get you, huh?"

Jack poked his chest out farther than it already was. "She didn't get me. I know these cars like the back of my hand," he huffed.

"Well, your hand must be amputated, because your pockets are about to come up short . . . real short."

"The day a broad beats me at anything, let alone fixing a Maserati, I'll eat shit and die."

"That's a pretty funky way to go, but suit yourself," Mickey said. "If Rydah put her money down, trust me, there's no ifs, ands, or buts. Don't let the estrogen fool you; Rydah knows cars like a gynecologist knows pussy." To Rydah: "No offense intended."

"None taken," said Rydah, knowing that Mickey wasn't throwing shade.

Mickey continued, "If she says the car needs a blood transfusion, the only question you need to ask is where to hook up the damn I.V. Let's get this over with." Mickey scooped up the money, stuffing the bills into his shirt pocket, and motioned for Jack to pop the hood.

Rydah turned her cap to the back and began to remove the plastic wrapper from a cherry Blow Pop. "I'll hold the job of the banker."

Fifteen minutes later, Mickey came up from under the hood, examination complete. "Let me guess: Rydah said it was the fuel strainer and you said it was the fuel pump?"

"That's right." Jack put his hand out to collect.

"Not so quick." Mickey looked at Jack with a small touch of sympathy. "Did you say it was a fuel strainer?"

Jack, who still hadn't got the memo, blurted out, "Fuel pump! I said it was the fuel freaking pump."

"Then you won yourself a losing bet." Mickey gave Rydah her winnings.

Rydah took her money with a smile. "Well, Jack, special thanks to you. Drinks will be on you tonight."

Chapter 2

Ace of Spades

The heels of the nude red-bottom shoes were the first part of her body that he saw after the valet attendant opened the door of the Lamborghini Gallardo. By the time both 6-inch heels kissed the pavement, people were outright gawking. Pockets of bystanders, tourists, and would-be club-goers in line waiting to get into the club were trying to figure out which was more astonishing: the rebuilt custom yellow Lamborghini, or the lady who'd gotten out of it.

God damn she was bad!

She was tall, sophisticated, and overflowing with sex appeal. She carried a red and nude clutch bag under her arm that perfectly matched the form-fitting nude cat suit that clung to every curve of her body. Her gait was as fluid as a fashion model as she strutted past the club's bouncers and velvet ropes, straight to a VIP booth at the hottest party in Miami.

Another stunning woman, wearing a tur-
quoise sequinned dress, reached out and gently
grabbed the catsuit-clad woman's arm in a hasty
attempt to get her attention.

Rydah stopped to see what she wanted. The
girl wasn't a friend, but she'd seen her out often.
They had conversed on a few different occa-
sions. "Hey, Sky. What's up?" The music—a
Chris Brown song—was so loud that it was hard
to hear.

Sky looked Rydah over as if she were a delectable piece of meat, similar to the stares she'd gotten when she got out of her car and entered the
club. Sky admired her. "As always, you're looking like a million dollars, girl. Have you decided
to date women yet? Because when you do, I'm
available." She moistened her lips with the tip of
her tongue, which had been pierced with a flawless 1-carat diamond.

Rydah thanked Sky for the compliment.
"You're not looking too shabby yourself. I love
that dress. However, I'm still strictly dating
men right now. But if I ever decide to change
lanes, I'll keep you in mind." Rydah had never
been with a woman, but several of her friends
did. Some went both ways, not sure which team
they wanted to suit up for. While others, mostly
chicks that had been burned badly by a guy or

two, now only strictly dated girls. Either way, Rydah didn't judge.

Sky winked. "You do that. I promise you won't regret it. The grass is fo sho mo' green and mo' wet on the other side."

Flattered, Rydah was unsure how to respond. Sky was cute and all . . . but so was her Bengal cat. But she wasn't interested in dating either of them. Before departing she said, "Keep it sexy, Sky." The music engulfed her as she walked away.

Twenty minutes later, Rydah enjoyed the view and the sounds from one of the ten private VIP balconies which overlooked the main floor from 25 feet above the action. The owner of the club was a friend of a friend, and he comped Rydah the highly sought after spot whenever she wanted it. She was swaying her hips to a Future song when a text notification flashed on the screen of her iPhone 6Plus.

Buffy: Hey girl.

Buffy and Rydah were friends and had met each other about a year ago. The two met in Bal Harbour Mall—both were shopping and had so much in common. Immediately, the two ladies hit it off and had been thick as thieves since.

Rydah: Where R U?

Buffy: On the dance floor w/ a girlfriend f/ church

Is it cool for us to come up & kick it w/ U?

Rydah: Sure. Give the bouncer my name and take the stairs.

Rydah watched Buffy snake her way through the crowd. A gigantic bouncer wearing a tight black T-shirt blocked the door to the stairway. He had to be at least seven feet tall, with a tree trunk for a neck. It would have taken a very determined person—and an M104 Wolverine army tank—to move the bouncer off his square if he didn't want to be moved. Buffy quickly gave him Rydah's name as she was leaning on the rail, looking down. When the bouncer contorted his massive neck to look up in her direction, Rydah nodded her approval, then looked away to make another call.

Upstairs in the posh VIP section of the club, Buffy greeted Rydah with a smile and a hug. "You look great," she said. Rydah returned the compliment. Buffy, staring at Rydah's rear, said, "Girl, your ass looks too perfect to be real," smacking Rydah's backside.

Rydah wasn't wearing any panties, and the playful smack on the rump stung and made her butt jiggle like jelly. Rydah wondered how Buffy would like it if she returned the favor with an open-handed smack to one of her cheeks, and not on the ass. But the thought dissipated as quickly as the sting.

"I don't know how perfect it is," Rydah said modestly, "but it's definitely real." Nothing about Rydah was artificial, including her hair, nails, or demeanor. She had nothing against girls that rocked that way, but she chose not to. Rydah was more than satisfied with the gifts God had blessed her with. Why fuck with God's work?

"I know that's right," said Buffy, stroking her 27-inch copper weave.

Buffy had yet to introduce Rydah to her girlfriends, when some no-manners-having busta-ass dude decided to pour himself a drink from Rydah's freshly-opened bottle of champagne. The drink thief was with a male friend and two females, and the four of them were obviously with Buffy, but Rydah didn't want to assume.

She asked Buffy, who was cheesing ear-to-ear, "Do you know them?" pointing to the drink-stealing busta and his sidekick.

A day and a drink later, as far as Rydah was concerned, Buffy introduced her entourage. "Oh," she said, "that's Lisa from my church and my friend Charlotte who I think I told you about." Lisa and Charlotte were gawking at the lavish suite as if they'd never been off the block. "That's Charlotte's boyfriend, Ken. It's Ken's birthday." Ken was the drink thief. "And that,"

Buffy continued, "is Ken's boy Jake." Buffy ran it all down extra cavalier-like.

Before Rydah could voice her disapproval of Buffy's arrogance, Buffy tried to clean it up. "I know Wolfe always makes it his business that he hooks you up with this huge VIP suite, and it's always hardly anyone in here with you, so I thought it would be cool. . . ."

"Cool to do what?" Rydah asked, watching Buffy's friends snap selfies and pictures holding her bottles of Ace of Spades. "Take the liberty to invite folks into my space without asking me?"

"It wasn't even like that," said Buffy. When she saw the unyielding look on Rydah's face, she tried to laugh it off. "The more the merrier, right? Live a little. We need to get this party popping! It's not like you don't have enough room, or drink for that matter."

Is she serious? At the moment, Rydah wasn't feeling the excuse or the messenger.

One of Rydah's pet peeves were leeches, especially leeching-ass so-called grown-ass men. She was all for women's liberation and all, but she also felt that a man should be a man and hold his own weight. And the fact that Charlotte's boyfriend had helped himself to a bottle that had been, in fact, gifted to her, was a problem.

"What I got has nothing to do with them," Rydah said. She hated inconsiderate people. She'd seen alley dogs with more manners than Buffy's present company, who had yet to even say hi and were just about finishing the bottle off. She considered calling the bouncer, booting everyone out of her shit. However, she said to Buffy, "Let Ken know that I said happy birthday and all, but he needs to be a gentleman and order himself bottle, and at least offer us ladies some as well."

"Girl." Buffy sucked her teeth. "It's the man's birthday and you got two bottles over there. You very seldom even drink anything. Always having water in your glass, faking like you sipping on something."

"It's principle," she said. "Men need to be men. That's the problem with these new-wave-age dudes."

Ten minutes hadn't gone by and every drop of the champagne was gone. "Ayo, Buffy, can you get more of this where that shit came from?" Ken asked in earshot of Rydah.

Rydah was about to snap, but before she could, Ken's homeboy, Jake, spoke up and said, "Man, don't worry. It's your birthday. I got us! Allllllll of us," he said, putting emphasis on the entire group.

"Very gentlemanly of you." Rydah smiled at Jake.

The server crept into the area almost embarrassed, with two bottles of Absolut vodka, which were the cheapest bottles in the club.

Just then, the sparklers lit up a path heading straight to Rydah's VIP area, and the sexy bottle girls came in toting five more bottles of Aces of Spades. Jaffey, the owner, had comped Rydah since she was low.

Before she knew it, Jake was in the ear of her cocktail waitress, asking for a refund on the cheap bottles of Absolut vodka. Ivy, who was always Rydah's waitress and took great care of her when she came there, didn't want to make a big deal. Besides, Rydah, always tipped her extremely well. Ivy could see the disgust on Rydah's face, and she wanted to defuse the situation before Rydah had the bouncer toss them on their asses.

"Don't worry. I'm going to have Jaffey comp it for you."

"No, don't do such. Make them motherfuckers pay for it," Rydah said.

"It's okay," Ivy said. "I don't want a scene. It's no problem."

Though Rydah never took advantage, she really did have full access to anything she wanted in the club. And Jaffey never spared any expense when it came to showing her a nice time.

"It's the principle," Rydah said to Ivy, and Ivy just looked at her with a coy smile.

"It's nothing. Trust me," Ivy said. "In fact, that slime-ball Jaffey needs to eat something. In my opinion, you never spend enough when you come in here."

"A'ight." Rydah smiled. "Thank you so much. And have the big Wolverine tank bouncer move them motherfuckers outta of here. "

"Gladly!" Ivy smiled.

Her song came on. Rydah used it as a welcome distraction and tried to focus on the lyrics and beat of the tune. She was upset but determined not to let a handful of freeloaders ruin her night.

Rydah began dancing and sipping, intoxicated by the music. Dancing was her second love, after working on cars and bikes.

Ken got the message from down in General Admission. He and his boy ponied up to buy a bottle of Ciroc. They were hugged up with Charlotte and Lisa, acting like big shots.

Buffy, who was tipsy, posted an endless stream of selfies. When she wasn't posting pics, she was banging out texts and what she thought were clever captions for the photos.

Rydah loved to laugh and have fun. She was a closet party animal and free spirit who loved cars, music, and life. A couple of satisfied big spenders approached her about future car projects they wanted her to tackle for them. Others just wanted to show their respect, talk shop, or just flirt. She was a confident man's dream girl: independent, beautiful, and could build a car from the ground.

Buffy, checking for someone to leave with, asked for Rydah's opinion. "What you think about the guy over there?" She nodded. "The one with the big diamond earring and necklace, wearing the red hat."

Rydah looked in the direction where Buffy had nodded. "The Spanish dude?" she asked.

"I don't think he's Spanish," Buffy said. "I think he's light skin. You think I should talk to him?"

Rydah looked more closely. "He look like he's either Spanish or a hip white boy. But he's definitely not black."

"Well, should I go talk to him?"

"Not my style, to go approach. But if you think he's cute, go for it."

Buffy said that she definitely thought that he was cute.

"Then claim him before someone else does."

That's all Buffy needed for encouragement. That . . . and all the champagne she'd drink, courtesy of Rydah.

Rydah watched Buffy half stagger down the stairs through elbow-to-elbow clubbers on a packed dance floor, to the other side of the club to introduce herself. Damn, had Rydah known the girl was feeling the alcohol like that, she wouldn't have even let her go over there.

Meanwhile, Rydah kept sipping and turning up by herself. Before she knew it, Buffy was back, introducing her new friends.

"Rydah, this is Mike and his boy Tiger."

Tiger looked familiar to Rydah, but she couldn't put her finger on where she knew him. Tiger said, "Nice to meet you." And then she remembered. He was one of the dudes eyeing her out front when she arrived. And nothing had changed; he was still staring.

"Sorry. I can't stop admiring you. I saw you the second your feet hit the pavement. You look nice fo' sho. But I bet people tell you that all time, huh?"

"Compliments never get old," she said with a coy smile.

He offered to buy her a drink. "What you sipping on?"

"Water, now."

"In a champagne glass?" he asked as if he didn't believe her.

She seldom drank more than one glass of champagne, and when she did, two was her absolute limit. "I'm a grown woman," she said, "in case you can't tell by looking at me. And I have no reason or inclination to lie, especially to anyone other than the police or a judge, and when I have to, I will do it very carefully."

Tiger stammered. "I–I didn't mean to insinuate that you were lying."

"Yet you did, all the same," Rydah poked, not letting him off the hook.

Tiger recovered well. "Then allow me to make it up to you," he offered. "How about breakfast?"

Naturally, Rydah refused his invitation, but out of courtesy, she allowed the small talk to continue for a while longer. Tiger asked for her number. She gave him a Google number that she used on her business cards.

A drunk Buffy leaned in. "Sooooo fucking out of your reach. Just orbits out of your reach."

He had a stupid look on his face but smiled it off. "I always get whatever I want. Just that simple."

After a few more songs, Rydah danced into the wee hours of the morning and was ready to call it a night. The club was still going strong when she left. Outside, she approached one of the valet guys. "Can I have my keys, please?" She pointed to her car. Since the Lamborghini was parked in front of the club, the only thing the attendant had to do was retrieve her keys from the lock box.

The attendant nodded. "Of course."

Rydah waited, and then she noticed a really familiar face. "Jimbo!"

A five foot tall, flamboyant guy with more gold than Mr. T from the A-Team turned to check out Rydah. He hesitated at first, as if he didn't know who Rydah was, and then he got closer, straining his eyes to make her out, and then said, "Rydah?"

"Ummmm . . . yes?"

"Daaaamn, girl. I ain't even recognize you." He was shocked. "And I ain't even drinking tonight, on antibiotics and shit. And that shit don't even mix."

"How are you?" she asked. "Is everything okay?"

"Yessss, everything cool. Winter cold, and it has been so hot here this winter."

"I know that feeling," she said, towering over him.

"Girl, you look good. Damn good. Your work suit hide a lot," he said, checking her out. "Still loving my Shelby edition you did for me, but wanted to talk to you about making me a bullet-proof mobile."

"I can definitely do that, for sure," she said.

"Yeah, I heard you did something similar for them crazy-ass Haitian niggas. I'm like shiiiit . . . let me make sure I don't get caught slipping."

"I got you. Come by the shop tomorrow and let's talk."

"For sure. I'ma get me a suitcase of paper together and be by tomorrow. That's good," Jimbo said with a smile as he walked off.

After a couple minutes, the valet attendant handed Rydah the key to her car and a bottle of water with the club's logo. He shut the door for her once she was in.

Rydah peeled off, going south down Collins, across the Causeway to Biscayne Boulevard. She was about to make the left on Biscayne when the blue lights bounced from her dashboard and rearview mirror.

Whoop-whoop!

"Aw, shit," Rydah said aloud. *The motherfucking police. I wasn't even speeding.*

"License and registration." The officer had blue eyes and red hair.

Rydah had no idea why she'd been stopped. She wasn't speeding. She knew better than that, especially at this time of the morning, after she'd been sipping. "Officer, do you mind telling me why you stopped me?"

If the officer heard her, he showed no indication of it.

"License and registration."

Okay, Rydah thought, *one of those*. This wasn't her first time being pulled over by a racist or overzealous cop. Most police were cool, but certainly not all of them. Rydah put her left hand on the steering wheel, while slowly using her right hand to get her registration from the glove box. Next, she removed her license from her purse, giving both the license and the registration to the officer. She then placed her right hand back on the wheel, next to the left one.

The red-haired officer looked at her picture. "You don't look like your picture, Ms. Banks."

"I guess you could say that I clean up well, Officer. But you still haven't told me why I'm being pulled over, sir."

For the second time, the police officer ignored her right to be told why she was being pulled over. Instead, he zeroed in on the registration of the yellow Lamborghini Gallardo.

"And you are Rydah Banks, the owner of this car?"

The man had her license and registration in his hand, which plainly contained the answer to both his question. Not only did he have selective hearing, Rydah thought, but his eyes must not be all that sharp either. Deaf and blind. She knew she had to be extra careful, or this stop may not end well for her.

She politely said, "Yes, sir. That's correct."

"Are you carrying anything illegal inside the vehicle?"

"Excuse me, sir?"

Now the officer looked at Rydah as if she were the one who was deaf and dumb. "Are you carrying drugs or guns?" he asked.

Here we go, she thought as she blew a long breath of hot air. "No, sir."

When she put her hands in her lap, the officer whipped out his gun as if he'd been waiting for the opportunity to do so all night.

"I didn't say move your hands, did I? Put both hands back on the steering wheel! Now!" Rydah did what she was ordered to do, all while silently praying to God that this stop ended well.

"So," the officer asked, "this engine is rebuilt?"

"Yes, sir. I rebuilt it myself."

"You mean you paid for it?" He said it as if he'd caught her in her first lie. And where there was one lie, there were drugs and guns.

"No, sir. I said what I meant. I rebuilt this engine from start to finish with these two hands."

She nodded to her hands, mindful not to move them from the steering wheel until Officer Gung-ho said that it was okay.

"Really?" he said as if he still wasn't completely buying it. "I'd like to see that."

Two more cruisers rolled up on the scene, lights flashing.

Officer Gung-ho said, "Where's the stash box located?" He was cocky.

"There isn't one."

A lot of drug dealers used stash boxes—secret compartments built into the car, usually connected to the electrical system—to transport drugs, guns, and money. Sure, she knew how to do it and was the master at them, but what did that have to do with the cost of gas in Dubai? Absolutely nothing.

"If you're smart enough to rebuild this whole car from top to bottom, how come there's no stash box?"

That's when an officer from one of the other cruisers that had just arrived slammed his door and began walking up to Rydah's car.

The new officer said, "Ma'am, will you please step out of the car." It wasn't a request.

Finishing off the last swallow of water in the bottle, she unbuckled her seat belt and opened the door. Then she slowly stepped outside the car.

"I'm going to ask you to do a few things for me," the new officer said. "I want you to do exactly what I ask, okay?"

Rydah faced the traffic and, as the cars drove by, their headlights beamed into eyes, causing her pupils to retract. People slowed down and stared out their car windows as they passed by the scene, curious but mostly glad it wasn't them being scrutinized by the law.

"Sure." She just wanted to get this shit over in one piece.

"Good," said the officer, as if they were friends. "I want you to hold your arms out like this"—the officer put his arms out like an airplane—"then touch the tip of your nose with the pointer finger of each hand." He demonstrated what he'd just said, and then asked if she could do that.

Rydah quickly and easily completed the task, just as she did the next four tasks after that one.

For the sixth sobriety task, the officer asked her to recite her ABCs, backward. Rydah noticed that the officer didn't bother demonstrating this time. That's because it was called a "sucker's task." That wasn't the official name, but it was called that because the average sober person couldn't do it. An intoxicated person wouldn't stand a snowball's chance in hell. This was the task dirty police asked a person to complete when they wanted to set someone up. Good thing she wasn't drunk. At least she had that going for her.

Rydah began with, "Z . . ." She took a deep breath, thought for a second, then said, "YXW. . . ." She silently replayed the alphabet in her head and said, "VUT . . . S. . ."

Rydah was trying desperately to locate—in her head—the letter that came before *S* when, from a ways up the street, a gold 1978 Cadillac Brougham burled down Biscayne Avenue. The car was almost identical to the one Madea used to elude the police in Tyler Perry's *Madea Goes To Jail*.

Rydah found the letter she was looking for: "R . . ."

The roar of the engine growled louder as the antique car neared the scene where Rydah and the cops were standing.

"Q . . ."

Being that Rydah was facing the oncoming traffic, she could see the imminent collision before the moment of contact. The officer administering the rigged sobriety test to her wasn't as fortunate. The Brougham seemed unsteady, seemingly picking up speed as it got closer. Rydah desperately wanted to get farther off of the side of the road, but she was afraid that if she made any move other than what the officer told her to make, he might shoot.

Because of the light in her eyes, Rydah couldn't see the driver of the old Cadillac, but it was obvious that whoever it was, they were out of control and probably needed to be in her place taking the sobriety test. The car was traveling at 1.5 times the speed limit and swaying. Rydah had a choice: stand there and get hit by this monster on wheels, or move out of the way and maybe get shot. Her heart pounded so hard that if she didn't get hit or shot, she may have a heart attack.

At the last moment, Rydah attempted to jump out of the way to avoid the collision. Officer Gung-ho drew his weapon.

One of the backup officers yelled, "Watch out!" But the warning was too late. The gold hog, being driven by an 88-year-old lady with a bad case of indigestion, ran smack dead into the police cruiser. The impact caused the back end of the cruiser to swing around into the officer, knocking him forty feet into the air. After mowing the police officer down, it spun directly across the spot where Rydah had been standing.

"Oh, shit."

Thank God she wasn't like a deer in headlights. She would've been dead if she had waited one more second before jumping out of the way. Besides the side of her Lamborghini needing a fresh coat of paint, she was good.

The old lady driving the Cadillac was also okay. Not a hair out of place on the gray fox. She straightened up her bifocals, reached in the glove box, and fumbled for a bottle of Tums. She opened it, popped two of the chalky discs into her mouth, and chewed. After swallowing, she said, "That's the last time I'm eating pig's feet. They nearly killed me."

Chapter 3

The Perks

5:37 a.m.

Rydah barely beat the sun home, but not by much. As she stepped through the door of the condo, her phone rang.

"Hey, babe." It was Wolfe, checking to make sure she made it home safe. "How was your night?"

"Great." She didn't bother wasting his time with the stunt Buffy and her so-called friends had pulled. "As always, thanks for the setup."

"It was nothing." Jaffey, the owner of the club, owed him a boatload of money and an even bigger boatload of favors, so copping the VIP whenever he wanted didn't cost Wolfe a dime. But it wasn't like Wolfe was hurting for bread. If he had the inclination to, he had enough money to buy that club and several more of them.

Next month this time, Rydah and Wolfe would have been dating for a year. Once a week, without fail, Wolfe made it his business to take her out on a date. He did everything from a simple movie at his place to a private flight to Vegas for dinner and a show. Rydah wasn't sure how Wolfe stacked so much paper, and she never asked, but whatever he did, he was really good at it. She was sure that it was illegal.

If Rydah was to believe what the streets were whispering, Wolfe had a mean streak. For every dollar of financial stability he possessed, when provoked, he was equally as unstable as a batch of nitroglycerine. It was safer to cross Satan than it was to cross Wolfe. But Rydah had never seen that side of him

She reciprocated by asking how his night was.

"It was uneventful," he said. "So I guess you could say that it was a good night"

"No excitement at all?" she questioned with a raised eyebrow. "Sounds boring."

"Boring is sometimes good," said Wolfe, neglecting to mention using the barrel of his Desert Eagle to play patty cake with a man's tonsils for coming up short with his money. Dude had a temporary lapse of memory that Wolfe's .44 down his throat quickly got rid of.

Wolfe changed the subject, asking, "Do you need anything?"

"Yeah. Two quarts of paint for the Lamborghini."

"Huh?" Wolfe sounded confused. "I thought you were done working on that car."

"Long story," she said. "I'll fill you in over breakfast. I'm cooking. How long before you can get here?"

"I'm going to need a rain check on breakfast, babe. I've been in the same clothes for three days. I smell like a ripe chicken coop. But if you want, on your way to work, you can drop by and pick up this bread that I got for you."

Wolfe was always giving her things. She appreciated it, but she didn't want him to think she dated him for his money. She could take care of herself quite well. She told him, "I don't need any money."

"That's good to know. However, I didn't ask if you needed it. I want to give it to you," he said. "You're not going to deny me the privilege to do that, are you?" Wolfe made it sound as if she were doing him a favor by accepting his money.

"I hope you don't mind me dropping by in my work clothes."

***

One week later

After hours, Michelob allowed her to have free reign to use anything she needed at the shop. The paint got delivered this morning, a few days early, so she stayed to spray the Lamborghini.

Rydah stopped to admire her progress. She was almost done. Just a few more touches, and when it dried, the car would look as good as new.

She was cleaning the nozzle on the spray gun when her ringing phone broke the silence. She hated being interrupted when she was working. As she was about to pushing the IGNORE button on the screen, Rydah peeped the caller ID.

Damn. She'd been so focus on finishing up the car that she'd almost forgotten that it was Sunday morning.

"Hello, Mom."

"Praise the Lord, doll baby. This is the Lord's day, so let's be happy and rejoice in it."

Every Sunday morning Rydah had breakfast with her parents and faithfully attended her father's church. She said, "God is good."

"I'm making your favorite for breakfast, strawberry pancakes with that special whipped cream you like."

"Thanks, Mom. You're the best," Rydah said as she shut the hood on the car. It went down louder than she would have liked it to.

"Baby, are you still at that shop working on that car?"

"Busted. But I'm just about done with it now. I have a few more little things to do that will take no more than an hour."

"Well, baby, this is the Lord's day, and you need to be praising and thanking Him that it was only the car that was hit and not you. You know God is such a faithful God."

"I know, Mom." She respectfully changed the subject before the sermon began. "I'll be out the door in a second. I'm going to run home to take a shower and grab some clothes, and I'll be there by the time you finish making breakfast. I can do my hair, makeup, and get dressed for church over there."

"Sounds divine," her mother said. "I'll see you shortly then, sweetheart."

Rydah was the only God-begotten child of Evangelist Amanda and Pastor Maestro Banks, and they thanked the Lord every day for blessing them with her. Amanda and Maestro married 48 years ago. For nearly the first two decades, they had tried to give birth to a child, but it just wasn't to be. What a struggle it was for them, as people of such strong faith, to stand before the church and tell the people of God that they can have all the desires of their heart if they just ask

God. Well, God knows they had been asking, and yet they kept witnessing the gospel and standing steadfast of God's promises. Then, on their twentieth anniversary, God blessed them with Rydah. Maestro loved the testimony.

"God doesn't always give you what you want when you want it, but he's always on time," her father would say. He'd been preaching the gospel for years, talking to his congregation about trusting God and asking and seeking to receive the desires of the heart. All the while God had yet to bless him and Amanda with a child. Back then, his faith had been tested and was getting weary. But Maestro knew that he and his wife had to be steadfast in God's words and trust him.

Miraculously, on the morning of their 20th anniversary—which happened to be on Easter Sunday—the phone rang. Maestro's mother was on the other end. His mother, Gladys, explained that her sister's daughter Deidra was en route to the hospital to give birth to a bastard baby that she couldn't take care of. Gladys said that Deidra would allow them to have the baby for $10,000.

Maestro was skeptical. He was desperate to be a father, but he didn't want to do anything that would put his faith in question. He asked, "Will my name be on the birth certificate?"

Gladys said, "If you hurry."

Maestro drove his 1988 Bentley to the Miami International Airport, and three hours after the phone call, he and Amanda were on a flight from the Sunshine State to Richtown, VA. The entire time, Maestro, who was a man's man, secretly asked God for a boy, but as long as the child was healthy, he swore that he would be grateful. He got the latter, a healthy baby girl.

Deidra was not only an unfit mother, but she was also an opportunist. When she saw how well-to-do Maestro and Amanda seemed to be, she had a whole new set of demands: "I want twenty thousand for my baby. Twenty thousand. Not an iron dime less. And I get to name her," she said. "Or no deal."

It was two times the amount they had agreed upon. Maestro had no problem coming up with the extra cash, but he was set on giving the child a biblical name. "We've been thinking about the name Hannah," he said.

Amanda, soft-spoken with warm eyes, said, "It's from the Bible." In case Deidra didn't know.

Deidra nearly exploded. She yelled from the hospital bed, "Hell no! Fuck no! No goddamn Bible fucking names for my seed! I suppose you want to turn the child into a fucking nun, too."

Gladys, Maestro's mother, felt badly about the confusion Deidra was causing. As a compromise, she said, "What about Madison?" Madison was a nice wholesome name, and it wasn't from the Bible.

Deidra sucked her teeth. "'Manda, Maestro, and Madison. Oh, what a happy fucking family that will be." There was brief silence, and before anyone else could speak, Deidra said, "I think fuckinggggg not!"

Deidra's mother was also in the hospital. Me-Ma was a God-fearing woman herself and never really saw eye to eye with Deidra, but it was her only daughter. Deidra's behavior at the hospital embarrassed Me-Ma. She'd always tried to be understanding and loving of Deidra, but there was no way to understand Deidra's outlandish actions and inexcusable behavior. Deidra continued to show that the only thing the two had in common was their blood. And if Me-Ma hadn't pushed the heifer out herself, she would have questioned that. But for the sake of her sister Gladys and her nephew, Maestro, Me-Ma tried to intervene.

"Deidra, honey, it's bad enough that you are insisting that our own flesh and blood pay you for taking on a child that you spread your legs to have, but now don't want, but now—"

Deidra was like a child spawned from Satan himself. She cut her mother off with a harsh look before she could verbalize the rest of her thoughts. "You have nothing to do with this, Mother. None whatsoever! This is my business and my decision." To Maestro, Deidra said, "It's my way or no way and you can hit the highway."

Amanda and Maestro looked at each other. Maestro's eyes were saying *What should I do?* while Amanda's eyes conveyed the message, *You better not fuck this up. Do whatever she says. Let's just get our baby and get the fuck outta here.*

It took almost everything Maestro had in him to swallow his pride. He told Deidra, "Okay. We'll do this on your terms. What name did you have in mind?"

"That's what I fucking thought," Deidra stated arrogantly. She didn't have an ounce of humility in her selfish body. She didn't even know what the word meant. "Tell me, where did you guys come from?"

Maestro thought: *What does that have to do with anything?* But he answered, "Hollywood. Hollywood, Florida."

No one said anything for at least five minutes.

Then Deidra pierced the bubble. "Her name will be Rydah." No one had a clue as to how she came up with the name Rider, but no one dared question it. "Spell it: R-Y-D-A-H."

Maestro said nothing, though he thought it was a ridiculous name. He quietly prayed that God would let this blessing of their baby go through.

Amanda, not wanting to rock this crazy lady's boat anymore than it was already, said, "Oh my goodness. I love it."

Deidra took a sip of water, piercing her eyes at Amanda, knowing good and well that Amanda couldn't love it.

"What a beautiful Rydah she will be," Amanda said.

"Don't play mind games with me, you fucking homely church lady."

Had it been years ago, Amanda would've mopped the floor with Deidra, but God had her heart and conscience these days. "Honey, I love the name, and I know this little beautiful girl will be a trailblazer and such a blessing to us. We thank you and appreciate you," Amanda said, as nobly and humbly as she could.

"You're welcome," she said. "Now give me my motherfucking cash and take the little bitch with you before I change my mind."

"Oh, my!" Maestro's mother said.

Amanda shot her mother-in-law a look that said, *Please don't piss this girl off.* Nobody wanted a child more than Amanda.

When Maestro wrote the check, Amanda saw demons and dollar signs in Deidra's eyes, and he took full advantage. He signed the check and looked up. "Let us first pray, and then get this birth certificate signed."

Deidra started to spit some disrespectful venom out of her mouth, but she realized that the check wasn't yet in her hand. "Make this prayer bullshit quick," she said under her breath.

Maestro let God lead him in a long prayer.

Not a second after the Amen came, Deidra said, "Okay, enough of all this bullshit. Run me my motherfucking money, because all of this prayer and Saviour bullshit going to seriously make me change my motherfucking mind."

After Maestro and Amanda took the baby, the first second they were alone with their bundle of joy, they prayed the blood of Jesus over her. Regardless of how they'd gotten her, they both knew that Rydah belonged to them.

This morning, church was wonderful, and Rydah enjoyed spending this time with her parents. It was their family ritual; she'd always eat breakfast with them on Sunday morning, attend church, and then have an early dinner. And no matter how old she got—she was 28 now—her parents still felt blessed to have Rydah as their daughter.

Rydah felt the same way about them. Although they weren't her biological parents, she inherited parts of each of them. Rydah learned to appreciate nice things and everything about being a lady from Amanda. Amanda sometimes wished that Rydah was a little more conservative, but she loved the fact that her daughter was more edgy than she ever dared to be, with a twist of class and pizazz.

Growing up, her father took her everywhere with him. Fishing. Ball games. But she especially liked spending time in the garage with her dad, where he tinkered with his cars and built things. That's where she got her passion for rebuilding cars.

Her parents poured every ounce of love they had into her and, in her own way, she made them proud.

Amanda, in her late sixties now, had aged well. If she was the example, the saying was true: "Black don't crack." She was a silver fox.

The lecture that her mother was giving fell on deaf ears, but she pretended like she heard them, and she knew what she had to say to shut her mother up.

"Mommy, I know you disapprove of me going to the club and hanging out, but God protects me. He always has me in His keeping care. And though I wish it were, my work isn't in the church. It's in the streets, and it's in the trenches. I'm looking for the lost, the hurt, the confused, the broken-hearted. And some are, but most of the lost souls are not in the church already. The bewildered in the wilderness."

"Come on now, tell it, baby." Her father egged her on like the members of his congregation did to him. Though her way of doing God's work was unconventional, he was proud that she was there for the young people who didn't know their way to God to point them in the right the direction.

"Those are the ones who need me, and it's up to me to be in these streets and trenches to lead and bring them to church, and then it's up to you all in the church to welcome them with open arms and to save them." Then she looked up at her mother. "Mommy, sorry I'm just not the traditional preacher's kid, that I don't dress like them or pretend to be something I'm not, but one thing's for sure: This heart of mine is pure."

Rydah's speech made her father smile. "That's right, baby."

"God sees all and knows my heart."

Amanda heard her daughter and knew she was preaching the truth. "Well, I just want you to be careful, and Pastor, let's pray over our baby girl for protection and wisdom while she's out in the trenches doing God's work and to save his people."

After praying with her parents, it was time for her to head home to chill out, get some rest, and get ready for work in the morning. Her parents walked her outside to a beautiful purple custom El Camino. Of course, Rydah had done all the work herself.

"Baby girl, this right here is your God-given talent." Her father shook his head in admiration. "What year is it?" he asked, walking around the beautifully crated piece of machinery. "Lord, have mercy. Umph, umph, umph." Maestro and his daughter shared the same deep passion and love for cars.

Rydah, proud of her handiwork, said, "It's an eighty-eight."

Even if he tried, Maestro wouldn't have been able to keep the smile out of his eyes as he nodded his approval. "Is there a particular reason you chose an eighty-eight to restore?" he asked, already knowing the answer.

"Eighty-eight was the best year," Rydah said. Finding one had been a lot of work, almost as difficult as rebuilding it.

"You got that right," Maestro agreed.

"That's the year God delivered you to us," Amanda said, intervening into the subliminal car chat of the two people she loved most in the world. "A blessed year indeed." Amanda gave her only daughter a hug. Rydah squeezed her back.

Like she did every single Sunday, her mother gave her a reusable grocery bag filled with plastic containers—more food than Rydah could consume alone. Thank God she didn't have to. Wolfe always stopped by on Sundays for some of her mother's "gourmet leftovers," as Wolfe called them. Rydah was no stranger in the kitchen, but there was no way she could compete with her mom in that arena. She didn't even attempt to try.

"Amen to that." Rydah tossed the keys to the El Camino to her father to crank it. The engine roared to life. *Vrrrooommm!*

"Music to my ears," he said. "Where's the Lamborghini?"

"I'm not finished touching up the paint," she said. "Couldn't miss our Sunday ritual, so I will finish it up tomorrow after work."

Amanda rolled her eyes. She never cared for the expensive yellow sports car. She thought it was too flashy. Besides, the car had a bad omen about it, she thought. One week, the electrical systems went out on her for no apparent reason. The police stopped her for no reason. And then she was side-swiped by a runaway tank driven by a woman high off of pig's feet.

"I think you should get rid of that car," said Amanda. "It's just not good for you."

"I'm going to get out of here and get ready for work." Rydah knew exactly where this was going, and she wasn't going to in that direction with her mother.

Though Amanda believed in God, she still had always been superstitious about "signs," and Rydah had learned long ago not to argue with her when they disagreed with one of her omens, auspicious or otherwise.

"Get rid of that car, baby girl. I know you could get good money for it."

"Call you once I get home, Mommy! I love you, Daddy!"

Chapter 4

Wheels Up, Guns Down

Miami

Li'l Kim's epic "Not Tonight" blared from the newly installed 1,900 watt stereo that included two shallow 10-inch subwoofers and a complimentary compact class-D amp neatly installed in the bulkhead behind the seats. It was a tight fit, but Rydah fabricated the installation herself. She'd done a total modification of the stock factory system in.

Tell him I'll be back, go fuck with some other cats

Flirtin', gettin' numbers in the summer ho hop

Raw top in my man's drop . . .

Bass hit like a rhythmic explosion as Rydah, along with an army of bikers and hot rods, maneuvered through the holiday-weekend traffic. It was epic.

The Fox Channel 7 news helicopter hovered above the swarm of bikers, broadcasting live. They'd come from all over the country for this: Cali, Baltimore, Richmond, and D.C. were just the tip of the iceberg. The visual could have easily been mistaken for a scene from a summer box-office action movie. For some, the MLK ride was a beautiful sight to behold, while others thought the bikers were a menace to the public roads. Perspective was determined by position. But there was one thing that everyone agreed on: the scene was buck wild.

There was nothing that the police could do about it. The law was clear. Law enforcement weren't allowed to chase the riders through the streets of Miami, and the riders weren't inclined to stop and talk. They came to ride, and that's what they did.

Two of Rydah's cousins, Ronnie and Floyd, flew in from Baltimore to participate in the festivities. They paid a friend to drive their bikes down a day in advance on an enclosed trailer. They would've driven the trailer themselves, but Ronnie, the younger and the flashier of the two, was a self-proclaimed boss and, according to him, "bosses must floss."

The event was billed to promote non-violence and was cleverly coined "Wheels Up, Guns

Down." No one was sure exactly who came up with the slogan, but it stuck like cheese grits to a hot skillet.

This was Rydah's type of hype. Her toys were up to par and, if faced with a choice, Rydah preferred breathing the exhaust of a finely tuned engine than smoking a blunt. Any day. The decision wouldn't have been close. Having the opportunity to share the fun with her cousins, who she hadn't seen since they were kids, made it all the more fun. She was down like four flat tires.

Rydah popped the Lamborghini's clutch, dropped the leather gearshift into place, and mashed the gas pedal. Seamlessly, the transmission of the Italian-crafted machinery slipped into third gear, spinning the wheels and snapping her head back as it rocketed forward. She weaved in and out of the traffic like a seasoned pro as bikers among bikers were popping no-hand wheelies, spinning doughnuts, standing on the seats, and at least a dozen other dangerous stunts. She stopped the ongoing traffic so that the three hundred street motorbikes and four-wheelers could have the space to show off.

With the eye in the sky watching down on them, it was open season. Cousin Ronnie threw the front wheel of his Ducati in the air. One foot was on the seat, while the other was on the handlebars. He nailed the trick for two blocks before putting it down.

Damn. Rydah had no idea that her little cousin could ride so well. She was impressed with his skills.

Watching the bikers brazenly display their talents, risking life and limb, got Rydah's juices flowing. Her need for speed and love of motor vehicles ran deep, and the countless crazy colors and engine sizes of the bikes zipping around got her wet between the legs. Rydah was in her element. She was where she loved and wanted to be.

After a few minutes, it was time to move on, not just for the chopper in the sky but for the riders as well. Rydah drove alongside the bikes for a couple of miles, cruising. When she got the signal, she sped a few blocks past all of the illegal bike riders and stopped in the middle of the intersection. Then three more cars, a Mustang (Shelby edition) GTO, '68 Plymouth Roadrunner Hemi, and a 1970 Chevrolet Chevelle SS, followed suit, paralyzing the traffic of any pedestrians or vehicles trying to get by. The only thing the oncoming traffic could do was stop and either be amused or frustrated as the riders showcased more death-defying stunts and tricks.

Rydah's phone rang, but she was too con-sumed with watching out for the po-po and enjoying the show to answer.

More ringing.

It wouldn't stop.

Fuck!

The annoying phone wouldn't shut up.

Not wanting to take her eyes off the action for even a second, Rydah picked up the jack without giving the caller ID a glance.

She shouted into the phone, "What! This isn't a good time!" She could hardly hear herself speak over the cacophony of screaming engines. She was in ecstasy.

"I've been calling you all weekend, guurrrlll. I want to know when we doing dinner?"

Vrrrrrooooommmm . . . Vrrrrrooooommmmm.

"What you say?"

"Dinner!" Buffy was shouting as loud as she could. "When are we going?"

Rydah heard nothing Buffy said. Not a word.

"Let me call you later?"

Vrrrrrooooommmm . . . Vrrrrrooooommmmm.

"I'm with my li'l cousins on bike patrol."

Buffy ignored the noise, desperately trying to get an answer to her question. "You promised that we'd sit down and talk," she screamed, "so that I could explain. I even bought you an apology gift! I feel really bad about the other night, and I want to make it up to you! We need to talk! You been putting me off for a minute, and I feel bad and really need to talk to you."

Rydah had heard enough to get the gist of what Buffy was saying. "I know!" Rydah shouted back into the receiver as the bikers continued to do their thing. "I know!"

Vrrrrroooooommmm . . . Vrrrrrooooommmmm.

She had been blowing Buffy off ever since the situation they had at the club, but she had promised to meet with Buffy for dinner. She tried to stand firm on her word, even if she didn't feel like it.

Vrrrrroooooommmm . . . Vrrrrrooooommmmm.

Buffy wasn't trying to take no for an answer. "You already know you're going to be good and hungry after all that riding. I know you could use some girl time."

Vrrrrrooooommmm . . . Vrrrrrooooommmmm.

Buffy added, "All that damn testosterone. Come on now, time to transform."

Buffy had a point. Rydah had been working around the clock at the shop, and when she got off, she stayed at work, fixing her own car. This was the fist day the Lamborghini had been on the street since it was sideswiped.

"Are you still there?" Buffy asked after Rydah didn't respond.

Vrrrrrooooommm . . . Vrrrrrooooommmm.

"Yeah! I'm here!"

Vrrrrrooooommmm . . . Vrrrrrooooommmm.

"So where do you wanna go?" Buffy wasn't going to hang up until Rydah gave her an answer.

"I'm not sure," Rydah told her, "but we will figure it out."

"Okay. Then I'll call you back later?"

"Any time after nine. I'm going to have to go home and clean up."

"Cool! Talk to you later."

Rydah clicked off just in time to see two riders flip a four-wheeler, trying to ride it on its hind wheels. Amazingly, they weren't hurt.

As the day went on, Buffy didn't let an hour go past without calling to keep Rydah on task. Evening came fast. Hours of stunt riding, driving, and holding up traffic quickly turned into nightfall, and it was time for Rydah to say bye to her cousins and head home.

On the way, of course, Buffy called again.

Rydah quickly answered. If she didn't, Buffy would just call back until she did answer. "I'm on the way home," she said before Buffy could ask.

"Great. Did you figure out where you wanted to eat yet?"

All the phone calls were starting to blow her high. Rydah wanted to reschedule, but she knew she'd promised. "No. Not yet. I'll call you back once I get home." Rydah hung up.

Rydah's condo, overlooking the Biscayne Bay, was small but chic. Being home only reinforced the fact that she didn't want to go back out. It was after 10 p.m. and she was tired. Her next thought was to call Buffy and inform her that she'd do dinner with her another day, but she knew that Buffy would not only be disappointed, but she would also keep calling her until that day came. It was probably better to get it over with, Rydah thought. On that note, she married the idea that she was going to hear Buffy out.

Rydah was about to jump in the shower when her phone rang again. *This bitch can't be serious,* she thought. Rydah picked up.

"If you keep calling, I won't have time to get ready," she quickly said.

"What are you talking about, babe?"

"My bad." It was Wolfe. "I thought you were someone else."

"I get it." Wolfe's voice was always low and raspy. If you didn't pay attention, you would miss what he was saying. And he rarely got excited, even when he said he was excited. He was odd like that.

"Are you done riding with your peoples and 'em?"

"I just got in. I'm supposed to be having dinner with Buffy later. I'm trying to get ready now."

"Maybe I could come over and take a shower with you before I head up the road?" He was driving to Jacksonville take care of some business.

"Sounds good to me." Rydah was already hot; might as well put out the fire. "How far away are you?"

"Fifteen minutes."

"I'll make sure the water is hot."

"You do that."

Rydah smiled. She absolutely treasured times like these, when Wolfe dropped by spontaneously to spend real quality time. It was the small things that Rydah enjoyed the most about Wolfe. Based on Buffy's clock, Rydah knew that she didn't have much time, but she couldn't care less. This was about the fifth time today that she strongly felt like postponing the dinner with Buffy.

Rydah lit the fresh cotton–scented candles that she always had around the house and then went into the bathroom, where she ran water into her oversized Roman tub. After getting the temperature just right, she added bubbles, grabbed clean towels, and put them near the tub. As the bubbled water filled the Roman tub, Rydah used the time to run to the kitchen, to her fully stocked bar, and she grabbed a couple bottles of water, a can of Coke, and bottle of Hennessy Black. She put everything on the stand in the bathroom next to a silver ice bucket and two designer champagne flutes. After arranging the items the way she liked, she cut off the piping hot water.

The doorman rang her house phone. He asked if it was okay to let Wolfe up.

In a flash, Wolfe was at her door, carrying an MCM studded backpack on his left shoulder. The smile was the first thing she saw, though. It was a gesture few people got from Wolfe.

When she tried to embrace him with a hug, he quickly pulled away.

"I stink," he said. "I smell like the city. You know how I am about that type of shit. Let me clean up first."

Rydah assured him, "You know I don't care about any of that, baby." Rydah didn't care how Wolfe smelled, But she also understood how he felt. She hated being around people after working on cars all day. The only thing she wanted to ever do was hit the shower and get fresh, so she respected Wolfe for that.

He took his shoes off at the door and then peeled off his jeans and shirt and walked, naked, straight into the kitchen, where he dumped the contents of the backpack on the glass-top table. There were only three things in the bag: a pair of new Versace boxers folded up into a small square, an EBT card, and bundles of cash. The cash covered the table.

When Rydah walked into the kitchen behind him, Wolfe pointed to the food stamp card. "It's like three hundred ninety-four dollars on the card now. Get some groceries. Use it tomorrow for sure. Oh, and if you remember, get me some of that water I like to drink."

"Don't I always?"

"You do." There was that smile again. "And it's supposed to be a fresh four hundred fifty-seven on it on the sixth of each month. The access number on that shit is 2007."

"It'll definitely come in handy," Rydah said. She stole a kiss on his cheek. She didn't cook much, but she still liked to keep the things she liked in the fridge.

Rydah picked up the Versace boxers. "I'm going to put these in the drawer with other ones that I washed, okay?"

"Baby, you're too good to me," he called out.

"Nope. Just good enough," she said back. "The water is hot. Once you're done counting your bread, come on and get in the tub."

"Anything you say."

"Yeah, so you keep telling me," she countered back to him, knowing that that wasn't exactly 100 percent true. Wolfe let her do whatever she wanted to do, within reason, and have whatever she wanted to have, but Rydah had no illusions about who wore the pants in their relationship. That would be Wolfe. And she didn't mind it at all.

While she waited for Wolfe to give her a holler that he was ready, Rydah tried to figure out what she was going to put on for her dinner date with Buffy. While standing in the closet, she yelled back into the kitchen, "Maybe you should help me pick out something to wear."

"Maybe you should model for me? Or maybe you should blow off the dinner date and just lay up with me?"

"You staying in?" she asked with a raised eyebrow. That would've definitely been different, because Wolfe ripped and ran the streets on a consistent basis, chasing money.

"I hadn't planned to. But plans can change. No big deal. Money don't get old," he said, "but people do. If you want, I could stay for a while. Your decision."

It seemed like a good idea: spend the night laid up with her boo. She and Wolfe didn't live together, so sleeping in the same bed together was always a treat. Yet she didn't want to distract him from doing what he loved to do. She was conflicted. On the one hand, something inside of her was saying that it was a good idea. On the other hand, she didn't want to infringe on his plans. If the tables were turned, she wouldn't want him infringing on hers.

Wolfe walked into the bedroom holding a handful of money. "Buy yourself something nice," he said, tossing the stack of money onto the bed.

"I keep telling you that you don't have to keep giving me money. You know I'm an independent bitch, right?"

"That's why I fucks with you," said Wolfe. "But I also don't want you to want for anything. Can you juggle being an independent bitch while acepting an occasional bankroll from her dude? Besides, you do so much for me."

"I do what I do for you because I want to. However, I don't want you to ever think that I'm with you for your money or what you can buy me. It isn't like that," she said.

Wolfe laughed at the irony of her logic. "You make sure I'm good because you fucks with me, but I'm not supposed to do the same thing. Stop playing." Wolfe swatted her on the butt. "Fair exchange is no robbery. That's not just a street maxim. It holds true in relationships also."

Rydah knew there was no need to keep going back and forth with him, because at the end of the day, he was going to do exactly what he wanted to do. She threw her hands up in mock surrender.

"Okay," she said, "you win, Wolfe. Buy me whatever you like whenever you like."

Wolfe compromised. "We're both winners. Another reason why I'm with you."

"Thank you, baby." She smiled. "Give me two seconds to make sure everything's straight in the bathroom."

He walked behind her to the bathroom.

Rydah dimmed the lights and lit the rest of the candles.

Sitting on the top of the commode, Wolfe unstrapped his prosthetic leg and removed it.

Ten years ago, his leg had been removed. The amputation began just above the right knee. What would have been a disability for some people only made Wolfe stronger and so much more ruthless. Losing a leg didn't cause Wolfe to lose any confidence or cockiness. People that didn't know Wolfe before the amputation couldn't tell the leg was missing. He didn't walk with a limp. And for those who had known him over the years, he was so big and so treacherous that they simply forgot or didn't mention it.

Every time he took the prosthetic off, it reminded him of what had happened. As crazy as that night was, Wolfe was grateful it was only his leg. Shit, he'd trade a limb for his life any day.

Wolfe had been in Overtown to drop off some work—two keys of uncut cocaine—to a guy called Panama Jack. Way above the ubiquitous palm trees, the sun shone brightly on blighted stucco and brick houses. It had only been 30 minutes since the sun rose, but the temperature had already reached 82 degrees. This day was going to be a smoker, Wolfe thought. And he only wanted to have his workday over and be home before noon, before the sun was at its peak.

Wolfe preferred to make transactions with weight at this hour because the police were usually worn down from chasing the youngsters around all night. By this time, they just wanted to get off work and go home to their families in one piece.

Panama Jack stayed in a small bungalow-type house in the bad part of the city that, like most of the houses in this neighborhood, was in need of some major repairs. The steps squeaked from

Wolfe's weight as he made his way to the porch carrying an army-green knapsack on his right shoulder. No lights were on inside the house, which was odd. Wolfe tapped the door three times then stepped back and waited. The heft of the burner resting on his waist, a 12-shot .40-caliber, pulled at his jean shorts.

Several seconds later, a light flipped on inside the bungalow and the door swung open.

"Aye, boy. I've been waiting on you. How you be, friend?" He spoke English well, but it was laced with a heavy Panamanian accent.

Wolfe had been dealing with the dude for eight months. In that time, Panama Jack was always on time with his bread, and it was never short. Just the way Wolfe liked it.

"I be just great," Wolfe said.

Panama Jack stepped to the side, and Wolfe walked inside the bungalow. The moment the door closed behind him, his instinct told him shit was rotten, and his gut had never deceived him. Wolfe knew he'd been lined up to be robbed.

Wolfe heard a floorboard squeak in the hallway and pulled out his burner just in time to fire down on the two goons bending the corner.

Pop! Pop!

He hit one of them flush in the chest. The other fired back.

Boom!

Wolfe was sandwiched between the remaining goon in the hall and Panama Jack. The living room was tiny, with not much furniture to use for cover—an old sofa, a worn table, and a frayed chair. Wolfe dove behind the sofa and then swung the gun on Panama Jack, letting off two shots. Both shots hit home, slamming through Panama Jack's chest and jaw. He died instantly. Wolf wished the pussy motherfucker had suffered more.

One left.

It only took Wolfe four shots to do it, and he had eight more left in his gun. He slung two more shots down the hallway, just to let the goon know that shit was still hot, and if he wasn't careful, he could revisit his two partners in crime in hell.

Pop! Pop!

The third gunman got bold—or desperate—and advanced forward.

Boom! Boom! Boom!

Pop! Pop! Pop!

The old sofa caught two of the shots. Wolfe's leg caught the third one. It felt like someone had stuck a hot fireplace poker in his leg, but Wolfe ignored the pain for now. He had to get the fuck out of there. Only God knew what other perils were lurking.

Two of the last three slugs Wolfe squeezed off caught the goon in the chest. Wolfe put two more in his head, just on general principle, before leaving.

Back in the car, his leg was in excruciating pain, but he couldn't go to the hospital. Not if he wanted to stay out of prison, anyway. The hospital had to notify the police of all gunshot-wound victims, and the police would quickly connect Wolfe with the three dead bodies he'd left behind. So, he got drunk and dug the bullet out of his thigh on his own. Unfortunately, two weeks later, the leg got infected with gangrene. He got a friend to drive him to a hospital in Alabama, where the leg was amputated.

Three dead bodies on the head of an already convicted felon, even with a shitload of cash, meant he wouldn't be able to dodge that 5x5 prison cell, so considering he was able to buy the best prosthetic leg that money could buy, he considered himself blessed.

Chapter 5

The Big Bad Wolfe

Rydah attempted to help Wolfe slip into the tub.

"Please, don't do that," he said. "I'm not help-less." Wolfe hated being treated like he was helpless because he lost a stupid leg. He had his life,and that was more than he could say for the cats that took his leg. A life for a limb; he'd make that trade any day.

"Tell me something that I don't know, Wolfe." She helped him anyway

"I don't need to depend on nobody."

"Except for me," she said, holding his arm as he eased into the hot tub. Once his body was submerged, she gave him a deep kiss that got his dick hard.

That was the thing about Wolfe: he had a major complex about people helping him or seeing him as handicapped. He didn't expect or want folks to treat him any different because he had one leg, and he definitely didn't want to depend on anyone for anything.

His take on folks was: he knew that people came and went into his life, especially chicks, so he made it his business to never depend on anybody. He strived every day to do everything on his own. He put himself through a rigorous physical therapy workout every single day without fail.

There was something about Rydah that allowed him to feel comfortable accepting her help, showing his vulnerability, but he didn't want to slip and make it a habit.

Wolfe said, "You know I appreciate you, right?"

Rydah nodded. "Yeah. I do. But you don't have to keep telling me."

"Fair enough," he said. "But that's the reason why I do so much for you." Though he'd undressed thirty minutes ago, he never shed his confidence. It radiated like the morning sun, along with the 10 carats of flawless diamonds set in the necklace he wore.

Rydah watched as Wolfe adjusted himself in the tub to sit up comfortably. He had perfect posture.

"Make me a promise?" he said to Rydah

"What is it?"

"Promise me that you will never look at me like a crippled, trick-ass nigga who tries to buy affection. The minute I think that, I'm out."

"Wait a second!" Rydah said abruptly and then lowered her voice, letting her eyes meet Wolfe's. "I don't see you as no cripple anything." She was buck naked, standing next to the tub. "And you're far from being a trick-ass nigga, because for one, I don't trick, and I don't fuck with niggas. I date men—not niggas. I care about you because of who you are, not what you have or what you can do. My love for you is genuine. And if you don't get that," she said, turning the tables on him, "then you won't have to leave, because I'll be the one that's out."

Wolfe admired her spunk, her curves, and her confidence as he searched her eyes for deception, larceny, or bullshit. But all he saw in her eyes was love.

"I'll never doubt you again," he said.

She punched him. "You better not." Wolfe could be a bipolar, moody-ass motherfucker sometimes, but she loved him.

Wolfe reached out to her. "Com'ere, baby. When was the last time I told you how beautiful you were? I'm glad you mines." He pulled her closer, coercing her in the tub with him.

Once he had her in the tub, Wolfe leaned into her, licking and sucking on Rydah's perfectly round breasts. She stroked his already rock-hard manhood. Looking in his eyes, she sat down on his dick for a few minutes, gyrating. The tub was big enough to hold the both of them easily, with room to spare. After about and twenty strokes, Wolfe busted inside of her.

"Damn," he said bashfully, "the pussy is so good I'm firing off like Quick Draw McGraw."

"It was mind-blowing while it lasted," she said.

No matter how hard he tried, Wolfe couldn't control himself when he was inside of Rydah. "I'm going to get some of those pills," he said. "I hate getting mine before you get yours."

Rydah rolled her eyes. "Bump that Viagra shit." She had a girlfriend that told her about the effects. "I don't need nobody fucking me for hours on top of hours, stretching my shit all out of proportion. I don't need any highway miles on this." She laughed. "I love the intensity of the sex we have. It's everything."

They kissed.

"Play with my pussy."

He did.

Rydah closed her eyes, enjoying motion of his fingers inside of her. "Besides," she said, "I think I'm getting too old to be getting fucked for hours. It's perfect the way it is."

Wolfe knew that she was stroking his ego, but he smiled anyway. He planned to get the pills first thing in the morning. *I should've been copped them,* he thought.

After Wolfe's fingers accomplished what his dick hadn't, Rydah kissed him. *There's more than one way to skin a cat.* She kissed Wolfe, soaped up the wash cloth, and began washing his chest. She asked if he wanted anything to drink.

"I have water, wine, and cognac."

"Hennessy."

"Coming up." She reached over to the stand beside the tub and poured the drink, and a glass of wine for herself.

Rydah took her time washing him up, and Wolfe was enjoying every second of it. When she was done, she quickly bathed herself, hopped out of the tub, and grabbed two towels—one to dry off her body and the other for her hair. Then she reached for the other towels she'd laid across the chair for Wolfe.

When she tried to dry him off, he said, "I got it. I can do it myself."

"Really, Wolfe? Why do we have to keep going through this?"

"Old habits are hard to break. Work with me," he said.

"I will. Now let me dry your crazy ass off."

"I thought you had to get dressed for a dinner date with what's-her-name?"

"Buffy. Yeah, I do."

"You know you are amazing, don't you?"

"Yes. Among other things." She giggled.

"You got that right. Who other than me has a girl that rebuilt a car for them?"

They made their way to the bedroom, and as soon they were near the bed, Wolfe aggressively took control. He surely wasn't acting like a man with one leg.

Chapter 6

Pimp Or Die

Zzzzzzz . . . zzzzz . . .

Wolfe's phone vibrated.

"Duty calls."

Rydah removed herself from Wolfe's arms.

Wolfe reached for his phone and looked at the screen. "Damn. Forty-seven missed calls," he said.

"You're a busy guy." As soon as the words left her mouth—*riiinnggg*—it was her phone.

Wolfe said, "No more busy than you."

"It's nobody but Buffy."

BUFFY: What's yo status?

RYDAH: Another hour, just out tub.

BUFFY: Cool

Rydah asked Wolfe, "What do you think I should wear? Shorts, jeans, or a dress?"

Wolfe said, "Shorts. And those come-fuck-me boots I just got you."

"The Tom Ford thigh-high ones."

"Those ones."

Rydah pulled out the boots, a pair of cut-off Daisy Duke shorts, and a bedazzled baby T-shirt. "Thanks for the help, babe." She leaned in and kissed him. She got up got dressed and then did her makeup and hair.

Wolfe left the same time as she did, and they both headed out into the world to hold up their ends of the bargain: him business, and her social.

Rydah got in her car then realized that she wanted to change her purse. Instead of the crossbody bag that she first decided to wear, she ran back in to get her big Birkin bag. She changed everything out and headed back to the car. Then on the way downstairs in the parking deck, she brushed against some wet paint from the maintenance man who'd painted earlier.

"Shit." She shook her head. Changing clothes would make her run late, but she had to, or not go. She ran back upstairs and changed into some short jean shorts, a black top, and tall thigh-high Tom Ford lace-up-from-the-front-to-the-thigh 6-inch sandals.

Just then, Buffy called, "Girl, where are you?"

"On 95. Where are we meeting?"

"We will decide once we together. Come to The Burger Chef on Sixty-ninth. It's right off the highway."

"Sixty-ninth?"

"Yeah, like I'm right there now."

"Girl, not really feeling that area."

"It's on and off the highway, and I'm right here. Soon as you jump off, I'ma be right there."

Rydah was feeling a bit off beat, and something in her told her not to, but she went ahead and agreed. "A'ight, be there in less than five."

"I'ma be right here waiting."

"Cool." She disconnected the call, and all of a sudden an awful headache came on.

Rydah pulled into the parking lot, which was crowded with a lot of people hanging out. It was Negro Central. Hordes of people were hanging out or soliciting illegal merchandise in the parking lot.

Damnnnn! she thought. *It's a lot of motherfuckers out this bitch. And no fucking Buffy! She said she was here already. I need to get the fuck up out of here!*

Just then, the phone rang. It was Buffy. "Girl, where the hell are you?"

"Right here at the light."

"Girl, I'm leaving."

"Nooooo! Don't! I'm literally right here at the light. And I can't turn on red. Just get you a water or soda from the drive-thru, and as soon as you wheel out, I'm going to be there."

Rydah hesitated. She was thirsty and knew that she should just leave and go back home, but she agreed.

Not even a full 90 seconds had passed before a guy somersaulted into the passenger's seat of her car, Dukes of Hazzard style. All she heard was him hit the leather bucket passenger's seat.

Rydah looked over at the young black guy in her car with his hoodie on. Her first thought was that it was one of the Bike Life guys playing a trick on her. "Who the hell are you?"

Hooded Guy flashed a shiny silver handgun and uttered, "You know what's up. Drive, bitch." He cocked the gun.

Rydah knew by the look in his eye that he meant business. Caught off guard, she couldn't think on her feet. All she did was put the car in gear.

"Bitch, put the top up."

"I can't. It's T-tops," she lied.

"Bitch, stop lying. Don't fucking play with me."

Rydah's hands were tied. She slowly pulled out of the drive-thru. Things seemed to move in slow motion. For a few seconds, she couldn't think straight.

"Turn left and then right. Don't make any crazy moves. And don't try no stupid-ass shit, bitch."

She followed instructions, looked straight ahead, and then took a deep breath. Rydah remembered what the news said about being kidnapped, and those do's and don'ts kept running through her head.

If the kidnapper moves you from one location to another, the odds of you being killed increase.

Yeah, bitch." He smiled and nodded. "I'm going to get a lot of money from you, ho-ass bitch," he spit out with venom.

A lot of money? Hells naw. You's a mother-fucking lie, nicka! That was the initial thought that ran through her head. That's when the skid marks went off in her head. She knew she needed to get out of that situation, and quick.

"Turn right at that light, bitch," he demanded.

She looked over at him, and he spit, "Bitch, what the fuck you looking at?"

That was the last *bitch* she was going to be.

It's pimp or die! Kill or be killed! It's survival of the illest!

Indeed, she would make that right turn as instructed.

It was a delayed response, but all of a sudden, she had to take her life back or she was going to die trying. That's when she put the pedal to metal. The CEO of Lamborghini would have been proud how she handled the German engineering and 175 horsepower like a seasoned Lamborghini pro, pulling off a processioned right turn.

SKIRRRRRRRRD!

She slammed on the brakes, bringing the car to a sudden, complete stop. She hit the seat belt and the button that released the door and was making a mad dash like Jackie Joyner Kersey in her Tom Fords, getting down the street, screaming and literally running for her life.

Rydah had about a five-second head start before the kidnapper knew what had just happened and could regroup. He stood on his knees in the car and let off a couple of shots. Then he jumped out like Magic Mike in his Jordans and began to run after her, gunning and unloading the rest of his clip.

Pow! Pow! Pow! Pow!

Chapter 7

When God Got It

Rydah stumbled. She heard the tires on her Lambo speed off. She turned to look and saw her car swerve across the street. He had almost lost control but quickly managed to grab the wheel and took off down the street. The last thing she saw of him were the car's brake lights.

She started creaming at the top of her lungs. "Help! Help! Help!"

"What happened?" a concerned bystander asked.

"I was robbed and my car was stolen," she managed to get out in a panic. "Call 911."

Before she even finished her sentence, it was apparent that someone had called them already. She could hear sirens getting closer and closer, and in the blink of an eye, they were on the scene.

The corner was full of detectives, officers, and bystanders. In the midst of everything, a man brought her phone to her. It had been on her lap and fell out of the car when she jumped out. The screen was shattered, and it wouldn't power on.

Seconds later, Buffy showed up. She seemed distraught. "Oh my goodness. What happened, doll?" Buffy ran up to Rydah and hugged her, sidestepping an officer who tried to keep her away while he asked Rydah a million questions.

"Did you know the person who tried to abduct you? What was he wearing? How old was he? What was his nationality? Have you ever seen the perpetrator before tonight? Would you recognize him if you saw him in a lineup? Do you think that this person was after you, or your automobile? Where did you get an expensive car like that?"

The questions were endless, and the scene quickly turned into a circus.

Someone amongst the growing crowd screamed, "Are you okay, baby?" It was Amanda. Rydah's mother didn't play when it came to her baby. She couldn't give a damn what police had to say. She pushed her way through the thickly congregating group of people.

When she finally reached the front, a police officer stopped her. "I'm sorry, ma'am, but you can't come any closer."

"That's my daughter over there, Officer . . ." She read his tag. "Officer Piper. I have to make sure she's okay."

Officer Piper looked to Rydah for confirmation. Rydah ran over and gave her mother a hug.

"Are you hurt?"

"I'm fine, Mom. Just a little shook up. That's all."

Her father, Maestro, made his way through the crowd after parking the car. After seeing that she was alive, he looked up at the sky and screamed, "God is great! God is great!"

Maestro had the entire set of bystanders coming to Jesus. The makeshift crime scene turned into a praise party.

Amen!

And when it was all said and done, he cursed the person who did this to his daughter.

"May God have mercy on their soul . . . because a wrath is coming!"

Chapter 8

Meet the Parents

"Take me home."

The police were finally done questioning her. Halfway through, the so-called questions began to feel more like an interrogation, and Rydah felt more like a suspect than the victim of a crime.

"The only place you're going is to our house," said Amanda.

Rydah's father seconded his wife's motion.

"We need to spend the rest of the night praising God for sparing your life. It's the least that we can do for our Lord and Savior, Jesus Christ."

Rydah grew up in the church, but unlike her parents, she sometimes questioned *why* or *if* God did all the things people gave Him credit for. For instance, if it was truly God who saved her life, then who was it that tried to take her life away?

Rydah rode in the back seat of her father's Bentley, thinking about what had happened.

She reran every detail of the ordeal through head over and over. Maestro was behind the wheel, praying, while Amanda fidgeted with the small gold and diamond cross that she always wore around her neck. The dainty cross hung from a thin chain that she'd had since childhood.

Rydah believed it was her quick thinking and the carjacker's bad shooting that saved her life, but she knew better than to argue with her parents, especially about anything they deemed religious. Instead, she sat in the back seat of the car and thanked God for her life. It must have been her good karma coming back.

Maestro's Bentley pulled into her parents' driveway, and the second they were through the front door, Amanda's phone rang.

"Blessed be the Lord. This is the Banks residence, where we serve an awesome God. Sister Banks speaking."

Rydah smiled. Her mother had always taken great pride in her phone etiquette and salutations.

Rydah watched as her mother carried on a conversation that was obviously about her. "Why, yes, she's alive! A little shook up, but she's so resilient. By the grace of God, my baby had God's favor and was in His keeping care . . . so yes, I'm blessed."

Rydah rolled her eyes.

"Why, yes, he's right here. I'll let you men handle that part. Here, honey." Amanda passed her cell phone to Maestro. "Someone wants to speak to you." Maestro raised an eyebrow. His wife said, "It's William. Rydah's friend."

Maestro put Wolfe on speakerphone and cordially asked, "What can I do for you, Brother William?"

Rydah held her breath as she listened to her father on the phone with her man.

"I know we've never met, Mr. Banks, but I'm a good friend of your daughter's."

"So I hear," said Maestro."

"And I've been looking forward to meeting you."

"Likewise."

"But for now," said Wolfe, "I would like to know if anything was taken from Rydah besides her car." Wolfe had heard about the carjacking from the streets. He tried calling Rydah, but her cell phone kept going to voice mail. He knew she was supposed to be meeting Buffy for dinner, so he retrieved her number from a guy he knew that fucked with her off and on, then gave Buffy a call. A shaky-sounding Buffy was the one who told him that Rydah was okay and had left the scene with her parents.

"Not much," Maestro said to Wolfe,. "I think she said she left her pocketbook behind when she jumped out, with her iPad, camera, wallet, gun, and all the other contents." Maestro looked back at his daughter. "Isn't that right, honey?"

Rydah said, "Yes, sir."

The handbag alone was worth ten stacks.

Wolfe said, "If the cat who stole her car has her keys, though security in that building is tight, she still need her locks changed immediately. I can head over and take care of that now."

"That's very nice of you, young man. I'll tell you what—I'll meet you there and give you a hand. I'll also have Rydah alert her security to the situation."

Maestro was a lot like Wolfe in that way. Looking at them, people wouldn't think so, because they seemed so opposite on the surface, but Maestro and Wolfe shared many of the same qualities. For starters, both men were strong, powerful leaders. Maestro led from the pulpit, while Wolfe led from the streets. Each was well respected by his peers, although for Maestro, that respect was manifested by love, whereas Wolfe's was manifested by fear. But respect was respect, and the way it was obtained didn't change the fact that it existed. And both men would do anything for the women in their life. Also, Maestro was much more street savvy than people gave him credit for.

Wolfe insisted he could handle the lock change alone. "No need to bother you with it."

"It's no bother at all," Maestro insisted. "She will need a few items of clothing anyway. Under the circumstances, I think she should stay with us for a couple of days. I'll pick up the clothes."

Rydah felt funny listening to them speak about her as if she weren't there, but she knew that they were only trying to do what they thought was best, so she let it go.

Wolfe agreed. "Not a bad idea. I'll see ya when you get there. Tell Rydah to please give me a call."

"As soon as I get settled in," Rydah said loud enough to be heard over the speaker phone

Wolfe rang the bell.

Since her parents weren't letting her out of their sight, even though Rydah didn't want to, she invited Wolfe over to their house—provided he and her father were still on speaking terms after they met up for the first time at her house.

Amanda answered the door, wearing an apron. "Hello. You must be William?"

Wolfe wore a pair of jeans and a T-shirt with white Gucci sneakers and a matching cap with a blazer. "And you must be Rydah's sister," he said.

What woman didn't like to be complimented? And Amanda was no exception. She ate it up.

"Flattery will get you far in this world. Come in. I'll get my daughter. I hope you're hungry."

Wolfe took off his hat. "Actually, I haven't eaten all day. I'm hungry as a wolf," he said, pun intended.

The foyer led down a hall that opened to a large, beautifully furnished family room. Wolfe said, "You have a very nice home.

"Thank you." Amanda asked Wolfe to take a seat while she went to get Rydah and check on dinner.

Rydah walked into the room, barefoot. Wolfe almost didn't hear her approach. Almost. But slipping wasn't something that he could afford to do. Slipping is kin to sleeping, and everyone knows that sleep is the cousin of death. Wolfe wanted no parts of that family tree.

Rydah had on a pair of jeans and a tank top that her father had picked up from her house. They hugged; a long hug. She didn't want to let him go. Wolfe's body felt both hard and warm in her arms. He asked if she was okay.

"I'm fine."

"Dinner's ready." Amanda asked everyone to come to the dining room. She'd made enough food to feed a troop of Boy Scouts, and everything looked delicious. There was grilled salmon, baked chicken, potatoes, seasoned broccoli, shrimp, rice, and some other things that Wolfe didn't recognize right off top, but he was willing and ready to sample everything.

Once they were seated, Maestro said grace.

"Thank you, Father, for providing this food for us to nourish our bodies. Father in Heaven, may you bless those who are about to partake in this meal. Father in Heaven, may you bless the person who prepared the wonderful meal. Father in Heaven, we thank you for sparing my daughter's life as you see fit. In Jesus' name we pray, and let us all say Amen!"

Amen!

The food tasted even better than it looked sitting on the table. And as promised, Wolfe tried it all, including dessert—a flaky-crust apple cobbler that was still warm from the oven.

"Ms. Banks . . ." Wolfe wiped his mouth with a linen napkin. "I can't remember when I've had a better meal."

Maestro wiped his mouth with a linen napkin. "I see the man has good taste. Can't take that from him."

Amanda said, "Thank you. I learned to cook from my mother."

"Well, she taught you well." After a couple of minutes of small talk while their food digested, Wolfe and Rydah excused themselves from the table.

"If anyone wants me," Rydah said to her parents, "I'll be in the den." She then led Wolfe downstairs.

The moment they were alone, Wolfe asked, "Give me some good pictures of that bitch Buffy and that ho's address."

"What for?" Rydah asked.

"Because the bitch set you up, and I don't intend to let it slide, by no stretch of the imagination."

Rydah thought about what Wolfe had just said. She'd thought about the possibility of Buffy being responsible also, but in the end, she had dismissed it.

She said to Wolfe, "I don't think she's smart enough or crafty enough to orchestrate something like that. And it doesn't make sense. Why would she do something like that?"

"Never underestimate what anyone will do at any given time." Wolfe put his hand on Rydah's leg. "And it doesn't matter why," he said. "It only matters that she going to pay for her sins."

"No, Wolfe." She thought about his reputation and some of the things she'd heard about him, and she didn't want that karma to come back on her. "Vengeance isn't mine."

"You right, it isn't yours. . . . It's mine."

Chapter 9

A Vessel of Blessings

Richmond, VA

"Great morning, sunshine."

Gladys Banks was dressed in a long black pleated skirt and flat-heeled leather ankle boots. The fur at the top of the boots complemented the mink mid-length swing jacket. Despite having been on this earth for nearly a century, Gladys was still young at heart and bubbling with energy. Though many of her childhood friends had gone on to see their maker, she remained upbeat and positive about life. A beautiful fall Tuesday morning was as good a reason as any for Gladys to be dressed in her Sunday's best when she strolled into the United Negro Bank of Virginia.

She figured, why deprive the world of getting the very best version of herself, each and every day, regardless of her age or circumstances? She may not be able to always control what happened around her, but there was one thing that she could control. Nobody knew when his or her time on Earth would come to an end, and if that day came sooner rather than later, Gladys wanted to be remembered at her very best. Especially on the first of the month, when it seemed like everybody and their grandmother's mother was at the bank, cashing their social security check.

"Good morning, Ms. Banks." Kim was the head teller at the bank. "I love those boots you're wearing." Kim had been employed at the bank for two decades. She tried to make it her business to get to know all of her customers, and Gladys and her husband, Malcolm, were no exception. In fact, Kim practically knew Gladys's entire family. She considered Gladys—who was quick-witted and still drove a brand-new Cadillac—to be one of the last of the old-school black Southern belles.

The compliment from Kim brightened Gladys's eyes even more than they already were. She said, "Thank you, darling." Her voice was angelic. "You're always so sweet and considerate. I tell my granddaughter all the time that the prettiest girls are the nicest girls."

Kimberly displayed two rows of even, white teeth before Gladys went on about her health and overall wellness.

"I'm doing splendid for an old lady," Gladys told her. "I've had better days and I've had worse days, but as long as I keep on seeing 'em—good or bad—I can't complain." She added, "Never seen complaining help no one get through tough times, no how." Enough about herself, Gladys took a seat at Kimberly's desk and asked, "How was your vacation?"

"The vacation was wonderful. We went down to our rental house in Hilton Head for a few days."

"Well, I'm sure that it was very lovely. Did your children join you all?"

All of Kim's children were grown. "My oldest boy, Shawn, brought his new wife, and Christina and her husband gave us the news that they are expecting."

"Congratulations!" Gladys's face illuminated with adoration. "I'm so happy for you. It seems like it was not too long ago that you were pregnant with Christina. Now she's giving you your first grandbaby."

Kim agreed. "It seems like yesterday."

"Time flies, sweetie." Gladys locked eyes with Kimberly and spoke from the heart. "So always be good to people and, most importantly, be good to yourself. You make sure you enjoy every precious second God gives you, because there isn't a day that's ever promised to any of us. God can take us home at any given time."

"I'll be sure to remember that," said Kimberly. She loved when Ms. Gladys came in. She was a ray of sunshine. But Kimberly also liked the fact that Ms. Gladys didn't accept any wooden nickels. She was the spunkiest, sassiest, sweetest eighty-nine-year-old she'd ever met. Kimberly prayed that her skin looked like Ms. Gladys's when she got to that age. The maxim "black don't crack" was alive and well.

"How's your son?"

"He's wonderful," she said with even more animation in her voice. She dug into her leather pocketbook and searched for her phone. "He's still in Florida, preaching the gospel and saving souls. Here are some pictures of him." Ms. Gladys retrieved the album folder she wanted and then passed the phone to Kimberly. The album contained fifty-six photos: pictures of her son's church; Maestro on the pulpit; Maestro with his wife, Amanda; the two of them with their daughter, Rydah.

Kimberly had a confession. "I watch your son all the time on television. Every time I watch him it seems as if he's talking directly to me."

"He inherited that from his daddy. Maestro is the spitting image of Malcolm." Malcolm had died in a car crash thirty years ago. Gladys never remarried. "I wish Malcolm could've been around to see the man that his son has become."

"I'm sure Malcolm is looking down on him from heaven, Ms. Gladys."

Gladys looked up at the ceiling and then changed the subject. "I spoke with my son yesterday. He insisted that I spend next winter with him down there in Florida."

"That would be wonderful," Kimberly said. "You get to stay in that beautiful house of his and escape the cold. Sounds like a great time."

"He didn't have to do a whole lot of convincing, I'll tell you that. I love spending time with him and his family, especially my granddaughter."

Kimberly watched Gladys's eyes light up when she mentioned Rydah. "That's one beautiful girl," Kimberly said. "How has she been doing since the carjacking incident?"

Ms. Gladys looked surprised that Kimberly knew about that. She was curious. "How did you hear about that?" The story didn't make national news, thank God.

"Your son talked about it during one of his sermons," she said. "So sad. I also saw some stuff on saw Facebook."

"Facebook? Why would something like that be on the Internet?"

"People were asking her if she was okay, so she addressed it to stop all the rumors, I guess. She said that she gives all praises to God."

Ms. Gladys made the sign of the cross over her heart. "If something would have happened to that gal, I don't even want to think what it would've done to our family. But she's okay now. Rydah is amazing. She's so brave and resilient."

"A lot braver than me," Kimberly said. "I don't know what I would have done in that same situation. But I probably wouldn't have had that kind of quick thinking." And on that note, Kimberly changed the subject. "So . . . how's your sister Mildred? I haven't seen her in quite some time."

Mildred Banks—AKA Me-Ma—was Gladys's younger sister, and the two were tight as a fat baby in a leotard. They shared everything, but Mildred drew an angry line in the sand when it came to her daughter, Deidra, and her grand-kids. Me-Ma loved those girls to death, and in her eyes they could do no wrong. In that sense, Me-Ma was a lot more gullible than Gladys was.

Like Gladys, Mildred was very religious. The only differences were that Mildred was com-pletely indoctrinated by the church and believed nothing was right if it wasn't in the Bible or quoted by her pastor. Gladys, on the other hand, loved the Lord as much as anyone, but she strongly believed that church was just a building where people came to rejoice in the Lord, and the people inside the building were sinners. She knew there were a handful of saints, but for the most part, people had plenty of shit with them. Being a first lady for over twenty-five years, married to a good man of God, Gladys had witnessed it all: saints, sinners, whores, liars, cheaters, thieves, murderers, gossipers, and plain-old miserable people.

Although Mildred was both a wonderful and great woman, her blind faith in people made her gullible. Mildred only looked for the best in people, even if that person was evil to the core.

Gladys dropped her head and took a deep breath. "God called my sister home about three months ago. She dropped dead while doing what she loved best, praising the Lord. However," Gladys added, "I think it was that goddamn daughter of hers that sent her to yonder. Excuse my language, but that damn niece of mines makes me want to do more than cuss."

Kimberly had her own thoughts about Mildred's daughter, Deidra, and none of them were good. But she kept them to herself.

"Deidra ain't never been worth more than two pennies, but Mildred didn't want to see it. And I believe in every fiber of my body that Deidra and all of her bullshit is what killed Mildred."

Kimberly didn't know what to say.

"I'm so sorry about your sister," she said. "I didn't know." In an attempt to comfort Gladys, Kimberly rubbed Gladys's arm.

Gladys thanked her. "Since Mildred passed away, everything has gone sort of haywire. Some would say it's gone to hell. The pastor at the Baptist church that she was attending convinced Mildred to sign some papers over to him. For the life of me, I don't know why she would think that was a good idea. It goes without saying that the pastor was as crooked as that road in San Francisco." Gladys was referring to Lombard Street, which is notoriously known for its hairpin-winding curves. "Then my nephew, Ginger, you know that was my favorite, outsmarted the preacher at his own game. Did I tell you that the preacher was gay?"

"No, you didn't." Kimberly was thoroughly intrigued with the story, and the bank wasn't too busy this morning, so she listened intently.

"Well, I'm not one to gossip, but you need to take a look at that porn Web site you young kids look at." Gladys leaned in and whispered,

"That pastor on there doing all kinds of nasty stuff to both men and women. Almost gave me a heart attack when I seen it. I'll tell you that."

Kimberly whispered, "I think I heard something about Ginger and a preacher." It was impossible to miss. Everyone in the city was talking about the preacher having sex with a known tranny. "But I haven't seen the Web site," she lied.

Ginger was one of Deidra's four kids that were left with Mildred to raise. "Well, it got them their house back. If that child hadn't blackballed that preacher, they would be homeless."

Deidra had four kids—three girls and a boy that wanted to be a girl—whom she abandoned and left Mildred to raise.

Kimberly corrected, "I think you mean blackmailed."

"Whatever. I know he had a set of black balls all up in places where they had no business being. I'll tell you that."

"Well, how are the rest of the girls doing?" Kimberly had attended high school with two of the Banks sisters, Bunny and Tallhya.

"Well, Tallhya went a little crazy for a while, but she's feeling better now, thank God. And poor Simone got breast cancer."

"I'm sorry to hear about their hardships. It sounds like they're really going through tough times."

"God works in mysterious ways. And when it rains, it sometimes come a-pouring. But God don't give us no more than He knows we can handle. Sometimes things have to fall just about to the gates of Hell, and as long as you stand on God's word, He will bring you right on back out that fire."

Kimberly let Ms. Gladys's words marinate as she thought about a few of the things that were going on in her family. "Amen to that," she said. Kimberly punched some keys on her computer. "Hmm. . . ." Something wasn't right.

Seeing the puzzled look on Kimberly's face, Gladys asked, "Is there a problem?"

"Well, there hasn't been any activity on Ms. Mildred's accounts here. No one closed them or anything, and usually—"

Ms. Gladys cut in. "Because that slimy, fake prophet didn't know about that account. That's why. Forgive me for my language, but every time I think about either of them, that no-good pastor or Mildred's trifling daughter, my pressure goes through the roof."

Mildred had opened an account that no one knew about: neither her family, nor her pastor.

"I can imagine. Just take a deep breath and calm down, though. We don't want anything to happen to you."

Gladys followed Kimberly's advice. After taking a breath, she asked, "Who was the beneficiary of this secret account?"

"Well, let me see." Kimberly's eyes bounced from one screen to the other. "There are five beneficiaries. Let me see. . . . Okay, here we go." Kimberly read from the screen. "Simone Banks, Boniqua Bunny Banks, Natallhya Banks, Gene Banks, and Rydah Banks. They will all have to sign, and the money will be divided up and disbursed in equal parts."

Next, Gladys asked the million-dollar question. "Well, how much money is it?"

"Oh." Kimberly said, "I'm not supposed to say."

"Who's going to know? I won't tell. And Mildred is dead, so she certainly can't rat you out." Gladys raised an eyebrow as if to say, *So what's the hold up?*

Kimberly glanced around to see if any of her coworkers were paying attention. After seeing that they were all dealing with customers or minding their own business, Kimberly said, "I can't give you the exact number, but it's north of one hundred thousand."

Gladys wasn't surprised that her sister had so much money squirreled away in a secret account. She confided in Kimberly that, "Mildred was always good with money. She lived like a miser. Me," she said, "I couldn't do it. I'm going to save what I can, but I like to see my money on my fingers, ears, in my house, and in my driveway."

Kimberly said, "You're not too bad at squirreling away money yourself."

"Yeah, but Mildred would rather live like a peasant so that damn grown-ass daughter of hers can live like a queen."

Kimberly said, "Do you mind if I ask you a question, Ms. Gladys?"

Mildred said, "Sure. You're like family. You can ask me anything."

"Why are you smiling? All of a sudden you started smiling when I told you how much money it was."

"I'm just thinking about my sister," she said. "Our momma used to tell us to never let your right hand know what your left hand is doing. I guess Mildred was listening. Everybody thought that she did all of her banking over at Consolidated Trust and the Credit Union, and all the time she was hiding a fortune right under everybody's noses." *Mildred was smarter than we gave her credit for,* she thought. "That ol' false prophet done spent every dollar that was in the Consolidated Trust account."

"Well, thank God he didn't know about this account. Maybe it can help the girls get back on their feet."

"For sure." Gladys was pleased. "At least something is the way Mildred would have wanted it to be." She was delighted to discover that Pastor Street wouldn't be buying more G-strings and dildos on her sister's dime, but she also had her own business to take care of.

Kimberly handled all of Gladys's regular monthly transactions: she deposited her social security check and her late husband's pension, then wired funds to pay each of her bills. Gladys was never late with paying a bill. It was something she took pride in.

When it was all done, Gladys shook Kimberly's hand and said, "I'll see you next month." Then she adjusted her mink hat, cocking it to the perfect angle.

Before she left the bank, Kimberly asked Gladys to do her one favor.

"Sure," Gladys said. "What is it?"

"I want you to quietly find a way to let the girls know about. . ." Kimberly looked around to make sure no one was listening before continuing. "The new developments."

"Don't worry. I surely will. I will get in touch with them and ask them to call you directly."

"And I can take it from there," Kimberly assured her then turned to go help another customer, her heels click-clacking against the hardwood floor as she strutted away.

Gladys wasn't barely past the door of the house before she called her son down in Florida to let him know what was going on.

Chapter 10

Not A Good Idea

Weston

Rydah loved her parents more than anything in the world, but living under their roof for the past three weeks had been tougher than a microwaved two-dollar steak. She wasn't sure how much more of it she should or could take.

For starters, Rydah was expected to follow the same house rules she had to abide by when she was growing up. According to the church's schedule, dinner was served at 8 p.m. sharp, every single night, unless there was a conflict in her father's calendar. Everyone sat at the table at the same time and held hands as Daddy said the grace. This was non-negotiable. They ate and discussed current affairs and how everybody's day was. There were no phones allowed at the table or television going in the background, only quality time with the family.

Wolfe wasn't even allowed inside of her bedroom. Her parents seemed oblivious to the fact
that she was a 28-year-old grown woman with a
place of her own. Under their roof, she'd follow
their rules and knew better than to even try to
request any amendments to their rules.

Rydah felt like she'd forfeited her independ-
ence and her privacy at the front door, along
with her sex life. When Wolfe ate dinner with
them, Rydah could tell that he was tight and
uncomfortable, but he'd rolled with the punches.
One night after they'd eaten, she told Wolfe that
she was horny.

Wolfe replied, "I may be a sinner to the core,
but ain't no way I'm fit to get caught with my
pants down in Bishop Banks' house."

On top of it all, Rydah was still mildly trauma-
tized. Since the carjacking, she'd yet to drive, and
she met with a therapist twice a week. Amanda
and Wolfe took turns driving her to the sessions.
On Wolfe's days, afterward he would take her
out for lunch, sometimes a movie or shopping,
just anything he could do to try to make her feel
better.

In the evenings, he would come by around 7
p.m. and usually stayed until 11 or 12, chilling
with her in the family room, playing backgam-
mon or chess. Tonight they were watching
Family Feud when the phone rang.

"Hello."

"O-M-G! You finally answered." The high-pitched voice on the other end of the phone belonged to Buffy. "I've been so worried about you," she said, trying her hardest to sound sympathetic. The only thing that transmitted through the phone line was disingenuousness.

"Is that right?"

Nosy-ass Buffy inquired about her whereabouts. "Are you at your parents' house?"

Why the fuck this bitch wants to know where I am? Rydah was about to tell a lie, but didn't. "Yep!"

"Can I come over?"

For a second, Rydah regretted admitting that she was at her parents' house, because she didn't want her bringing any B.S. over there. Then she thought again. She could send the dudes if she wanted to. However, Maestro, a gun collector, had an arsenal of assault rifles and though a churchman, he believed in "Stand Your Ground." Not to mention Wolfe, who'd been itching to murder the culprits. However, she knew that wasn't going down. Buffy had to know better.

Rydah cut her wandering thoughts and came back to the phone call at hand.

"Rydah, you there? I'm going to go ahead and head over that way."

Again, Rydah was honest.

"That probably wouldn't be a good idea," she said.

Buffy asked, "Why not? I want to come and check on my girl."

This bitch can't take a hint.

Rydah looked out the corner of her eye to see if Wolfe was paying her any mind. He was still watching Steve Harvey. "Honestly?" she said. "I just don't think that that would be a really good idea."

"Of course it's a good idea. I wanna come see you. We can have some girl talk. Maybe even drag you out to go to the club tonight."

Like, what the fuck?

"In case you didn't get the memo, Buffy, I just got carjacked three weeks ago. You and me going to a club together is a super long shot."

Turning away from the TV, Wolfe gave Rydah a *who the fuck is that?* look. She acted like she didn't see him.

"Well," Buffy said, "I don't wanna sound insensitive, but do you think you could get me on the guest list?"

Rydah chuckled a little longer than she meant to, because she was honestly at a loss for words.

Buffy was relentless. "No need for you to let your VIP connect fade away," she said, laughing.

Rydah looked at the phone as if it were a serpent, ready to strike. She was speechless, just holding the phone in disbelief.

"So unless you have a damn good reason," Buffy said, "no matter what you say, I'm coming over."

There was a list of things that Rydah wanted to say to Buffy, starting with, *Bitch, you must got bull nuts hanging between your legs.* And *you need to stay as far away from me as you can before Wolfe plants you in someone's flower garden.*

But instead, she said as easily and kindly as she could, "Because my mother thinks you set me up. So it goes without saying that you're not welcome at her house right now."

Buffy was momentarily as quiet as a cat burglar. Finally, she said, "Yeah! You right. Your mother gets real gangsta when it comes to her baby girl. Mad protective." Then Buffy asked the million-dollar question: "So do you think I had something to do with it?"

"I don't want to," Rydah said honestly.

Wolfe attempted to wrestle the phone away from her, but Rydah stood up, moving out of his grasp. They playfully struggled for it again. She mouthed the word *Stop.*

Wolfe was about to put her on his shoulders when the house phone rang. The call was from Virginia.

Rydah said to Buffy, "Hey, girl, I just got a call from my grandma in Virginia. I'll hit you back later." It was a perfect excuse to get off the phone.

Buffy got the last word in. "You know that I would never do anything to hurt you, right?"

Rydah acted as if she didn't hear her.

Click!

Then she answered the house phone, and the call from her Grandma Gladys would change her life forever.

Chapter 11

Out of the Cuckoo's Nest

Chesterfield, VA
AKA: Arrest-erfield, VA

Shit! What the fuck am I really doing? Tallhya asked herself. *I know this shit ain't right, but what else am I supposed to do?* She pulled up beside the bank in a car she'd stolen from the valet at a Jehovah's Witness convention. *Bitch, you ain't got shit . . . therefore, you ain't got shit to lose.*

The Last Union Federal Bank. . . .

Tallhya looked at the time of the dashboard clock: 1:38 p.m. This time five days ago, she was in the nut house being fed anxiety pills, tranquilizers, and green Jell-O. When she found out that the hospital couldn't hold her against her will, she checked herself out immediately. Next, she called her sister Simone to get her share of the bank robbery money, only to find out that her cut was severely diminished.

Simone, who had been recently diagnosed with breast cancer, needed money desperately for the doctor and treatments. Simone hated stealing from her sister—especially after using the Baker Act to have her committed into the Westbrook Mental Hospital—but she had no choice. It was literally a life or death decision. She chose to live. Simone used the remainder of the money to do renovations on her late grandmother's house, which Simone and her cop husband were now living in. She would have to make amends with Tallhya later.

Tallhya didn't mind Simone using the money to get treatments and doing the necessary repairs on her childhood home, but she was pissed that Simone hadn't used any common sense and put away any of the hard-earned, ill-gotten money for her. Did Simone think she was never going to get out? However, she tried not to flip out too much, because after all, her sister was doing chemo and fighting for her life. At the end of the day, it was only money, she reasoned. It comes and goes. Simone would be her sister forever.

Besides, Tallhya blamed herself for allowing her sorry-ass, cheating, soon-to-be-ex-husband, Walter, to drive her crazy enough to have to be put in the nut house in the first place. If she hadn't flown over the cuckoo nest, she could've held on to her own cash. *Lesson well fucking learned.*

In the meantime, she had nothing, and in two days, she wouldn't even have anywhere to live. Going back to the house she grew up in to live with Simone and her new husband, Chase, wasn't an option she wanted to entertain. There were too many memories in that old house. Me-Ma was dead. Ginger was dead. Bunny was dead. She would go crazy for real, talking to the ghosts of all of her family members.

Tallhya had met a nice lady who was volunteering at the hospital. Her name was Dorsee Jackson. Tallhya and Dorsee hit it off immediately. She was the one that told Tallhya that the hospital couldn't keep her if she didn't want to be there. Dorsee also told her that, in her opinion, she didn't need all those drugs that they were feeding her. Tallhya stopped taking the pills and a week later checked out. Dorsee offered to give her a place to stay until she could get on her feet. She just failed to mention that room and board would cost $100 a week. Although it was not a lot of money, when there was no money, something as small as $100 seemed to be big. Tallhya had not one iron dime. Besides rent, she needed a phone, transportation, and new clothes. She'd lost a cool twenty pounds in the hospital—the one good thing she got out of being there—and could no longer fit any of her old things.

Tallhya wanted to kick herself for letting Walter swindle her out of her lottery winnings. The moment the money was gone, so was he, and that was the moment she went crazy. It was too much to handle at the time; seeing her husband hugged up with some bitch—a skinny bitch, at that, after he told her that he liked his women with some meat on them. *Just another one of his countless lies,* Tallhya mused. Life sucked, and she had no one to turn to, except doing what she knew how to do.

She pulled the ski mask down over a blond wig and then blew into the plastic gloves she'd swiped from the hospital before snapping one onto each shaky hand. As ready as she would ever be, Tallhya pulled the stolen Toyota in front of the small branch of the Last Union Federal Savings Bank, blocking the doorway. She sucked in on deep breath and hopped out the car.

As soon as she stepped her feet through the double doors of the Last Union Federal Bank, it was on and popping. Feeling invincible, she waltzed into the bank with a BB gun that looked real enough to get the job done—or get her killed. In her fragile and desperate state of mind, Tallhya was cool with either outcome. If she were dead, she would no longer have to worry about money. Heaven didn't charge for things like rent and wings, she hoped.

Inside the bank, there were only three customers. Two of them patiently waited in line while the only teller helped a lady in front. There was another bank employee, dressed in a neat little business suit, sitting in a glass cubicle. Tallhya surmised that she was the bank manager.

"Okay, bitches, get on the fucking floor!" Tallhya waved the BB gun around. "Don't make me say that shit again!" she shouted. "Next time I'm going to pop somebody in the ass to show you that this ain't no fucking joke." Her adrenaline pumped blood through her body like crazy. But no one thought that she was joking. Her eyes, big and wild, weren't the eyes of a person trying to get a laugh. They were the eyes of a person that had nothing to lose.

Once the customers, the teller, and the manager were on the floor, Tallhya leaned over the counter and grabbed a handful of cash out the first drawer. But that wasn't enough. "Get up!" she said to the customer that the teller had been waiting on when she walked in. Tallhya gave her a bag. "Empty both drawers and put the money in here. And don't get stupid over someone else's money. You understand?"

The customer shook her head. She was in the bank simply trying to cash a check; she didn't want to die for anybody's money. Not even her own. "I'll do whatever you say. Just please, please don't hurt me."

"Bitch," she said to the teller, "step away from the damn counter. You ain't setting off no silent alarm today." She saw the teller out of the side of her eye with a stupid look on her face, like she had been busted. That didn't stop Tallhya. She was on a roll.

"You?" She motioned to the lady that had been sitting in the glass cubicle. "Go to the vault and fill this bag up." The bank manager caught the bag that Tallhya had tossed to her. Tallhya walked with her to the vault to keep her honest. Petrified, the bank manager did exactly what Tallhya instructed her to do.

Once both bags were filled, Tallhya took the money and headed for the exit.

Everything went over smoothly. In less than four minutes, she was back in the car. Tallhya tossed the bags on the floor and peeled off.

"Thank You, God!" She didn't find it odd at all to be thanking God for a successful bank robbery.

Driving, trying not to get noticed, she turned up the spiritual music and began to sing a Kirk Franklin song. Until that moment, she hadn't even known that she knew the words, but she sang it like her life depended on it.

"Thank you, Jesus," she said, praising God.

Then, the dye-pack went off. The noise startled her.

"Oh, shit! God damn! What the fuck?" She couldn't help herself, screaming over the gospel music.

In a blink of an eye, the car was inundated with a pink dye. It was everywhere. Smoke took over the interior of the car, even inside Tallhya's mouth and nose, making it difficult for her to see or breathe.

Endless coughing turned into choking, and her eyes were burning. It was unbearable. Tallhya couldn't see where she was going, because the dye had smeared on the windshield like blood. The smoke and the dye did their job overtime.

BOOM!

There was a hard bump, and it felt like the entire bottom of the car fell out. Unbeknownst to her, she had driven the car up on the sidewalk and ran head-on into a blue US Post Office mailbox. After she realized that she was okay, she thanked God it wasn't a person she'd hit and that she wasn't dead.

Struggling with all her might, she forced the door open and ran for cover. She was sure the car was going to blow up. She ran into the nearby woods and kept running. She thanked God for Daylight Savings Time and that it was getting dark early.

She disappeared into the sunset and the deep forest, took off her coat and wig. Once she was deep into the trees, she peeled off the gloves and got out of dodge. The blond wig kept the dye out of her real hair, but she still desperately needed a shower.

An hour later, Tallhya checked into a seedy hotel on Jefferson Davis Highway that supplied rooms to crackheads, dope fiends, and prostitutes turning quick tricks. Tallhya took so many showers that the hot water ran out.

Having to leave the bags of money from the bank in the car and only having the cash that she leaned over the counter and took herself, Tallhya had only $210 to her name. She used the money to purchase another week at Dorsee's and get a few groceries.

And the circle was complete. She was back where she started when the day began: broke as joke.

She thought about all that she'd been through, and an overwhelming flood of emotions hit her.

She tried to keep the tears from rolling down her face, but the effort was useless.

"God . . . why me?" Tallhya stared upward, toward the cracked ceiling. "I wanna do right," she said to whoever was listening. She dropped to her knees, onto a cheap, worn-out red carpet and said, "Help me, Lord! Help me, Jesus! Jehovah! Father, in the name of Jesus, help me." A steady stream of tears stained her face. "Lord, help me!"

Her prepaid cell phone rang, interrupting her monologue with the All Seeing. When she answered, an automated message said, "You have six minutes remaining."

"Fuck." Could she catch one break? Just one?

"Hello . . . Tallhya?

"Gladys?"

"Don't you recognize your aunt's voice? Lord have mercy," said Gladys, "it hasn't been that long, has it?"

"Of course I recognize your voice, Aunt Gladys. I was just distracted by something."

"Girl, you too young to be distracted by anything but one of them fine young men out there with a good job and love for the Lord. I wish I was your age again."

Tallhya cut her off. "I only have a few minutes, Auntie. I'm on a prepaid."

"A what?" Gladys had no idea what that meant.

"I only have five minutes left on my phone before it cuts off. I have to put some more money on it."

"Well, I have good news."

Chapter 12

Remembrance

Glenn Allen, VA

Established in 1958, Roselawn is a fairly modern cemetery. The lush, manicured grounds, which are aptly named Memory Gardens, have a spiritual air about them. It's a certain peacefulness that helps to comfort the mind and soul of the deceased and their visitors. Those were just a couple of the reasons why Mildred "Me-Ma" Banks, while she was alive, chose this particular cemetery for her body to rest once she was ready to embark on her pilgrimage to heaven.

Chase wheeled the black SRT Grand Cherokee onto the cemetery grounds. Simone sat quietly in the front seat of the SUV, looking off to her right, staring out the window. The cabin of the truck was quiet; the couple hadn't spoken for the past 45 minutes, since leaving the house this morning.

After pulling into a parking spot, Chase held Simone's hand. He could feel the perspiration. He asked, "Are you ready to do this?"

She wasn't. This was her first time here since Ginger's funeral. Ginger and Bunny were buried right next to Me-Ma. Simone had seen to it. After all, she knew that family meant more to Me-Ma than anything in the world, next to God.

The two got out of the SUV together. Simone exhaled. The morning was mildly pleasant; the temperature was hovering around 76 degrees, capped with a beautiful azure, cloudless sky. Birds sang as they foraged for food and crickets chirped, trying not to become breakfast for their feathered foe.

She said, "Yes. As ready as I'll ever be."

Chase got out and went around to the passenger's side of the jeep and opened the door for Simone to exit the vehicle. Once she did, he opened the back door, too, and reached into the back seat for the picnic basket Simone had prepared last night. Together, they held hands and walked side by side toward the graves. They'd been married for only a couple of months, but their love was as strong and authentic as a couple that had known each other all of their lives. Love is not measured by time, but how that time is spent together. At least that was the way Simone felt about the subject.

Less than twenty-five yards from where they parked, Simone laid a quilt on the freshly-cut grass, wet with morning dew. It was one of Me-Ma's quilts, hand sewn. From the basket, Simone removed Me-Ma's leather Bible. It was visibly aged, like she was, but strong and dependable, also like she was. Besides the Bible, she removed a single flower from the basket: a purple daisy.

"This is for you," she said, laying the flower onto the headstone. Daisies were Me-Ma's favorite blossom, and purple was symbolic of royalty. Without question, Me-Ma had been, and always would be, the queen and matriarch of the Banks family.

Simone opened the worn Bible and leafed through the pages until she came upon the passage she wanted: Psalm 91. She read the full Bible passage to her grandmother. When she was done with the reading, both she and Chase, in unison, said "Amen." Simone then kissed her hand and caressed Me-Ma's stone.

Bunny's grave was to Me-Ma's immediate right. When it was time to show her respects to Bunny, Simone put the Bible away, replacing it with an expensive bottle of red wine and three crystal goblets. Simone opened the wine, pouring the fermented grapes into each of the glasses.

She set a glass on Bunny's stone, along with a red rose, kept a glass for herself, and handed the last one to her husband.

She toasted: "To family and bad bitches."

Chase touched goblets with his wife. "Amen to that," he said. "Family and bad women. But none finer than my wife," he added, with a consoling kiss on the lips.

Simone sighed. "Bunny loved life so much . . . and so hard," she lamented. "It's hard to believe that she took her own life."

Chase shook his head. "She was so young, also." He was the one who'd found her. He stumbled upon the body in a hotel room while investigating another case. She'd apparently overdosed on a handful of pain pills after finding out that her boyfriend had been murdered and then getting revenge on the person she felt responsible for taking his life.

Chase shared a private thought with Simone, one he'd had on more than one occasion, but never shared, until now. "Sometimes I wonder if somehow I could have saved her. . . ." he said. "If my investigation would have drawn me to the hotel sooner."

Simone thought about what he said. She'd had similar thoughts about ways things may have been different, but deep down, she knew that there was nothing anyone could have done.

She told her husband, "I don't believe that God makes mistakes. He makes things happen exactly the way He wants them to happen. So there was nothing that you, me, or anyone else could have done to change the outcome of what happened."

Slowly, Chase nodded his head. He wasn't a big church guy, but he believed in God. "I guess you're right."

"To my sister Bunny, I don't know why you would do this, in this way. You leave me with so many unanswered questions." Tears formed in her eyes. "But I hope you are at peace finally!" She cried as she poured the rest of the bottle of wine out.

"Baby, don't cry. She's okay. She's with Me-Ma and Ginger."

Not wanting to cry, she tried to suck it up. Simone smiled. "I know that's right. Let us pay our respects to Ginger and get out of here before we guilt ourselves into having a bad day." She was already going into the picnic basket.

Chase said, "Cool. Let's do that."

Simone had brought a rainbow-like Cattleya orchid for Ginger's grave. The flower was indigenous to Costa Rica. It was exotic, over the top, and bold: all the things that made Ginger who she was. Along with the flower, Simone had a copy of *Vogue* magazine with her favorite celebrity donning the cover: The original Don Dada herself, Mrs. Beyoncé Knowles-Carter. Simone read the interview to Ginger before packing up.

As she was putting the things back into the picnic basket, she couldn't help but think if it was symbolic that she was there because she would be joining them soon. After all, she was in the middle of having chemo treatments, and at this point, it could very much go either way. Before she got into feeling sorry for herself, she decided to say a few final words and get out of there.

"To missing my family," Simone said. As she zoned out at her sisters' and grandmother's grave she added, "I have no one but you, Chase."

"And I'm never going to leave you. You are my angel, and I love you more than life itself."

"Thank you, baby." Having him by her side was all she needed, though she really wished she didn't have to be there at all and that she had her sisters there with her. But it truly meant the world to her that he was so supportive and by her side.

The phone rang again, and she looked down at it. "Aunt Gladys?"

"See, I'm not the only one you have." Chase tried to make her feel better.

"Yes." She nodded with a smile. "Aunt Gladys is always right on time."

That she sure was!

Chapter 13

Glamma Gladys

Rydah took an Uber to her grandmother's house. It had been more than two decades since the last time she went there. When she was seven years old and school was out for the summer, Rydah's mother and father had taken her to New York to see the Broadway play *Annie*. On the way back from the Big Apple, they stopped in VA to visit Grandma Gladys. The house was just as she remembered it. White stucco with pink shutters and huge statues of Jesus and Mary standing vigilant in the front yard on either side of the stone steps.

Rydah rang the bell. Lights were on inside the house, but no one came to the door. She punched the button a few more times.

Ding-dong. Ding-dong. Ding-dong.

She thought that she heard noises coming from inside, but still, no one answered. Puzzled, she knocked on the door and rang the doorbell again. Nothing.

Maybe she'd imagined the noise, she thought. She was certain that this was the right address. A car was on the side of the house, covered up. She could tell from the shape that it was her grandfather's Thunderbird. The car was a timeless piece of history in their family. It was one of the reasons she had such a deep passion for cars. She wondered if it still ran. If it didn't, she would fix it.

In the driveway, a brand-new, shiny Cadillac was parked. The vanity plate read *MsG2U*. Rydah had to give it to her. Grandma Gladys never disappointed. The woman was the hippest senior citizen that she knew. This was definitely the right house, but why wasn't she answering the door?

She reflected back to her conversation before leaving Miami:

"Hey, Glamma."

"Hello, baby."

"I hate to wake you. I know it's super early." It was 7:10 a.m.

"I've been up for a couple of hours now, baby. Just sitting here, having my morning coffee, reading the obituaries. What time do I have to pick you up from the airport?"

"*My flight leaves in another hour. I should arrive at about eleven o' clock. But I don't need you to come and get me. I'm gonna get a rental.*"

"*I won't hear of it. I'll be there to get you.*"

"*No need, Glamma. I'm gonna need a car to drive around while I'm there anyway.*"

Gladys said, "*You will drive my car wherever you want to go. You can put as many miles on it as you need to.*"

"*And what are you going to drive?*"

"*Chile, don't back talk me. When I pass away, I'm leaving it to you. It's already in my will. So you might as well get used to it.*"

"*Don't talk like that, Glamma. You're not going anywhere anytime soon. Probably outlive us all.*"

"*Thank you, baby, but I'm still not allowing you to drive no rental car while you staying with me. You hear me?*"

"*Okay. Let's compromise then. I'll use my Uber app to schedule a ride from the airport, and I'll use your car once I'm there. But,*" Rydah said, "*that's only if you let me treat you to lunch today.*"

"*I guess I can live with those arrangements. But if you don't get that Uber, make sure you call. If not, you're going to be in big trouble. And trouble with me isn't what you want.*"

Rydah hoped her grandmother hadn't gone to the airport, but if that were the case, her car wouldn't be in the driveway. Rydah put her ear to the door. The TV was on. She knocked again.

When her grandmother finally answered, Gladys smelled like a mixture of White Diamonds perfume and cigarette smoke.

Gladys gave her a big hug. "Girl, you's as pretty as a flower. Let me look at cha."

"Glamma, you been smoking?"

"Nope."

Rydah followed Gladys through the foyer, past the living and dining rooms, and into the family room. The family room smelled like tobacco smoke.

Rydah gave her grandmother side-eye. "You know good and well that you not supposed to be smoking. "

"Now, listen. . . ."

Rydah wasn't trying to hear it. "If you promise to cut back, I won't tell my father that you been smoking like a chimney. And you know he's going to flip, and my mother will lecture you, so . . . oooh, you know how she goes on and on with those lectures. Trust me, you don't want that."

"Wait a minute, missy. I'm your grandmother."

"And I love you to life for being such a great influence on me. And out of respect, I won't give you a lecture on why smoking is like committing a slow but deliberate suicide. Don't you see the warning on the sides of the pack?"

Gladys said, "You a li'l sassy thing, ain't ya?"

"Yup! Just like my glamma," she said, trying to get back on her good side.

"Flattery will get you everywhere. Now, let me get myself dressed so we can start this process to get you your money."

"Thank you, Glamma." Rydah kissed her on the cheek

"Girl, you don't have to thank me. I'm just trying to make sure you get what's yours."

Rydah smiled at her grandmother then blurted out, "What are they like?"

"Who? Your sisters?"

Rydah dropped her head shamefully. "I've never wanted to hurt my parents' feelings by trying to push the fact that I do have siblings."

"Well . . ." Gladys sucked in a deep breath. "Baby, you should live for you. They will understand."

"It's just that I never felt like I was adopted. Ever. Like, never ever! My parents love and accept me for who I am, and the truth is, I've never really inquired about my real family, because I know for a fact that they could never be better than the one I have now."

"Hummmmmph. You got that right." Gladys started to say something, but then she remembered her promise to her son. Maestro made it clear that he wanted Rydah to make her own decisions and develop her own feelings about her sisters. Amanda, on the other hand, felt that Deidra was the scum of the Earth and didn't trust any of them. But Maestro had made his wishes final, and they both agreed that Rydah was a smart girl and that it was best for her to form her own opinion.

"But I do sometimes wonder what my birth mother is like."

"Chile . . ." Gladys chuckled, fanning Rydah off. "Now, my grandmother told me that if you can't say nothing nice, don't say nothing at all. So my lips are sealed tighter than a Ziploc bag."

"And you always told me that the least you could do for a person is to be honest with them."

"You too much, girl. You know that?"

Gladys had always thought her granddaughter was God's gift to the world, and being with her made her remember why she loved this little lady so much.

"Waaaiiiiting . . ." Rydah sang in her sweetest voice, batting mink eyelashes.

Gladys looked her granddaughter over and just admired her. She was beautiful, smart, kind, put-together, and most of all, she was nobody's fool. She knew what Maestro had requested, but at the end of the day, she was *his* mother and the matriarch of the family. And she was more concerned about the wellbeing of her granddaughter that any half-baked promise she may have agreed to.

"Well, Deidra . . ." she said with a disgusted look on her face. "Yuck!" she said in such a nasty tone, out of her normally loving, grandmotherly voice. "The monster that gave birth to you?"

Rydah didn't respond. She just looked at her grandmother and got a kick out of her rolling her eyes at the thought of Deidra, her birth mother.

"Humph . . ." She sucked her teeth. "Chile, please! That thing ain't worth the dirt on a snake's belly. And I'd trust my hemorrhoids more than I'd trust her."

Rydah laughed so hard she almost cried. "Glamma, you know you not right."

"I'm dead serious, girl. And I was being nice because the woman is your blood. Trust me, you don't want to know her. I never saw a wench so low down and dirty. She uses everybody in the most extreme way. Your *brista* was a scammer. Deidra got him to steal all this designer stuff for her and some man, then left him at the mall when he got caught."

"His momma did that?"

"That's not even a small slice of the shitty pie. Deidra never sent the boy one dime. And your no self-esteem-having overweight sister Tallhya . . ."

"Glamma, don't say that."

"Well, it's true. She pretty. All of them pretty. You look like them, too. Well, your mother slept with the fat sister's husband. That's what drove your sister to the crazy house."

"Are you kidding?"

"No, ma'am. I'm certainly not. I have to go pick her up to take her to the bank as well, so you'll meet her."

"I'm excited."

"She's actually sweet. Kind of gullible, but will give you the shirt off of her back."

Rydah asked, "What about Simone?"

"She has breast cancer and is doing chemo. I spoke to her husband, Chase. He took her to the bank this morning to sign her necessary documents."

"She's married? Does she have children?"

"No children. And I don't know why that girl jumped the broom so damn quick. Maybe she wanted those cop benefits. You know that the state has good insurance and such. I don't know."

"How long she been married?"

"Not long at all. As soon as she got sick, she got married a few days later. She went to the Justice of the Peace, which was very surprising to me, because she's always been a high-class kind of girl. Her daddy—God bless his soul—Simon raised her like her farts never stank. And when he passed, her stepmother took everything she had, including the underwear out her dresser, and sent her packing to Me-Ma's."

"That's sad." Rydah's heart went out to Simone, and she hadn't even met her yet.

"Maybe so, but it made her wise up. And you know how they say so-and-so beat somebody like they stole something. Marjorie did steal something, and I heard that Simone beat the break dust off of that child."

"What about Bunny?"

Gladys dropped her head. "Bunny and Gene both passed away. Gene is your brista—sometimes your brother, sometimes your sister. But I will let Simone tell you about that."

"And Bunny?"

"She took her own life."

"Why?"

"Because she was into a lot of deep, dark hell and . . . I think depression over the guy she was dating or something. It never made any sense to me, but I'll let Simone tell you about that when she has enough energy. Just was very sad."

Rydah was temporarily quiet. "She committed suicide?"

"I'm afraid so." Gladys dropped her head. "Umph, umph, umph! She was such a beautiful girl, so full of life."

"Okay. Yes, ma'am." Rydah accepted the info her grandmother shared with her. She didn't push, but she really wanted to know more.

"Well, I will call and check on Simone and see if she is up for dinner. And if she is, I will make you all your favorite things and you can have some personal, quality time bonding with Simone—and Tallhya, too, if she can come over after. So for now, let's get pretty and get to the bank before it gets too late."

They got dressed, and her grandmother stopped her at the door. "Where is your jacket?" Gladys asked her granddaughter as if she were still seven years old.

"I didn't bring one. Guess I wasn't thinking." With the need to explain herself to her grandmother, she said, "It was ninety degrees in Miami when I left. And it's March. Shouldn't winter be gone?"

Gladys shot her a look. "Girl, that's Miami and this is Virginia, two entirely different worlds. You will not get sick on my watch." Gladys did a beeline to her cedar walk-in closet. "I think

I have a mink wrap you can throw over your shoulders so you won't catch a cold."

"Glammmmmm. . . ." Rydah felt like a little girl in the Barbie store. All of the endless furs, in all styles, colors, and shapes. "O-M-G! If I die, just bury me here. Glam, did you will me these, too?"

"Sure did," Gladys proudly said. "A couple to your mother, but most of them to you."

"Put this wrap on and let's get to the bank."

Rydah picked up a beret-style mink hat that matched the wrap her grandmother suggested she wore. "Is it okay for me to take this?"

"That old thing is older than you, sweet pie, but you can help yourself to anything you like."

"Well, here's to vintage." Rydah adjusted the mink beret over her hair, which was styled in Indique tresses that fell down her back. After getting the angle just right, she said, "I've got unfinished business with this closet when we return." The thought of scavenging through her grandmother's closet excited her as much as the perfectly rebuilt engine of a 1970 Mercury Cyclone GT.

Chapter 14

Identical

"Why is Tallhya staying here?"

The parking lot of the hotel was littered with needles and crack vials. Gladys pulled into a parking space near the front. A prostitute, walking with a trick, strolled by the car. The prostitute glanced nervously into the window of Gladys's Cadillac, making sure it wasn't the vice in an unmarked car. Satisfied that Gladys and Rydah weren't po-po, the prostitute—wearing a purple wig and a tight-fitting purple polyester dress, with concave cheeks and dark, lifeless eyes—pulled her trick along by the hand. She was Tallhya's age. Six months ago, before getting hooked on smack, she was a young fly stallion with all the answers. Now she was not only out of answers, but she was also devoid of hope.

Gladys said, "Don't make me into no liar."

Tallhya popped out of room 218 looking tired and disheveled. She waved down below, then took the stone stairs to the parking lot. When she climbed into the back seat of the Caddy, Gladys said, "This is your sister, Rydah. Rydah, this is your sister, Tallhya."

The siblings looked into each other's eyes for the very first time, and both girls instantly felt a familial connection. For a moment, Tallhya thought that she was on the brink of really going crazy again. Not only did Rydah have the Banks sisters' piercing grey eyes, Tallhya observed, but she was also the spitting image of their elder sister, Bunny, who had recently committed suicide after her boyfriend was murdered. Tallhya had to pinch herself to make sure she was awake. But would that work if she were seeing a ghost? She didn't know.

Rydah said, "Nice to meet you, finally."

Tallhya was still trying to discern whether she was smack dead in the middle of a bad dream, or if things were possibly turning around. First, Gladys had called her about some money that Me-Ma supposedly had squirrelled away. God only knew how badly she needed the money. And now she was sitting behind a sister that she never knew she had, that just so happened to look exactly like a sister she'd just lost.

Tallhya was mesmerized by the likeness. Bunny was drop-dead gorgeous in every conceivable way, yet somehow, Rydah was ten times finer . . . more polished. She was stunningly beautiful: skin that looked as if it could star in an Oil of Olay commercial without filters, teeth straight from the Colgate box, hair spun like silk, and the aura of a movie star. Tallhya couldn't pull her eyes away.

Although Rydah and Bunny looked so similar, Rydah seemed to be sweeter, and her confidence was through the roof. She was everything that Tallhya dreamed of being. There was something about Rydah's energy and personality that motivated Tallhya, making her want better for herself. Her feelings weren't motivated by jealousy, envy, or sibling competition. She just wanted what her sister had, but in her own way.

Tallhya was a little nervous when they went into the bank, but Kimberly made her feel comfortable. The formalities of signing the paperwork went over that easily.

Kimberly's eyes were glued on Rydah. "It's unbelievable how you two look alike." Kimberly and Bunny had gone to school together. "Other than your hair being different, the two of you could be twins."

That's when the light bulb went off for Tallhya.

All of the Banks girls had similar characteristics. Even her brother, Ginger, was gorgeous. Tallhya figured that all she had to do was lose weight—a few pounds gone and she would be fine as well.

At that moment, she decided that regardless of what it took, she was gong to get slim.

Chapter 15

Reunited

"This calls for a celebration!" Gladys said. Her skin was glowing. "I got a real nice bottle of wine chilling on ice, and I've set the table with my good China." She admired her spread.

Gladys had cooked everything herself. All the food was placed down the middle of her Mahogany formal dining room table, which sat twelve people. Lobsters, grilled and blackened salmon, shrimp prepared three different ways (fried, steamed, and grilled), scallops, mussels, mixed vegetables, corn on the cob, sweet and baked potatoes ...

"Looks like Versace china, Glam."

"You already know," Simone said, taking a seat. "Aunt Gladys has always been over-the-top fancy. You can't tell that lady nothing when it comes to some fly shit."

All Tallhya noticed was the food. While her mother often looked hungrily at things with dollar signs in her eyes, there were shrimp in her eyes, telling the story of how she was about to devour that food.

"You got everything!" she said, joining her sister Simone. "Aunt Gladys, you know you shouldn't be doing this to a fat girl."

Rydah said, "Girl, when you go with me back to Miami in a couple of weeks, I got a doctor that's going to fix you right up. He's the same doctor that those celebrity chicks are going to. So you might as well indulge, girl." Rydah admired the food. "Glammmm, this is too fab. You really outdid yourself," she said, giving her grandmother a kiss on the cheek.

Gladys started serving the food. "I ain't outdid nothing," she said. "Glad to do it. Like I said, we're celebrating. You girls only get to meet each other for the first time once. Shoot, it's the least I could do. I'm happy that you girls are united and love each other and all that good stuff. So enough with the thanks, let's just enjoy ourselves."

The girls ate until they felt as if they would pop. Once they were stuffed, Gladys told Rydah to take them to the den. However, Simone insisted that they go out on the screened-in porch so she could smoke her medical marijuana.

"The only perk of cancer," she said after inhaling her first toke of the night.

Gladys came out with a tray of glasses filled with wine and limeade, then doubled back to get chocolate cake, sweet potato pie, and apple pie. "For the munchies," she said.

"Glam, what you know about some munchies?"

"They ain't just start smoking pot this decade, girl. Keep sleeping on your grandma if you want. I've been telling you for the last thirty years that I don't miss much of anything."

Rydah feigned an eye roll. "Excuse me," she said.

Simone got up and gave Gladys a hug. "We appreciate you."

Gladys fanned her off. "That's what family is for, girl."

"And these limeades are the best," Tallhya said. "Always have been." She looked up to the sky. "I know Me-Ma up there smiling at you, Aunt Gladys." Being with Gladys reminded her of how much she missed Me-Ma. Tallhya smiled and looked to Rydah. "Me-Ma knows you would have loved her."

"I know. My grandmother always used to talk about how wonderful she was," Rydah said as Gladys had exited the room.

It felt a little awkward to the girls that Rydah, who was their blood sister, kept referring to their grandaunt, Gladys, as her grandmother. She could see the looks on their faces, but it was her reality.

"Me-Ma was real churchy, but she had a heart of gold," Tallhya said. "She wouldn't hurt nobody, just better not mess with her grand-girls, I know that much! I swear, I miss her so much." Just the thought of Me-Ma made Tallhya's face light up.

"Makes me sad to think about her, she was so wonderful," Simone added. "Since I lived with my dad, I went over there on the weekends and every other Sunday. She made me feel like I was her favorite." She smiled.

"But in fact, she made us all think we were her favorites in her own way. We all accused each other of being her favorite, because she protected us like we were her own cubs." Simone took a pull of her weed. "Now that I think about it, it was probably because she knew Deidra wasn't shit."

"Where is Deidra nowadays?" Tallhya asked, holding her breath.

"Chile, please," she replied, sucking her teeth. "Nobody seen her in a few weeks now." Simone took a long pull of her medical marijuana and reveled in knowing exactly what had happened to Deidra's no-good ass. "Wherever she at, though, trust me, she better off there than here with us."

"It's her normal shit," Tallhya added, shaking her head. "Always have been. Dashing in and out of lives, disappearing—and when she returns, it's empty-handed. Probably somewhere scamming some damn body. Doing some fucking lowlife shit right now as we speak."

"Yup, that's Deidra for ya. Thieving and manipulating," Simone said, blowing the smoke out of her mouth.

"Deidra needs to stop that shit before somebody kills her ass." Tallhya put her two cents in. She hadn't the foggiest idea that her sisters had already whacked Deidra and had no remorse for it.

"Damn . . ." was all Rydah could say. "She sounds pretty bad. She can't possibly, *reallyyyy* be that bad?"

Both Simone and Tallhya said in unison, "Worse!"

"Unlike anything you would ever believe, and because this is supposed to be such a great moment of us being together getting to know each other, we won't waste any more of our time together talking about her. Let's just sum it up:

the best thing she did for us was give us life and our good looks, honey," Simone said.

"I concur." Tallhya raised her glass and handed Rydah hers. "To sisterhood."

"Sisterhood!" The ladies toasted.

Rydah was almost scared to tell the girls how great her mother was. She was secretly relieved that Deidra was the worst and she hadn't had the opportunity of meeting her own mother. *Damn shame,* she thought to herself.

"Consider yourself lucky that you never crossed your paths with that sorry-ass bitch," Tallhya said. "I told my therapist that that bitch is dead to me."

"You still salty about Walter's lying, cheating ass?" Simone asked.

"Yes, I am," Tallhya said bluntly. "I sure am!"

"Cheating with Deidra just put the nail in the coffin?"

"Yup. Sure did."

Simone just looked at her sister, and Rydah listened and watched them both. They had the same exact features, eyes and nose, just completely different weights, hairstyles, and personalities.

"I feel better about me, but . . . not him," she said matter-of-factly.

"And aren't you 1033 crazy?"

"Sure is!"

Like a tennis match, Rydah watched her two long lost sisters go back and forth.

"Meaning your crazy ass can probably kill somebody and get away with it?"

"Yup, and not do one day in the pen . . ." Tallhya nodded with a sinister smile. "I could kill your ass with my bare hands for taking me to a goddamn psychiatric facility and telling them people to Baker Act me. . . . Yup, sure could kill your ass dead!" She hit her sister with a playful punch.

"Ummmm . . . you can't beat on a sick woman." Simone tried to be quick on her feet, but she couldn't find the words.

"Oh. any excuse will do. Don't worry, you know-it-all bitch, I won't! I'm not going to kill you, or Walter, for that matter."

With a raised eyebrow, Simone asked, "Really?" She gave a sigh of relief.

"No, you safe. But don't worry, I'm going to get *his* ass. In God you trust, or bet your last dollar that I've got plans for Walter. He's going to pay for exactly what he done to me. . . ." The room was silent. "And he needs to be alive."

"Ummmm . . . do share with us what you're going to do to him."

"I'm going to give him and the world the very best version of myself. Going to be so damn fine, stomach going to be flat and waist going to be *snatched* to the motherfucking gawds, booty popping, boobs sitting up perky. That's what the motherfucker's punishment is going to be." She let out a bewitching laughter. "It gets me high just thinking about how he ain't going to never ever be able to smell the puss ever in this lifetime!"

"That's right, sister," Rydah added. "Sometimes you have to make them sorry, even if they never say sorry."

"Yes, that's why I really need you. I need you to take me to that doctor, you know the one on Instagram that all the celebrities and strippers go to?"

"Dr. Slim Jim or Dr. Snatch or somebody?"

"Yup, him. Sister, I really need you to do this for me. I just need you to give me a ride to the place, let me get my consultation and date, and take me back and let me stay with you until I heal." Tallhya was so passionate in her spiel.

Honestly, when Tallhya referred to Rydah as a sister, that was all Rydah needed to hear. There was something about the word *sister* that just warmed her heart. Growing up as an only child was always hard. Girlfriends who claimed that they were "sisters" came and went and took their sisterhood lightly. Inside, she had always yearned for a real sister, who, no matter what, was bonded to her by blood.

"I got you, sister. Trust me, with Dr. Snatch you going to give not just Walter a heart attack, but all these men and women alike."

"Yesssssss. Check can't clear fast enough!"

Simone gave her sister five. "That's right!"

"Yup, that motherfucker . . . the nerve of him . . . nope, not anymore." For a second, her mind started to venture off into those awful Walter memories, and then Tallhya had a light bulb moment, turned to Rydah, and asked, "As a matter of fact, you think if I ask Auntie Gladys to keep my share of the money, she would?"

"I'm sure she would. Why? What's going on?"

"This motherfucker won't give me my divorce, and he has my money tied up and is trying to come after everything I got. Being that Simone had me committed, it just didn't make me look good in the court's eyes, and they gave him control over my motherfucking money. Makes me so freaking angry every time I think about it. So, as soon as I get my money from the Me-Ma situations, what if I gift it to Aunt Gladys?"

"I'm sure it's no problem. But yeah, let's ask her."

Rydah ate, talked, and laughed with her sisters and grandmother. With all the post-traumatic stress and feelings after the carjacking, it was the first time she had laughed in a long time. There was something about smelling the Virginia air that made her happy, or maybe it was just the love of her grandmother and the feeling of having sisters. She sat and enjoyed the moment until they heard the doorbell. Honestly, the sisters didn't care who it was. No one else in the world mattered but them.

Then, Chase entered into the room, with a strange look on his face.

"Hey baby! What's wrong?" Simone noticed the stressed look on his face.

Chase was a really good guy and loved every single thing about Simone, even the toilet she shitted on. He was a police officer on the Richmond Police Department and had an idea about Simone and her sisters' shady past with the bank robberies, as he had been the head investigator. He loved Simone so much that he told her, "Listen, I'm not sure what your role was in this whole fiasco of these bank robberies, but I'm going to let it go. Just make sure it never happens again."

And since then, she had been keeping her hands clean. She knew that if he dug deeper, he could possibly put her in prison for the rest of her life, but once he found out that she had been diagnosed with cancer, he told her he didn't want lose her, and he had taken care of her ever since. If she survived cancer, and their relationship survived the treatments and the deadly disease, she would indeed marry him.

Chase insisted that they go to the Justice of the Peace and get married, and promised her a huge wedding after she beat cancer.

What did she have to lose? She had no family, really; no parents, and having lost a sister and a brother only days apart. The security of knowing she had someone in her corner who loved her to death was enough for her. But knowing everything that she and her sisters had done, and the things that she had manipulated and masterminded, the best thing for her to do was quit while she was ahead. She had a significant other on her side, and the fact that he just happened to be a cop in her pocket was the icing on the cake. Not to mention, the stability on his job and benefits and insurance didn't hurt at all.

"It's bad, babe," he said to Simone with a lump in his throat.

"What is it, honey?" Maintaining a poker face, Simone had all kinds of things running through her mind.

What the fuck is it? What could it be? Is he coming to lock me up? Has he found out about the banks me and my sisters robbed? Then she told herself, *Girl, keep it together. What's worse than cancer?*

"It's your mother." He cleared his throat. "It's Deidra."

"Deidra?" Tallhya asked, shocked. "Well, what the fuck that bitch done did now?"

"She's dead . . ." He paused. "We found a few parts of her body, but enough to identity her with dental records."

"Parts?" Rydah questioned. "Parts?"

"Damn, wouldn't you know it? All of Deidra's bullshit finally came around," Simone said, knowing good and well that she wasn't surprised. She tried hard to think about having cancer and the effects it had taken on her body so she could get some tears, but they wouldn't come right away.

Rydah sat, astonished, then asked, "Are y'all okay?"

Chase's eyes looked at Rydah. She was drop dead gorgeous and resembled the Banks sisters, but she had a certain hotness about her.

Rydah saw Chase looking at her. She had not been formally introduced to him, so she attempted to make light of the situation. "Hi. I'm

Rydah, from Miami. I'm their sister. Deidra sold me at birth, so we just met today, and we're bonding. Long story, but that just about sums it up. How are you doing?" She reached to shake his hand.

"Chase," he said, extending his hand. "I'm your brother-in-law. Sorry we had to meet under these circumstances."

"Right?" Rydah said, shaking her head.

"Damn, I knew this day was coming, but didn't think it would be this soon." Tears appeared in Tallhya eyes.

"I'm sorry, Tallhya." Rydah hugged her. "I'm sooooo sorry."

Simone got up and hugged her sister too.

Gladys came in to comfort the girls. On that note, Gladys said, "I know for a fact that Mildred had a life insurance policy on her, too."

Tallhya's tears dried up. "God be working in mysterious ways. He knew I needed this good news."

"Good news?" Rydah questioned. "I know Deidra was a bad excuse for somebody's mother, but her dying isn't good news, is it?"

"No, but if you knew where I was two days ago, how bad Deidra really was, and how bad off and desperate I was, then you would understand."

"She really was a greedy piece of shit," Simone said, "and nobody with a loving mother like what I'm sure yours is would ever understand a rotten woman of such magnitude of shittiness Deidra is or was. And when you look at how she reproduced such beautiful children, you would never understand the pain and let-down she took us through."

"She was really rotten to the core," Gladys co-signed, because it was the truth, but also because she didn't want Simone and Tallhya to look like heartless bitches. "She wasn't no earthly good, and I know she ain't heavenly bound. All that mess she put y'all through, she's going to have to account for that. Judgment Day."

"You right about that. God going to deal with her, then," Rydah said.

"Don't you mean Lucifer?" Simone asked. "Trust me, she ain't getting into the gates of Heaven, not by a longshot."

"Well, at least I know for sure I will be able to get my damn surgery, finally," Tallhya said.

"Damn, are you going to be okay?" Rydah was puzzled.

"Honestly, the best thing that woman could do was die. Trust me, she saved us a lot of pain and suffering. She's never done one motherly thing for us but give us life, because after she brought us into this godforsaken world, we were fair game. All she ever did was lie, steal, and pimp our asses in her own way. Bitch is better off dead," Simone said with malice.

"You got that right," Gladys said under her breath.

Tallhya busted out laughing, and everyone in the room turned their attention to her. "Now irony will have it that the bitch had to die for us to finally get a benefit from her ass."

"The benefit is a financial settlement from all the abuse," Simone added to what Tallhya was saying.

"You're so right, girl." Tallhya slapped hands with her sister. "I bet that bitch running through Hell, hot as fish grease that we get to collect that insurance money."

"I know that's right. Raising hell in Hell. Mad, looking for a reason to trick it out of us if she could." They kept the running sarcasm going.

"Chase, you see what you married into? This family crazy, right?" Tallhya said when she noticed Chase was speechless.

"It is, but it's mines though," Chase said with his chest poked out. He leaned in and kissed Simone.

"Well, I'm here to do anything you need. And I know I speak for me and my grandmother as well," Rydah said, trying hard to console her newfound sisters, even though they didn't seem too much like they needed consoling. "Yes, we are here and will give her a nice memorial. At least put her away nice," Rydah suggested.

Rydah felt as though they were blessed. Richmond had been a blessing. She was collecting money on her grandmother's and her mother's death. Or was it a curse?

"Memorial service? How much is that going to be?" Tallhya asked in a dead-serious tone. "I don't wanna be dipping into my surgery money. Shiiiit, she wouldn't even bury us if the shoe was on the other foot."

Simone spoke, knowing that she needed to cover her own tracks, since it was she, after all, along with Bunny and Ginger, who had killed Deidra, and she had helped them dispose of the body. "Cremate the bitch!"

Chapter 16

MIA

The first few days after returning to Miami went by quickly. There was something about going to Virginia and meeting her family that gave Rydah life and the will to put the memories of the carjacking behind her.

Rydah spent most of her free time preparing for Tallhya's arrival. The two sisters spoke on the phone several times a day.

"Should I get a car? What kind of car do you think I should get?" Tallhya asked.

Rydah tried to convince her sister that transportation would be the least of her problems once she got there. "How many times do I have to promise you that wheels are not a thing? You can borrow one of mines until we get you proper."

"You sure?" Tallhya didn't want to impose on her sister any more than she had to. Rydah had already got her the hookup with a five-star-rated doctor to perform her liposuction procedure. She not only got Tallhya pushed to the front of a 6-month waiting list, but Rydah also managed to negotiate a 30 percent discount. All that, plus, she said Tallhya could stay with her as long as needed.

"Because," Tallhya said, "I have no issues with getting a rental." Tallhya wasn't the freeloading type. She'd been drowning—emotionally and financially—before God answered her plea for help, sending her a much-needed life preserver. Her share of the money Me-Ma left them had literally saved her life. She could now afford the surgery, which would help with her lack of self-esteem, and she'd still have enough money get back on her feet.

"Will you just relax and let your little sister do her thing?" Rydah chuckled.

"What's so funny?"

"I can tell we share the same DNA," she said.

"How so?" asked Tallhya.

"Because I had almost the same reaction to Grandma Gladys when she insisted that I drive her car while I was in Richmond. I didn't want to impose—blah, blah, blah. But really, Tallhya, it's cool. You'll see."

"Okay, but eventually I'm going to have to buy one. I saw this li'l Kia with low mileage that I think I could get a good deal on, but I wouldn't try to drive it to Florida."

Rydah cringed at the image of her sister driving a Kia. She hated that South Korea crap. "Hold off on the Kia, sis. We'll get you whatever you need from down here, even if I have to build it myself," she said. "Hold on to your money, girl. All you need is an airline ticket for right now."

"I need new clothes," Tallhya insisted

"What for?" Rydah reminded her. "You're not going to be able to wear them after the surgery."

That was something Tallhya looked forward to. "But for now I have nothing," she said.

Rydah came up with a compromise. "Then pick up the bare necessities, but nothing more. We'll figure out the rest together after you get here. Just don't go overboard."

Tallhya currently wore a size 16. She had been considered "big boned" for her entire life. That was what the nice people called her. It was hard to envision herself a "normal" size.

"Thank you, sister. You're the best."

Rydah said, "There's only one catch. . . ."

There's always a catch, Tallhya thought. "What is it?" she asked.

"Every Sunday I have to spend the day with my parents. It's sort of like a tradition. We do breakfast, attend my father's church, and then have big dinner. It's non-negotiable. No ifs, ands, or buts. Just on general principle you're going to be expected to roll with the script."

Tallhya thought about her sister's request. Me-Ma was a Bible thumper. When Me-Ma died, they found out that the pastor at her church had scammed her into signing over her house and bank accounts to him, and was then on the down-low getting head and sleeping with her transsexual brother. But in the end, he would have to answer to God for that.

She asked, "Is that it?"

"That's it," Rydah said.

"For a second I thought I may have to sign over my first born or something," she joked.

Two days later, Rydah picked her sister up from Fort Lauderdale-Hollywood International Airport.

"How was your flight?"

Tallhya had taken her advice. She only had two bags: a carry-on and a small suitcase. This was her first time flying.

"The seats are way too small," she said. "Other than that, everything was Gucci."

Rydah put the suitcase in the back of the purple El Camino. The inside was white with purple piped-out seats. The headrests had her name embroidered into the white leather in purple script. When she turned the key, the engine roared like a cat out of the jungle. The five hundred horses under the hood were so powerful, Tallhya felt the vibrations penetrating her body. Rydah asked her if she was hungry.

"Yup! I could eat. The only thing they gave us on the plane was a tiny bag of peanuts and a half can of soda."

"Shit. You were lucky to get the peanuts for free." Rydah laid down on the gas, burning a little rubber, before peeling out of the airport like the police were hot on her trail. In a matter of seconds, the speedometer reached 60 miles per hour.

Tallhya buckled up. "You better slow your ass down, girl."

"This isn't fast." Rydah turned on the music. "Wicked" by Future blared from the speakers. Then she dropped a few ounces of pressure on the accelerator. The souped up El Camino jetted down the highway like it had wings.

Tallhya was amazed by all the different types of palm trees on the side of the road. They were everywhere.

Cruising at a smooth 85 miles per hour, Rydah navigated the purple rocket in and out of traffic effortlessly. An app on her phone alerted her to road hazards, speed cameras, and squatting cops waiting to make their monthly quotas.

The sisters met Wolfe for lunch at a seafood restaurant in Bayside. Wolfe was on his best behavior. He and Tallhya seemed to hit it right off.

When they were done grubbing out, Wolfe excused himself. "I got business to attend to. I'll have to catch you ladies later," he said. He paid the bill, kissed Rydah on the lips and her sister on the cheek, and bounced.

After lunch, Rydah drove Tallhya to Brickell.

They parked inside the high-rise and took the elevator up to the thirty-third floor.

"Damn, sis!" Tallhya had to pick her mouth up off the floor in order to speak. "Is this where you live?"

"You like it?" Rydah kicked off her shoes. She'd read that besides a lot of unwanted dirt, bad energy clings to the bottom of people's shoes and gets tracked through the house.

What is there not to like? Tallhya thought. The place was fucking amazing. Tallhya imagined herself living this way: three hundred and fifty feet in the air, overlooking the Atlantic Ocean. Right away, Tallhya knew that this was where she wanted to start over.

The two sisters sat on the balcony, talking. Rydah gave Tallhya the 411 on Miami, and Tallhya shared stories about Bunny and Ginger. She kept saying how much Rydah and Bunny looked alike. And the outrageous things she shared about Ginger were straight up made for TV. Before either of them knew it, hours had flown by.

Rydah's phone rang. "I had no idea it was this late," she said before answering it. "It's Wolfe, girl. He's downstairs, on the way up here."

Tallhya said, "I didn't know that he lived here."

"He dooon't," Rydah corrected. "He comes over when he isn't working, though. But he's always working."

Tallhya smiled. "It's good that y'all spend a lot of time together. I like Wolfe. He seems like he really fucks with you hard."

"I do." Wolfe took off his shoes at the door. "That's my baby. For real."

He joined the girls on the balcony with a bottle of gold champagne then went back inside to the kitchen for glasses.

"How romantic." Tallhya examined the bottle of expensive champagne.

"Girl, he trying to impress you," Rydah casually said to her sister.

"Hey, I heard that." Wolfe came up from behind and kissed her on the neck. Rydah took one of the three glasses from his hands. "And it's true," he said. "For you, my dear sister-in-law." He handed Tallhya a long-stem champagne glass. "And yes, I ended my workday early to come and spend time with you. What do you want to do tonight?"

Tallhya's face lit up. "What are our options?" she asked.

"Well, we can do whatever we want. The city is our oyster. You want to party? You want dinner? You name it."

"Hmmmm . . ." Tallhya thought about the choices she was offered. "Decisions, decisions, decisions. A party sounds good, but I would prefer to go out and celebrate *after* my surgery."

"I have an idea," said Wolfe.

Rydah took a sip of the champagne Wolfe had poured. "Do share," she said.

Wolfe told them what he had in mind. "We can have a chef come to us and fix a gourmet dinner here. And when you're healed from your surgery," he said to Tallhya, "I promise you an epic night out on the town to welcome you to MIA!"

Tallhya hadn't yet gotten past the part about the private chef. "Sounds good to me." She smiled, raising her glass for a toast. "To family."

A few glasses of champagne later and a couple of plates from the private chef Wolfe brought in, and the night was coming to a close. Everything was cleaned and put away, and Tallhya was about to wind down when she overheard Wolfe and her sister in a deep discussion.

"So what about that bitch, Buffy?" Wolfe's voice had lost most of its charm.

"What about her?" Rydah said.

"You asked me not to deal with her petty ass until you got back. You're back," Wolfe said. "And my patience is wearing thin."

Wolfe was convinced that Buffy was responsible for Rydah getting snatched, and he was a firm believer in retribution. Rydah was more forgiving.

"Let God take care of her," she said.

"God?" Wolfe laughed. "I'm told that God forgives. I don't," he said. "And neither should you." Wolfe spoke a little too loudly.

Tallhya walked into Rydah's bedroom. She asked, "What are you two lovebirds arguing about?"

Wolfe didn't take too kindly to people interfering in his business. Normally, he would have checked the violator with violence. He didn't discriminate on gender or kin—man, woman, child, mother, brother, or sister-in-law. His motto was that if you were able to commit the violation, you were able to pay the price.

However, he saw the reward in getting Tallhya to see things from his perspective. Wolfe asked Tallhya, "Did Rydah tell you about the girl that set her up to be kidnapped?"

Rydah rolled her eyes.

Tallhya looked from Wolfe to Rydah and then back to Wolfe. For the short time she'd been in Miami, it had been all fun and sunshine, but this sounded serious. "What happened?"

Wolfe gave Tallhya both the facts and his interpretation of the facts. Then he shared how he thought the transgression should be handled. "But Rydah thinks we should leave it in God's hands. I'm just afraid that if God takes too long to act, the bitch might try her hand again. Next time, Rydah may not be as lucky. What do you think?"

One of the main things Me-Ma taught the kids she raised was that if someone fucked with one of them, they fucked with all of them. That's the way the Banks rolled. Me-Ma ain't raise any punks, including Ginger.

Tallhya said, "I think we should beat that bitch's ass!"

Chapter 17

Not My Sister

"And I'm telling you right here and now," Tallhya said to Rydah, "that bitch needs to be dragged. And if you don't do it, I will. That's a promise. I put that shit on Mc Ma, Bunny, and Ginger's grave."

Wolfe got a better reaction out of Tallhya than he expected. She was a natural firecracker waiting to explode. But he played it cool.

"I can't let you do that," he said. They were standing in the entryway of the den, which doubled as Tallhya's bedroom.

Tallhya wasn't trying to hear it. "I'm telling you the God's truth," she said. Her eyes were on the screen of a laptop that Rydah had let her borrow earlier.

Wolfe was curious. "What're you looking for online?"

"Running through that bitch's social media. That's the best way to find out where a bitch at, what she doing, or where she plan to be."

"Word?" Wolfe liked her style.

"Dead ass," Tallhya said, continuing to drum on the keyboard. She was on a mission.

"What you going to do when you locate her whereabouts?" Wolfe asked

"I'm going to do exactly what I promised I'll do—drag the bitch! I ain't never really been much of a talker." Tallhya felt like this was her way of paying Rydah back for being so generous. Also, the way she saw it, in the hood, most big sisters fought at least a dozen battles for their younger sister before the younger sister's eighteenth birthday. Tallhya figured she owed Rydah about a dozen ass-kicking hands, the same way Bunny had kicked ass for her when they were growing up.

God forbid, what if Rydah had got seriously hurt . . . or died? she thought. They never would have met. Thank goodness nothing like that had happened, but at the same time, Tallhya felt that she needed to let these Miami bitches know that there were consequences and repercussions for messing with a Banks girl. Rydah had folks that loved her, folks that weren't going to stand by and let anybody try to fuck her over.

Wolfe loved Tallhya's energy. He wished that Rydah was more like her sister. She was the type of bitch that he needed on his team.

Chapter 18

April Fool's Day

Partygoers filled Club Hoax well beyond its 1,500-patron capacity. Buffy had been scamming, sucking, and saving all year for her mcga birthday bash, and the final results were even better than her expectations. Eighty-inch projection screens were positioned throughout the club, and the camera stayed positioned on the birthday girl for the entire night. Buffy hammed up every second of it.

The party was called "The Dirty Thirty," and the theme was the Wild, Wild West. Buffy lived on social media, and she blasted her favorite platforms—Twitter, Facebook, Instagram, and Snap Chat—advertising it as the party of the year.

There were mechanical bulls set up in the middle of the lower level. Anyone that could stay on the mechanical beast for a whole two minutes with the setting on high won a stack. A line of inebriated guys and a few chicks tried their hand at the prize. None of them got close to hitting the two-minute mark.

Half-naked go-go dancers stood on the bar, dropping it like their lives depended on it. You could rent the back of a stagecoach, furnished with a queen-sized bed, for thirty minutes at a time. Mock canons were shot off every half hour. Men walked around in chaps, women in Daisy Dukes, and almost everyone wore a cowboy hat and boots.

Buffy was excited to see her vision come to life. The only thing that excited her more was meeting her new mystery friend. Buffy hoped that the mystery girl she'd met on social media would be as hot as her pictures were. If so, Buffy planned to make love to her like a real cowgirl.

Tallhya walked into Club Hoax rocking black leather Daisy Dukes, ostrich cowboy boots, and a skin-tight, blinged-out T-shirt. Across her chest, she wore two bandoliers, fully loaded with bullets. And she carried two real-looking AK-47s. She gave the security guard her fake name and was escorted straight upstairs to VIP, to be formally introduced to the birthday girl.

Tallhya had successfully catfished Buffy on Facebook. Tallhya had used her real pictures, but said her name was Natalie.

Buffy gave Tallhya a long, thirsty look and nearly fell in love with the color of her eyes. "Thank you for coming." She hoped they were real.

Tallhya blinked, showing off her mink eyelashes. "I wouldn't have missed it for all the pussy in Bangkok," she said. Tallhya once heard the line used in a movie, but she couldn't remember its name.

Amused, Buffy took a harder look. "You remind me of someone I know," she said.

"That's not a very original come-on," Tallhya said. "But I'll give you a pass, because I hear it all the time."

The D.J. played a Trina cut and the girls went nuts.

"You are so pretty," Buffy said. She liked girls with a little meat on their bones, as long as they were cute. "Are you really into girls?" she asked.

"Not at the moment," Tallhya quipped. "But the night is young." She thought to herself that this shit was easier than she expected. She could just take the bitch home, get her drunk, and then slit her throat with a kitchen knife. But if she got knocked, she could kiss her surgery and her life good-bye. The only two states that executed more people than Florida were Texas and VA.

Fuck that!

"True." Buffy was clueless as to Tallhya's real intentions. "The night is young," she said. "And so are we. Young and free to do anything we want. Anything."

Tallhya smiled. This was the type of attention that she craved to get from men. But it no longer concerned her, because after her surgery, she would have to fight the guys off with a stick.

She didn't respond to Buffy's remark.

Breaking the momentary silence, Buffy said, "This shit is going to sound corny, but I was in love with the girl who you remind me of."

"Was?" Tallhya feigned like she gave a fuck. She asked, "What happened?"

Buffy contemplated the question. *After Rydah wouldn't give me the time of day, I got one of my homeboys to carjack her bourgeois ass.* Then she said, "She was straight."

Tallhya joked, "Don't ya hate when that shit happens?"

"In the worst way. But I never thought I'd rebound with one of my social media fans."

Did this bitch just call me a groupie? Getting this bitch drunk, taking her to a hotel, and poking her with a sharp knife is starting to look like a good idea again. Who the fuck does this ho think she is, a broke Nicki Minaj?

"Fan this!" Tallhya reared back and cold-cocked Buffy with one of the fake assault rifles. Buffy dropped like a thot's G-string backstage at a rap concert. She screamed, "That's for my sister Rydah, ho!" Then she commenced to ram her ostrich boots upside Buffy's head.

The one-sided melee was like something from an MMA fight, and the entire smackdown was being recorded live on 23 different projection screens.

People were screaming, "Stomp the bitch . . . stomp the bitch . . . stomp the bitch!"

And Tallhya didn't disappoint. She zoned out. She envisioned the faces of her cheating-ass ex, Walter, and his new bitch in place of Buffy's and got to whaling even harder.

"Stomp the bitch . . . Stomp the bitch . . . Stomp the bitch!"

Finally, security showed up. Better late than never, if you were the one getting your face stomped out. But Buffy would have given anything for them to have gotten this crazy bitch off of her a little sooner.

A big black guy wearing a tight yellow T-shirt, who looked like he came straight up off of WrestleMania, snatched Tallhya up like she weighed no more than a ham and cheese sandwich. He had her a good three feet off the ground, carrying her across club's floor, kicking and screaming. The next thing Tallhya knew, she was out the front door on her ass.

A stranger walked up. "Are you okay?"

Tallhya was out of breath. "I'm fine," she said.

The guy handed her a closed bottle of water. "You look thirsty."

She hadn't realized how dry her throat was until the cool water hit the inside of her mouth. *Damn, that shit taste good.* She'd been on an adrenaline rush, and now the rush was quickly turning into an adrenaline crash. She sat on the bench, drinking the cool bottle of water, smiling at how she'd kept her promise. She'd beat the brakes off a bitch at her own Dirty Thirty birthday party.

Thirty definitely had a dirty start for Buffy.

Tallhya was smiling at the ordeal when a massive headache came on. Tallhya took another long drag of water and she was done! She collapsed to the ground, out for the count.

Chapter 19

American Dream

12 hours later

Tallhya woke up on a pissy mattress in a small, dark room that—besides the urine—smelled like old clothes and mildew. She had no idea where she was or how she got there. The last thing she remembered was mopping the floor with that bitch Buffy and getting thrown out of the club. And then she recalled someone offering her a bottle of water. After that was a blank canvas.

She tried to wipe the mucus away from the corners of her eyes, but she was unable to carry out the task. Each of her wrists was encircled with a heavy plastic tie. The plastic ties were intertwined with one another, creating a virtual handcuff. The same contraption was used on her feet. Someone had made her a prisoner. When she attempted to yell out for help, her screams were shortstopped by a rag, which was packed inside her mouth. She had to breathe out of her nose

Click.

Someone cut on a flashlight and pointed the beam into her face.

"I see you're finally awake," said a voice from behind the flashlight. His accent was Haitian, and he spoke with the casualness of a friend or lover. "I'm going to remove the gag," he said, "but when I do, you must promise not to scream. Okay, Tallhya? Nod your head if you understand."

The bright LED light caused the decibles from the drum-like noise reverberating inside her head to increase two-fold.

If you get that fucking light out of my eyes I'll agree to whatever you want, she thought. But since, at the moment, she couldn't speak, she nodded.

The guy with the flashlight and the Haitian accent approved. "Good," he said, then: "I told you that she would be cooperative."

Tallhya and Flashlight weren't the only two in the room?

"They all cooperative when they tied up and shit," said his partner.

Flashlight: "Don't be so negative."

The partner said, "Whatever. Let's just move this shit along."

Flashlight removed the rag from her mouth. "Okay, Tallhya, I need for you to answer a few questions for me. Okay?"

Tallhya had few questions of her own, starting with, "How do you know my name?"

Flashlight said, "I'm psychic. I know many things." To prove his point, he said, "Your name is Natallhya Banks. You're thirty-two years old, and you're from Richmond, Virginia." Then he laughed. Tallhya missed the joke. "Besides," said Flashlight, "it's all right here on your Virginia ID."

Her predicament was getting worse minute by minute.

"What do you want with me?" she asked.

"What do I want?" Flashlight echoed. "Well, Tallhya, I want what everybody in America wants—money! It's the American dream, no? Okay," he said, "your turn is over. Now I ask questions. And your answers will determine whether or not you make it back to Virginia alive, or end up in Mexico selling pussy."

Tallhya said, "I don't have any money."

"Well, as you know, I've already been through your wallet, and based on the stuff I found on your person: two grand worth of hundred-dollar bills, a Consolidated Bank platinum card, an iPhone 6Plus with a Swarovski crystal custom case, Christian Louboutin lipstick, Chanel chain purse . . . Tell the broke shit to someone that don't know better," he said. "I'm sure there is more money somewhere."

Tallhya begged him to believe her. "Trust me," she said, "there isn't any money." After the $150,000 life insurance policy Me-Ma left was divided three ways, Tallhya had spent everything but the twenty thousand she had put up at Rydah's house. Most of if was for the surgery, and the other grand was for a good weave.

Flashlight said, "I'll be the judge of that."

"I take it you're out here on vacation," said the partner. "So if you wanna be back with your family and friends, you need to figure out where to get one hundred and fifty thousand dollars."

"I don't know anyone with that kind of money."

Flashlight wasn't buying it. "You better think about it real hard, then."

Tallhya, just a couple of weeks ago, felt like she had nothing to lose. In fact, she hadn't cared if she lived or died. Now, her life had changed. She had met her sister, who was kind and pushed her to win and wanted nothing less than the best for her. Her self-esteem was building, and finally she had the financial resources to change her lifelong battle with obesity. And after she got her lifestyle under control, she would help others as well. Ironic how at this very moment she wanted nothing more than to survive, to live, to be healthy, and to strive.

"So," the partner said, "who are you out here on vacation with? We take travelers checks." He had a mean look plastered on his face.

For some reason, when Tallhya looked at him, all she saw was his mug shot picture in her mind, with that mean and ugly disposition written all over his face.

Tallhya told the truth. "I'm visiting my sister."

The partner nodded his head.

"Now we're getting somewhere," he said. "What your sister do out here?" He took a not-so-wild guess. "She a dancer?" Half the street girls in Florida either danced or ran scams.

"No," Tallhya said, a bit too defiantly. "She works at a car shop."

"Fuck!" Flashlight rolled his eyes. "That shit no good. What about family back home?"

"Two of my sisters are dead, and the other one has cancer. My mother is dead—and when she was alive she never gave me a dime." Tallhya chose not to mention Me-Ma or the money she left behind. It would only complicate things more than they already were, she thought.

Flashlight or Mean-Mug didn't seem to be moved by her losses. "What about your nigga?"

"He left me for a skinny bitch and cleaned out my bank account before he dipped."

"Fuck! It must really suck being you," Mean-Mug surmised. "You may be better off to everyone selling pussy for a living."

Flashlight tried to make her better understand the predicament. "You know what it's like working whore houses in Mexico? Fucked up. Nigga after nigga, wetback after wetback. You'll be servicing about twenty to thirty smelly dicks each night. You seem like a cool person that's caught a few bad breaks. You've come through before, and I believe that you can get through this. Get us the money so that you can go on with your life."

Think, bitch! Think! Think!

Tallhya stared off into the darkness. A few weeks ago, she was in the crazy house being coerced to take meds she didn't need. That seemed like Disney World right now.

Mean-Mug got an idea. "Does your sister have a dude?" He held Tallhya's phone in his hand. "Who can we call?"

Tallhya started to lie and say no, but the fib died on her lips. "Yeah," she said. "She has a boyfriend, but I don't know him like that.

He may not care enough to pay the price for me. We just met a few days ago. I just met my sister for the first time not even a month ago."

A phone rang with a "We Are Family" ringtone. It was Talhya's.

The partner killed the call, got the number, and then Face-Timed the caller back. When Rydah answered, he pointed the camera toward Tallhya on the urine-saturated mattress with no sheets. He held it just long enough for Rydah to get a brief visual of Tallhya's predicament. Then, the kidnapper texted Rydah from Tallhya's phone

Tallhya: 150K to get her back alive!

On the other end of the phone, Rydah was speechless, but she texted back right away.

Rydah: I'll give you whatever you want. Just don't hurt my sister.

Flashlight's partner handed him the phone. "Look at this shit, man." After Flashlight read the message, they both thought the same thing: *Bingo*.

"I thought you said that your sister worked on cars for a living. What does her nigga do?" Mean-Mug was trying to hide that he wasn't pleased and now he wanted to know if there was a way that he could squeeze more.

"I don't know," Tallhya said honestly. "All I know is that his name is Wolfe and that he's from down here somewhere."

Neither guy could hide behind their poker faces how Tallhya's statement had surprised the hell out of them. The name Wolfe represented money and danger. Everybody in the streets knew that Wolfe was caked up. But the name also meant trouble. Wolfe was an egotistic, ruthless, certified sociopath.

Flashlight said, "Well, Tallhya, your sister seems to be more worried about you than you thought. She says that she's willing to pay to get you home safe. For that, I'm not going to put the rag back in your mouth. But if you act stupid, I'm not only going to gag you . . ."

The partner pulled a pistol from his waist and finished Flashlight's sentence. "I'm going to fuck you with this."

"I—I wont try anything," she stammered. "But I need to use the bathroom. Is it possible to untie me?"

"Piss on yourself, bitch. That's what you been doing."

"But since my sister is paying you, please cut me some slack," Tallhya calmly asked. "Honestly, you don't have to worry about feeding me. Just get my diet pills out of my purse and I will be okay," she said.

"She is human," Flashlight said.

"Get that bitch a bucket and give her them leftover bum-ass wings that I got from The Office the other night."

Mean-Mug looked like he was about to change his mind. He stared her in the face, and she looked as innocent and hopeless as she could. In return, Flashlight placed a bucket and styrofoam takeout tray of old chicken wings in front of her. However, Mean-Mug still studied her.

To reassure them that they were making the right decision by untying her, she said, "I promise I won't do anything crazy."

But she couldn't speak for Wolfe.

Chapter 20

The Shake Down

Tallhya was left alone in the room. She used the time away from her abductors to pray. One after the other, she prayed to God, Me-Ma, Ginger, and Bunny. It was the same prayer each time: *Please help me!*

She even asked (via prayer) for help from her no-earthly-good mother. Maybe the woman who gave birth to her would be a better mother from the grave than she was in real life. One thing for sure, Tallhya surmised, was that reaching out to her mother, whether she was in Heaven or Hell, couldn't make her situation any worse than it already was. Like Me-Ma used to say, "Closed mouths don't get fed."

To the best of her knowledge, it had been about two hours since Flashlight and his partner were last in the room. She couldn't be sure, because she didn't have a watch, and of course she didn't have a phone.

After praying, Tallhya used the time trying to utilize meditation techniques she'd learned from a psychologist while in the crazy hospital. It was useless. Each method required her to do two things: (1) Take deep breaths and (2) Clear her mind completely of all thoughts.

The first one was easy enough, but she didn't have a snowball's chance in Hell of clearing her mind. She was way too nervous for that shit, and there was no logical grounds to relax and clear her mind.

The small room was pin-drop quiet. For some reason, Tallhya's mind kept going back to when she was in that seedy hotel after the bank robbery. She was destitute of not only money, but of hope as well. She'd spent the few pennies she'd gotten from the robbery on the hotel room and food. She wasn't sure if the bank's cameras had captured a good image of her and if the police were hot on her trail. She'd only had six minutes on her prepaid phone, and with nowhere else to turn, Tallhya had cried out to God. Lo and behold, He had not only showed up, but He showed out! In what seemed like the blink of an eye, God had changed her life significantly.

Tallhya kept reminding herself that this was no different. If He thought that she was worth saving then, why would God allow her to be thrown to the wolves now?

Deep in thought, Tallhya began hearing voices. Was she hallucinating? What were audible hallucinations without images called? *Crazy*. Was God trying to speak to her, or was her mind playing tricks on her?

Turned out that it was neither. The voices manifested from the devils outside the room where their captive was tied up. Prince (AKA Flashlight), and his partner Abe (AKA Mean-Mug), weighed their options.

Sitting on a ratty sofa, Prince expressed his concerns. "I don't think it's the right move, trying to shake that nigga Wolfe down."

Prince and Abe had been friends since the sandbox and had always been tighter than fish pussy. They were like peanut butter and jelly, different but complimenting each other.

Abe wholeheartedly disagreed with his homeboy's rationality. "Fuck Wolfe! He not exempt from the game." Abe, sitting across from Prince in a mismatched corduroy recliner, was adamant. "It's 'bout time somebody man up and get at dude. Shiiiit!" he exclaimed. "Might as well be us."

Prince shook his head. He'd heard wicked stories about Wolfe—each more treacherous than the next. The man was not only vicious, but he was also relentless. Prince once heard that Wolfe waited a whole year to murk a dude who'd dinged the door of his new Bentley parked in a Wal-Mart parking lot. Wolfe investigated the indiscretion for months. He wrote down the plate number of every car parked in his section of the lot and questioned them all. When Wolfe finally found out the identity of the perpetrator, dude was serving a six-month skid bid in Turner Guilford Knight Correctional Center for driving without a license. When he got out, Wolfe gave the careless asshole the opportunity to pay what it had cost to get the ding out. He'd even saved the receipt. Dude made a fatal mistake of thinking Wolfe's request was optional.

"Wolfe isn't going to let no shit like that go without serious repercussions and consequences. You know that's right." Prince made sure his buddy understood what they were agreeing on.

"Like I said," Abe spit, "fuck that one-legged, cripple-ass nigga! You scared of a gimp? Just say you scared, bro," Abe teased. "A scared-ass nigga is what I ain't ever known you to be. Guess this some new shit you on."

"It's not about being scared," Prince said. He set the empty beer can down on the floor. "This chick was supposed to be a quick lick until we got all the details down on the armored truck heist. Get us enough cash to hold us over."

"Never count unhatched eggs," Abe sagely said. "That armored truck play is set to go in motion in a few weeks. This shit here . . ." he said, "is here and now. I'm not passing up on nooooo fucking bread, bro. This is how we play it. We call the sister back and tell her to tell Wolfe to cough up the hundred fifty K or we kill Tallhya. And after we kill her, then we gon' find his bitch and make him pay to get her back, too."

"Man, that's real ambitious, and I like your ambition," he told his buddy. "But the last thing we need is to be going to war with Wolfe!" Prince fully understood the dangers of fucking with a nigga like Wolfe, but all Abe saw was money signs. He felt that their team was invincible.

"Once we take the armored truck out, we'll have enough bread to go to war with whoever." Abe was sure about that. "Bet that, my nigga."

"That's not the point," said Prince, speaking with plenty of logic.

"Money is the point, my man. Always has been and always will be. Anything else is pointless. So let's just focus on the grind: one bitch, one truck, one lick at a time."

Prince chuckled. "Speaking of bitches," he said, "here comes yours."

"Heyyyyy, boo. I called your phone. Why you ain't answer?"

"Busy." Abe looked annoyed. "And didn't I tell you not to come over here unannounced?"

"What was I supposed to do?" Buffy said. "I needed to speak with you, and when I called, you didn't answer."

Abe was blunt. "What da fuck you want?"

Buffy shouted, "I want to kill that bitch!"

"So go ahead and tell the entire fucking neighborhood?" a twisted-face Abe said.

"I! Want! That! Bitch! Dead!" Buffy screamed, emphasizing each word to get her point across. "And I want her to die a fucking slow, painful death!"

In the other room, Tallhya could hear everything and recognized Buffy's whiny voice. Her heart dropped.

Fuck! Ain't this a bitch. If it weren't for bad luck, I wouldn't have any luck at all.

She didn't like the way this was going. When she first heard Buffy's voice, her heart dropped. Now it was racing 90 miles per hour.

"I want that bitch dead!" she heard Buffy scream.

Fuck, the feeling is mutual. She tried to be optimistic. *They won't kill me as long as they think they can get paid.* However, optimism was hard to maintain when one's survival hung in the hands of a bitch one just stomped out. After they got the money, what would keep them from killing her then? Her existence would no longer hold any value for them. In fact, it would be the opposite; she would be a liability.

Before she knew it, Tallhya began to hyperventilate. Tears and sweat rolled down her cheeks. Then she heard a voice in her head. This time it really did emanate from inside of her.

You got God!

The three simple words calmed her down.

You got God!

Then she heard Me-Ma's voice. *"And with Him, who can be against you?"*

Then came Bunny's voice. *"Bitch, if you don't drag that motherfucking bitch again and beat the living shit and fucking daylights out of her when you get out of here! Teach her about fucking with us Banks sisters!"*

Next was Ginger's voice. *"Biiiiiitch, you never crack under pressure! If you don't get your game face on! Focus on getting out of here in one piece and getting skinny motherfucking skinny and fly and stunt on all these motherfuckers."*

Then lastly, she could hear typical Deidra in her head. *"I know good and well you ain't stunting these motherfuckers. Focus on that money—play your role and figure out how to get their plans on that armored truck. Fuck everything! Fuck your feelings! Focus on that money!"*

"Calm the fuck down," Abe said.

"Calm down? Look at my motherfucking face." Buffy turned so that Abe could get a better angle. She turned the volume down on her voice a few notches, but she was clearly still angry. "That bitch fucked my face up completely."

Abe had to agree.

"Yeah, your face is fucked up." Her face was red and blue and swollen.

Prince said, "Day-um!" and turned away. "Bitch got a mean hook. Remind me of my sister!"

Buffy ignored Prince and whined to Abe, "I had to get stitches and everything . . . ." She was laying it on thick.

Tallhya thought, *Good for that bitch! A permanent scar! Bitch is going to always remember me and my sister, even if I'm dead! Mission accomplished.*

"I want y'all to handle that bitch," Buffy said. "I want her dead. She embarrassed me at my own shit. I want her and her sister Rydah to die! Both of them dead! I hate them bitches."

Prince said, "Ain't that the same chick you wanted to lick just a few months ago? Now you want her dead because her sister retaliated on some shit you instigated and lined up?"

Abe left the emotions out of the equation. Once the emotions were gone, all that was left was the money. He said, "Miss me with that shit,

Buffy. She's worth way more to me alive than dead, any day of the week. Matter of fact, I'ma hit you up later. Just go on home, lay low, and let your mug heal," he suggested. "Instead of running 'round these streets all destructive and shit."

"Go home and do what?" she questioned.

"For once," Abe said, "just do what I tell you to do. Go home. Stay off the phones and social media. Don't let nobody know shit. Just keep your mouth shut. Do everybody that justice, please."

"A'ight." Buffy acquiesced. Then she said, "Are you going to pick up when I call you?"

"Stop fucking playing with me, Buffy, and do what I say to do, a'ight?"

It seemed like hours, but it was only a few beats of silence. For a second, Tallhya thought that they were going to come into the room. Then she heard a door slam. Hard.

"That bitch is bad news, man . . . bad fucking news!" a disgusted Prince said to Abe. "She gon' get you killed before it's all over with. And me too, if I ain't careful. Shit!"

"At the end of the day, Buffy be 'bout that paper," Abe said. "How many of them fake, flossing-ass niggas has she lined up for us?" Abe asked. "A boat load. That's how many. A fucking boat load. More than you can remember. That's how many. As long as she keeps food on our plates, she's all right with me. So be grateful."

"For sure," Prince said. "She's come through in the past, but everything gets old sooner or later. I'm just saying that the bitch may have run her course. Bit by bit, you sacrificing pieces of your swag and your good sense fucking with this chick. You put too much faith in her. A snake is a friend to no one. It's only a snake. Just because it doesn't bite you right away doesn't mean that it never will."

"I have to admit," Abe said with a nod, "she is a heartless bitch. That's her best quality, though."

That was the first thing the two lifelong friends had agreed on all day

All Tallhya wanted right now was to be released and get out of there, get her surgery, heal, and start living the life that she should have been living a long time ago.

As time turtled by, Tallhya continued to lie on the pissy mattress, exercising patience and faith, and somehow tuning that smell out.

Suddenly, Abe walked in. Before she could sit up, he grabbed her by the hair with one hand and punched her in the face with the other. He hit her so hard she went out.

"That's for giving my bitch a black eye on her birthday." When she woke up, he wrapped his hands around her neck, choking her. That was all she remembered before blacking out again.

"Miss?"

Someone was trying to get her attention.

"Miss?"

When she came to, Tallhya only had vision in one eye. The other was covered with some type of bandage. She could barely see out of the one that wasn't covered. Everything was blurry. People were standing over her, but she couldn't make out much of anything else. A few beats later, she realized that the people standing over her were paramedics.

Everything seemed to move in slow motion.

Tallhya heard a lady with a high-pitched Spanish accent speaking to someone as the medics strapped her onto a stretcher.

Someone said, "They dumped her from a green van. I thought she was dead."

"Thank you, ma'am. Do you mind coming downtown to give a statement and look at a few photos?"

"I'm kind of busy."

"It wont take long"

"Well . . ." the Spanish lady reluctantly said, "okay. But I only have a minute."

"Yes, ma'am."

A paramedic with red hair asked, "Does she have a pulse?"

There were two fingers on her wrist.

"It's weak, but she has one!" He wore his hair in dreads.

Red Head said, "Thank God, ma'am, that you called when you did."

Tallhya could feel the gurney being lifted into the back of the ambulance. She felt sick to her stomach.

Speaking into the radio, one paramedic said, "We have a black woman in her late twenties, early thirties, possible heroin OD."

OD?

Other than the drugs administered to her at the mental hospital, Tallhya had never abused a drug in her life.

"No track marks," said Red Head.

"Probably a recreational user."

Tallhya tried to respond, but her body wouldn't cooperate.

"Vitals low."

"Oh, shit!"

"What?"

"Her heartbeat's dropping rapidly. She may not make it."

Chapter 21

Lunch Money

Rydah had wired the $150,000 to the bank account the abductors had specified. Wolfe came through with the cash like it was lunch money. He didn't want to give in to suckers trying to shake him down, but he felt bad for Rydah that these fools were holding Tallhya, doing who knows what to her.

Rydah felt horrible. God forbid if Tallhya didn't live. She would never forgive herself. She kept running everything through her head from the day of Tallhya's disappearance.

Wolfe took the phone away from his ear and said to Rydah, "Stop beating yourself up, babe!" He'd been on the phone with everybody he trusted, trying to find out how this had happened. Right now he was talking to a guy named Jack Fishy. Jack Fishy was an ex-bail bondsman and ex-bounty hunter turned private investigator. Everyone called him Fishy.

Fishy had a reputation of being able to find anyone, anywhere. People in the street joked that Obama had hired Fishy to find Osama Bin Laden.

"I need your services," Wolfe said. "Someone snatched my sister-in-law and shook me down for a hundred fifty G."

Fishy said, "I'm on it. It shouldn't be hard following a trail of money that large." Within five minutes, Fishy knew that the money had been transferred through a Bahamian bank. "As you know, peoples who transact a lot of shady money or just wants to duck taxes think of Nassau as a baby Swiss banking system. But it isn't as sophisticated as people think. I'm on it, Wolfe."

The street's lips were tight for the moment, or no one knew anything. And someone always knew something.

Vexed, he hung up the phone. "I promise, baby, when I find out who's behind this . . . I don't even want the money back," he said. "But on everything I love,"—which wasn't much— "they going to pay dearly."

Rydah knew better than to say anything to try to stop him. Nor did she want to.

Wolfe saw the anxiety etched in Rydah's face. "Baby, I promise you everything will be okay."

He took her into his arms. It hurt Wolfe seeing Rydah broken up the way she was. This was the very reason why he hated being in a relationship, because your enemies targeted the things you loved most.

"Why haven't they called? We paid them what they asked for."

Rydah had to ask her parents to use their account to wire the money. She didn't want to tell them, but she didn't know what else to do.

"They'll call," said Wolfe, but in his heart, he knew that it could go either way. They could kill her just as easily as they could release her. It was 50/50.

Rydah felt helpless and angry, and she secretly wished that Buffy paid for what had happened. Every time she thought of all the tragic ways she wished Buffy would die, Rydah had to ask God for forgiveness.

The text came from a private number

Unknown: Your sister is on the way to the hospital.

Rydah almost threw up. How bad was she hurt?

Chapter 22

The Lady Lagoon

"Someone probably slipped you a roofie," the doctor concluded. "You said the last thing you remembered was drinking the water, then waking up in a strange place?"

It had been a few hours since arriving to the hospital, and Tallhya was laying in the bed, trying to take everything in. She still couldn't believe what had happened, or that she was alive to tell the story.

"Yes."

"Do you remember being given drugs of any kind?" the young Spanish doctor asked with a raised eyebrow.

"Yes! Ummm . . . no . . . ummm, I don't know." Tallhya searched her brain but couldn't be sure. "I don't remember."

"Was there any kind of intercourse?" he asked.

"No!" A pause. "I don't think so."

The doctor patted her on the shoulder. "You are safe now. We will take good care of you."

Once the doctor left, Rydah said to Tallhya, "Miami isn't the place for you to be running the streets alone. What the hell were you thinking about? I work late for one night and everything goes to shit."

Wolfe said, "Let's just focus on the fact that Tallhya is here with us now."

"I guess you are right, but I still don't like what happened to my sister."

"None of us do. And whoever's responsible will pay for it."

Tallhya thanked Wolfe for coming up with the money. "I promise I will pay you back."

"Don't mention it," Wolfe said. "Just keep me out the doghouse with your sister," he half joked.

"I'll do the best I can."

Wolfe then asked, "Did Buffy have something to do with this?"

"She told them to kill me. But they said I was worth more money alive than dead."

"What else do you remember?"

"Not much."

Rydah's parents entered the room, and that was Wolfe's signal to exit, but he didn't want to make it obvious, so he stayed for a few minutes longer.

Maestro came with people from his church, rejoicing that Tallhya was alive and safe. Amanda couldn't stop talking about how the two sisters needed to be more careful and stop being so trusting.

Wolfe held face as long as he could, but it was time for him to leave. He needed to hit the streets and get to the bottom of things. He said his good-byes and left the room.

Wolfe was at The Lady Lagoon on business. The manager told him that the owner would be out to see him shortly. To pass the time, Wolfe copped a seat at one of the strip club's ten bars, nursing a Heineken and a double shot of Remy. On stage to his left, a half-naked dancer gave him the eye. She was mixed: half Chinese and half black, but it was obvious to anyone with eyes that the black genes were the more dominant of the two. The honey was as thick as a bowl of oatmeal and fine as a summer evening on a white-sand beach. Wolfe wasn't the least bit interested and ignored her advances.

The Lady Lagoon was open 24/7, had four stages, and kept at least forty strippers on payroll at all times, even on the slowest nights.

On the weekends, there were sometimes as many as two hundred girls making niggas throw money like it was water and they were trying to put out a fire.

The owner of The Lady Lagoon was a man named Jaffey Logan, a serial club owner and legend among anyone in that circle. He had a long history of owning spots throughout South Florida, mainly Miami, and he had his hand in every part of the industry, from clubs to liquor to promotions to prostitution. Jaffey knew as much about running night clubs as Sam Walton knew about retail. In the 80's and 90's when the nightlife scene was at an all-time high, Jaffey sat at the top of the mountain and collected an avalanche of money. Unfortunately, when the bubble burst, the paper evaporated as quickly as it came.

After finishing his phone call with the liquor warehouse, Jaffey exited his office donning a fresh pair green gators and a green linen suit. He was told that someone was waiting to see him, and that someone was no other than Wolfe. Adjusting the angle of his hat, Jaffey wondered what Wolfe wanted with him. Wolfe wasn't the type that frequented clubs of any kind, unless it was an absolute necessity. Never for pleasure.

Jaffey spotted Wolfe sitting at the bar and reluctantly began walking in that direction. He owed Wolfe a little over ten million dollars.

Wolfe was still facing the bar when Jaffey snuck up behind him. The music was blasting. Jaffey was about to tap him on the shoulder.

Wolfe said, "I wouldn't do that if I were you."

How the hell did he see me? Jaffey wondered.

"Have a seat." Wolfe finished off his cognac and placed the empty glass on the bar.

"What brings you to this side of the Intracoastal, my man?" Jaffey wasn't used to Wolfe just popping up. "I thought you said I could have until the end of the month to make that payment. After Memorial Day."

When the recession hit in '08, puncturing the real estate market, Jaffey reached out to Wolfe for help. Wolfe knew that Jaffey was a legend in the business, but he also knew that Jaffey had vices. If Jaffey hadn't been an owner, he would have been an owner's best customer. He loved women, gambling, cocaine, and flossing, a mixture that, more times than not, led to a dead end.

In all actuality, it wasn't a really good idea for Jaffey to have his own strip clubs, because he indulged with the help too much—but no one could deny that he knew how to get the people to come to not just the strip clubs, but the party clubs as well. That was why Wolfe floated Jaffey the first $2 million. He genuinely had love for the dude. Wolfe also believed in Jaffey, although he knew that he would probably never get all of his money back.

Jaffey always did what he could, and everything wasn't about money. Because Jaffey knew people in high places, he was better off to Wolfe alive than dead. So Wolfe continued to bankroll his clubs, but not lately—the buck had stopped, but the tab was still there, and Jaffey always paid something. He never wanted be on Wolfe's bad side. Who in their right mind would?

And this was why Jaffey rolled the red carpet out to Rydah at any club she wanted to go to. Most times she was treated better than a lot of so-called celebrities. Jaffey made sure that all of his staff knew who she was, and if they didn't damn near bend over to kiss her ass, they were fired on the spot. It was the least he could do considering the ballooning tab that he owed her man.

When Wolfe said, "I'm not here about the payments," Jaffey breathed easier. Until then, he'd been holding his breath.

"Then what can I do for you?"

"I need all of the surveillance tapes from Club Hoax."

Jaffey was both relieved and confused. He was relieved that Wolfe hadn't come for an early payment, and he was confused as to why Wolfe would want the surveillance tapes from Club Hoax. "Is there something I should know about? You never struck me as the type that needed to check up on his woman."

Wolfe said, "How and when I check on my lady is none of your business. But that's not the reason I'm asking for the footage. I got a hunch that the footage may clarify for me."

Jaffey knew better than to ask what the hunch was about. Wolfe was relentless and methodical when he had had a hunch. Best to leave well enough alone. "No problem," he said.

Wolfe made it clear what he wanted. "I need all the footage—from both inside and outside the club—for the past three weeks."

"It's going to take me a day or two to get it together, but you got it." He didn't want to make Wolfe upset. "And for the record," he said, "I always treat Rydah like the queen that she is, giving her carte blanche."

"Appreciate it," Wolfe said.

"Don't mention it. She's so beautiful and classy and carries herself as a lady."

"Yeah, she sure does," Wolfe bluntly said.

Jaffey nixed the ass-kissing and small talk and got straight to the request. "I'll make the call immediately. And as for the payment, I'll have it for you right after Memorial Day. It's always real fruitful for me around those times."

"For the entire city," Wolfe said.

Wolfe finished his Heineken, talked to a few people who were vying for his attention, and then kept it pushing. Business as usual.

Chapter 23

The Fonz

Tallhya was discharged from the Memorial Regional Hospital at 9:17. Rydah had been waiting there to pick her up since six in the morning. Outside, the sky was slate gray and gloomy. Tallhya thought it was apropos to the way she felt inside.

Due to the injuries she incurred—two fractured ribs and a bruised eye socket—the doctor informed Tallhya that any cosmetic surgeries she'd planned would have to be postponed for at least six weeks. Six weeks was the "if she was lucky" date.

The news hit her like a cement bag in the gut, knocking what little wind was left in her already nearly depleted sails.

Rydah decided to make a detour before taking Tallhya to her parents' house, stopping by a little trendy diner downtown, where the food was

always on point. Rydah ordered two of the spe-
cials: 2 eggs (prepared any way you like), home
fries, bacon, sausage (or ham), and buttered
toast with jelly. As always, the cook did his thing.
The food was delectable.

Rydah chomped off half a sausage link in
one bite and chased it with a forkful of cheesy
scrambled eggs.

Tallhya's plate went untouched.

"Why aren't you eating?"

"Don't have much of an appetite."

If she couldn't get her surgery, then Tallhya
figured she would starve herself to lose the
weight. She was tired of being labeled "the cute
big one" or "the fat Banks sister."

Rydah took another bite of the sausage. "You
should at least try your home fries," she said.

"At least be woman enough to stare," Tallhya
said loudly enough for the two women who were
stealing glances at her when they thought she
wasn't looking. "Bitches!" She said to Rydah,
"Can we get out of here?"

Pushing her plate away, Rydah said, "Sure.
If you don't want to be here, we out." Rydah
dipped into her purse, pulling out a couple of
twenty-dollar bills and a ten. She left the money
on the table.

Back in the Lamborghini, Tallhya said, "You
could've taken a doggie bag."

"Now you say that shit." Rydah jokingly rolled her eyes. "I didn't want to make you stay anywhere you didn't want to be. I just thought you might have wanted something good to eat after chowing down on hospital food for the past three days. And that place makes the best damn home fries in the city."

"My bad."

Rydah hung a left on Biscayne. "Nope. It's my bad for not asking if you were cool with being out so soon. We can hit 'em up some other time."

For weeks afterward, all Tallhya did was eat, sleep, and cry. When she wasn't sleeping, she was crying, and when she wasn't crying, she was sleeping. Once or twice, she managed to do both at the same time, eventually crying herself to sleep.

When she was asleep, she often dreamed about life after she got the surgery done. The image was the same every time she had the dream: a skinny version of herself rocking a tiny bikini on a sandy beach. And then she would awaken and start crying all over again. It seemed as if everyone in the state of Florida was thin, taunting her for being out of shape. Deep down, Tallhya knew that she was being irrational, but it was how she felt.

In her eyes, the only good thing that had happened to her since being released from the hospital was Aunt Amanda. Like the mother Tallhya never had, Amanda nursed and catered to her every need every single day. Tallhya secretly wished that Amanda had been her real mother instead of Deidra. That it was she who had been adopted by her Uncle Maestro, instead of Rydah.

Day by day, with Amanda's help, Tallhya recovered from her injuries. During this time, since Tallhya had seemed to sink deep into depression, Rydah and Tallhya barely spoke. Rydah hated it. She'd finally been reunited with one of her estranged sisters, and they weren't doing anything together. All Tallhya wanted to do was lay in bed, tuning out the world.

Rydah could no longer take it. She burst into the guest room where Tallhya was staying. "Enough is enough!" Rydah shook her. When Tallhya opened her eyes, Rydah screamed, "Bish, get out the bed and get dressed. And when you're done, put these on." She handed her sister a pair of big-framed Chopard sunglasses. "We're going out today, and I'm not taking no for an answer."

Tallhya looked at Rydah like she'd lost her mind. "Why you gotta be so damn loud—waking me up and shit?" With an exaggerated yawn and stretch, she said, "I was sleeping good."

"It's freaking one o'clock in the freaking afternoon," Rydah told her. "Time to get up."

Just then, Amanda came into the room, carrying a tray. "Time for brunch." Amanda had cooked French toast and bacon, and she'd put fresh strawberries and blueberries in a bowl on the side so that Tallhya would have the option to put the fruit on her French toast or eat it separately. Rydah swiped a piece of bacon as Amanda placed the tray on the night table beside the bed.

"Don't mess with my food."

"Oh," said Rydah, "now all of a sudden you full of energy and stuff."

Tallhya ignored her.

Rydah asked Amanda, "How does she just get to sleep the days away? Didn't you give her the house rules, the ones you implemented on me?" The house rules had always been, *If the banks are open, you should be out of bed.* "It's unfair."

"You treat her better than me," Rydah said in a little girl's voice.

Amanda waved off Rydah's complaints. "The girl is healing from a traumatic event. Wait until she gets her strength back."

The way she's being pampered, Tallhya may never get her strength back, Rydah thought.

Tallhya stuck her tongue out behind Amanda's back, teasing.

"Rules are rules. In this house, nobody is allowed to sleep past nine a.m.," Rydah said, pulling the covers away from Tallhya, almost forcing the linen to land on the floor. "Now get up!"

"Mother Amanda, she keeps bothering me," Tallhya complained. "Tell her to let me rest. And she's being mean to me, too."

"You a snitch now?" Rydah rolled her eyes.

"Rydah, that's no way to treat your sister."

Rydah sighed. "Mommmm. . . ."

"Especially," Amanda reminded her daughter, "the sister that you claimed to have been waiting your entire life to meet. Did you know that Rydah used to cry herself to sleep at night because she wanted a sister to play with?"

"And once she has one, she's mean to me."

"But she needs to get up," Rydah protested. "She just can't sleep her life away."

Amanda agreed with Rydah. "Some fresh air would do you good, Tallhya. But you girls have to promise to be safe and not overdo it."

Rydah quickly said, "We know. Now get up, my dear sister, so we can get some fresh air as our beautiful mother has requested." Rydah smiled, side-eyeing her sister. "Honor thy mother and thy days will be longer. Those are the Bible's words, not mines."

Tallhya tried one last excuse. "I have nothing to wear. Remember, I didn't bring any clothes because I thought I was going to be doing shopping for my flat stomach and small waist after the surgery."

"Mm-hmm. I knew you were going to try to pull that. That's exactly why I got you this." She went into her backpack and pulled out a Pink sweat suit. "You got thirty minutes to shower and get dressed. Hurry up."

Before leaving the room, Amanda suggested that Tallhya should put something in her stomach. "And drink some juice," she said. "Hydrate, dear, hydrate!"

Forty-five minutes later, outside in the driveway, Rydah had another surprise for her sister.

Tallhya was tongue-tied. Parked in the driveway was a white four-door BMW 645. "Stop playing, Rydah. This is for me?"

"It was a salvage. I redid the entire thing myself." Rydah handed her the keys. "For you, my sister."

Rydah shouted. "Oh! My! God!"

"Now let's go to the mall and get you a few outfits. My treat."

After a couple of hours of shopping and a few stores later, Tallhya said, "I'm hungry."

"Me too."

The sisters decided to have lunch at a place called Gourmet Dărê. It was a new chic restaurant that Rydah had been wanting to try ever since the doors opened to rave reviews six months ago. They were seated by their hostess near a 500-gallon aquarium that was home to a colony of tropical fish of every size and hue.

The two had been giggling and laughing since they sat down.

Rydah drank her lemonade from a crystal champagne glass. "Girl, you so crazy."

"Naw," said Tallhya, "that's you." At the table, they were discussing a multitude of topics like family, relationships, movies, and purchases they'd made earlier that day.

Rydah told Tallhya, "I think you should've gotten the silver Swarovski crystal shoes instead of the black ones."

Having a bit of buyer's remorse, Tallhya agreed.

"Don't get it twisted. You can never go wrong with black, but those silver ones were everything. Like, because you are my long-lost sister," she said, "I would've splurged for them both if you wanted."

Tallhya took another bite of her entrée; it was the best grilled salmon she'd ever eaten. She said, "You know you are more flamboyant than me. You're so much like Bunny it's scary. Y'all two would've stayed fighting over each other's clothes."

"For real?" Rydah couldn't help but get excited when she talked about the siblings she'd never met. "I wish I could've known her."

"I promise you would have loved her and hated her at the same time, because her paws would've stayed using her five-finger discount on your stuff," Tallhya said then changed the subject to something less sad. "Do you think that my feet will drop a size after my surgery? I read that somewhere online."

"Ummmm . . . I never heard that one before."

"Ladies . . ." A guy walked up to their table.

The two sisters eyeballed him.

"Not to intrude or be rude, I'm sure that you hear it all the time, but it's worth saying it again: you two are so beautiful. Are you twins?"

"Thank you for the compliment," Tallhya said. "And no, we're not twins."

"But we're sisters," Rydah chimed in. It felt good to say she had a sister. Plenty of girlfriends had come and gone, claiming to be her sister until they got bitchy and petty, but this was different. No matter what happened, good or bad, nothing could change the fact that their blood bonded them together forever.

"Really?" said the gentleman. "Your father must have strong genes."

"You mean our mother," Tallhya said. "We look like our mother."

"Well,"—he tipped his hat—"let her know that she did the world a real great service by giving birth to such beautiful beings."

Rydah was about to tell the stranger to fuck off, but in a nice way, when the waiter approached with the one-hundred-dollar bill, placing it on the table.

In true gentlemanly fashion, the stranger picked it up. "I would love the honor of taking care of the tab for two beautiful ladies." Before they could say no, he dug into the pocket of his linen trousers and came out with a black American Express card.

For the first time, Rydah checked him out. He was carrying three bags: two from Saks-Fifth Avenue and a Hublot watch boutique bag. His skin was smooth and brown like expensive chocolate. He was at least six feet tall with a short haircut, and he was very dapperly dressed in a linen button-down shirt, Louis loafers (no socks), and a diamond-studded Rolex watch.

Rydah knew that Miami was the hub for credit card scammers, AKA swipers, and she was well aware that they came in all shades, colors, and sizes. There was no stereotype to put them in. Miami was home to the most sophisticated scammers in the world.

Rydah studied him, knowing that in Miami there were three classes of people: the haves, the have-nots, and the haves who have not paid for a damn thing, AKA the scammers. If she had to bet on it, there was something and everything about this fella that said he was definitely a have.

Tallhya thanked the stranger for his generosity.

He smiled and said, "Mind if I sit for a second?" as he slid into the booth beside Tallhya.

"Looks like you already did."

"Forgive me if you think that I'm being too presumptuous. It's not every day that a man gets to sit next to a gorgeous lady such as yourself. I like to take advantage when life offers me opportunities as such."

Tallhya instantly noticed that his cologne was intoxicating and his swag was definitely on point.

Rydah said, "Thanks for picking up our bill, but um . . . I don't even know what to call you. My name is Rydah; and you are?" She extended her hand.

He cleared his throat. "My name is Alphonso. But my endearing friends call me Fonz."

"I'm Natallhya, and my endearing friends call me Tallhya.'"

"Well, Tallhya, I hope to one day be able to call you Tallhya."

This guy was really pushing it at Tallhya, hardcore, Rydah noticed, but Tallhya was being reserved. She wanted yell to her sister, "Don't let him get away!"

Tallhya was intrigued, but she was also skeptical. She asked, "Do you live around here?"

"On Sunny Isles."

"Fancy," Rydah said, knowing that Sunny Isles was dubbed the French Riveria of Florida, filled with high-rise, high-dollar condos on the ocean.

"I like it," he modestly said.

"And who are you shopping for?" Tallhya nodded toward his bags

Again, he beamed that enticing white smile. "I got myself a suit, a couple of shirts and a little watch."

"A Hublot is no *little watch*," Rydah said. "I think it would be better described as a time-piece," she said as her eyes pierced the bag.

Fonz turned to Tallhya. "May I ask if you're married or not? I mean, I don't see a ring or anything."

"Nope," Rydah answered for her. "She's not married."

"Relationship?"

"My sister is new to town," Rydah said. "She's been divorced for quite some time now."

"Well, this question is for you, Natallhya. Are you open for dinner with me, let's say, any time in the next couple of days?"

"Ummm . . ." Tallhya wasn't sure how to respond. "I don't even know you," she said. "And I'm not in the business of really hanging out with strangers."

"That's why we should go to dinner, to get to know each other."

"Well, ummm . . ." Tallhya hesitated, turning red. The truth of the matter was that she was a little intimidated. Walter was the only man she had ever really dated, and he stole all of her money and tore her self-esteem down to dust in the process. She couldn't believe someone as handsome as Fonz wanted to get to know her. What was his motive?

Sitting down, he must not be able to tell how big I am, she thought. *But what if he doesn't care?*

Tallhya wasn't ready to take the chance of entertaining the idea of someone actually liking her and getting her feelings hurt. It was almost easier not to open up that can of worms than to gamble with her feelings.

As if he could read her mind, before Tallhya could turn him down, he said, "Let's at least exchange numbers. Take it back to the old school. Get to know each other a little over the phone, and then dinner? Can you go along with that?" He was confident in his delivery.

Not nearly as confident as Fonz was, Tallhya said, "I guess."

Pulling out his phone, Fonz wasted no time. "So, what's your number?"

Tallhya gave it to him, and Fonz locked it in.

He asked, "Are you going to answer when I call?" Her phone rang. "That's me. Lock me in."

"I wouldn't have given you the number if I didn't plan to answer," she said.

"And what's your number, sister? Just in case Natallhya doesn't answer, I'm going to call you to get her on the phone for me. Deal?"

Rydah laughed.

Fonz said, "I'm dead serious."

Rydah could see that Tallhya was a little shell shocked, so she took it upon herself to ask the tough questions. "Exactly what is it that you want with my sister?"

Fonz responded by saying, "I'm not sure what your question is."

"What are your intentions with my sister?" she said, rephrasing her query.

"Just to get to know her better."

Tallhya interjected. "That's what they all say."

"Well, I'm not them all by a long shot," countered Fonz. "But if you don't give me a chance, I can't prove you wrong."

"Give the brother a chance, sis. And if he's full of shit, you already know we'll deal with him."

"I'm shaking in my boots."

Rydah said, "You should be."

"All I'm asking is to be given a chance," Fonz said. He stood up. "But I'm not going to intrude on your time or space too much longer."

Both Rydah and Tallhya were pleasantly impressed with him. Tallhya thanked him for paying their restaurant tab again.

"Hopefully it will be the first of many." Before parting, he said, "I'm going to call you tonight, okay? Pick up and hear me out."

Rydah assured him, "She'll listen as long as you're not blowing hot air."

"That's all that I ask of you. The ear of a good girl that's not all caught up in the streets."

When Fonz left, Rydah exclaimed, "Girrrlllll, he was fine! And he threw himself at you. You're sitting there acting all nonchalant and shit, like you a boss playa or something."

Tallhya wasn't as optimistic. "He's only seen me sitting down," she said. "He has no idea how big I really am."

"Girl, please. Dude sat beside you, checking you out like you was the last top model or something. He was so engulfed in you that he hardly even knew I was sitting over here."

"I just don't have the energy for all the bullshit, lies, and let-downs that come with an insincere relationship."

"I'm not asking you to marry the dude. Just go out to dinner and get to know him. See what he's talking about. Have a nice time. You owe it to yourself."

Tallhya nodded. "I'll do it." She giggled. "Dude was hella cute, wasn't he?"

"Like a cold drink of water. Now, let's hit up a couple more stores, sis!"

Chapter 24

Bad Time to Post

Good food, a handsome gentleman, and countless shopping bags filled with fabulous finds later, before they knew it, the time had flown by and the stores were closing. The shopping spree was nearly over as the girls headed to the car, giggling.

Rydah had never seen Tallhya so happy. "Today was definitely a good day," she said as they neatly placed their bags into the trunk of the BMW.

Tallhya couldn't front. "I had a blast. Thanks, sis—for everything. Who knew what some fresh air and a little retail therapy could do for the sick and shut-in?"

"Well, I'm not one to say I told you so, but . . ." Then her phone chimed. "It's a text from Mom. She wants me to remind you to take your meds."

"Damn! I'd forgotten, too."

Rydah said, "And you know it took her forever to compose that text message. She old school."

They laughed.

Rydah closed the trunk while Tallhya headed to the driver's side of the BMW. "You cool with driving still?" Rydah asked. "If you're tired, I can take the wheel."

"I'm good. You going to have to pry that steering wheel from my cold, dead hands."

"I hope not." Rydah was about to get in on the passenger's side before she changed her mind. "Let me go get us some bottled waters so you can take your meds. I don't wanna hear Mother's mouth," she said. "And trust me, you don't either." She laughed as she reached for a few singles out of her billfold. "Hydrate! Hydrate! Hydrate!" Rydah imitated her mother.

"I know that's right. You don't want her to beat your ass for not looking after her new favorite daughter," Tallhya teased.

Rydah said over her shoulder, "You wish," as she walked away from the car.

Tallhya cranked the engine and cut on the A.C. As she waited for Rydah to return with the waters, she checked on social media. It had been a while since she had been on any of the sites.

The moment she began scrolling Facebook, she saw it. Buffy had blasted her timeline with selfies, one after another.

Another one.

Who the fuck posts this many selfies wearing the same outfit, just slightly different poses? Tallhya answered her own question. *This bitch Buffy, that's who.*

For some reason, the pictures of Buffy smiling made her more furious by the second. She didn't think Buffy had a right to be happy, posting all over social media like nothing had happened. Tallhya looked into the rearview mirror. When she took off the sunglasses, though it wasn't as bad and it was healing, the bruise was still visible on her eye. Her blood rose by a couple degrees, instantly.

Tallhya slapped the steering wheel of her car. *This bitch ain't learned about posting yet! That was the way I got at yo' ass the last time.*

Tallhya studied the screen. Then it hit her. *Wait a minute!*

Buffy was at Bal Harbour Mall . . . the same mall she and Rydah were at.

God works in mysterious ways, doesn't He?

She zeroed in closer and studied the pictures. In a few of the photos, Buffy was with two other chicks. If the last couple of photos were an indication, they were on the second level parking deck, one level below where she was parked. It was indeed a small world, with so many big possibilities.

Tallhya looked over her shoulder. Rydah was making her way back to the car. Tallhya geared it into reverse as Rydah got in.

"Here you go."

Tallhya took a sip of the water. "Buckle your seatbelt," she said. "Tight."

Rydah's expression said, "What's up?" as she buckled her safety belt.

Tallhya simply said, "Today may be our lucky day." Then she smiled at her sister and tapped the gas. The engine of the Beamer purred.

On deck 2, Buffy stood in the middle of the lot, still posing and taking selfies, paying attention to nothing but the angle of her camera. Tallhya zeroed in on the little ho and mashed the gas. In her mind, she planned to kill Buffy by running into the bitch at 50 mile per hour, breaking bones as if they were twigs, killing her instantly. A hit and run.

The worst part of the whole thing would be that they would probably have to get rid of the car, at least for a while. But there was no reward without sacrifice.

The Beamer was five feet away. Just before impact, three words ran through Tallhya's head—*Slow. Painful. Death.*—causing her to stomp the brakes. She wanted Buffy to suffer.

The car slowed, but the at fifty miles per hour, the anti-lock breaks weren't designed to stop the car instantly. The Beamer clipped Buffy's side, knocking her off her feet. Buffy flew a couple feet into the air in one direction, and her blond wig in another.

A "What the fuck?" expression was plastered on Rydah's face.

With no time to stop, the driver of a Honda Accord ran into the back of the Beamer. Tallhya couldn't care less about the damage to the car or who saw what she did next.

Tallhya jumped out of the car. Rydah reached in her black Celine purse, came out with a .25-caliber pistol, and jumped out of the car, seconds behind her sister.

Tallhya stood over Buffy, who was bruised and bleeding. "Slow and painful, bitch?" Tallhya wasn't thinking straight. All she wanted was retribution. "Be careful what you wish on other people, because it may come back to bite you."

Buffy looked as if she wanted to cry, hoping Rydah would feel some semblance of pity and help her.

Rydah burst her bubble. "I don't give one solitary fuck about your tears, bitch." She pointed the .25 directly at Buffy's dome. "You set me up to die."

Buffy had a broken leg and a laceration on her forehead. "No," she said, still crying. "It wasn't like that."

Tallhya said, "Know this, bitch . . ." She didn't really care what Buffy thought it was like. "Every time I see you, I'm going to whip yo' ass. And I put that on my grandma's grave!" To get her point across, Tallhya punched Buffy in the face.

Two guys approached. At first they thought that it was the mall's security or undercover police, but then Rydah recognized one of them. They were Wolfe's people.

"Did Wolfe tell you to follow us?" she asked.

JoMo, the one she knew, nodded.

The other guy moved swiftly. He opened the trunk of the BMW and took the bags out, placing them in the back seat of the Benz that they were driving. JoMo instructed Rydah to take the Benz home. "Wolfe will call you shortly," he said.

"We don't want her dead," Rydah told JoMo.

"That's no longer your problem," JoMo said coldly.

"I'm serious," she said.

"I hear you," said JoMo.

Rydah searched his expressionless face for an indication as to whether he was lying. JoMo's reputation was as ruthless as Wolfe's, and that was scary for Buffy. Her last minutes amongst the living could very well be spent in the trunk of a car.

If it was true, there was nothing more Rydah could for her. She tapped Tallhya on the shoulder. "We gotta roll."

Buffy started screaming for help. JoMo's friend put a piece of tape over her mouth, silencing her.

Rydah gave her one last parting bit of advice. "You need to learn not to fuck with us Banks sisters," she said.

Chapter 25

Not Stable

Rydah knew better than to go to her parents' house, so she went home. Wolfe showed up a few minutes later.

When he walked in, the two ladies were sitting on the plush white leather sofa, talking. They got quiet when they saw Wolfe. Looking at each other, they both knew that they were in big trouble.

Tallhya took the blame. "It's my fault, brother-in-law."

Rydah was angry with Wolfe. "You had someone following us and you didn't even tell us?"

Wolfe was blunt. "Damn right. And it's a good thing that I did."

Rydah shook her head as Wolf poured himself a drink.

"So your first day out of the house," he said to Tallhya, "you roll over a bitch in broad daylight, damn near killing her?"

"Basically," said Tallhya, cucumber-cool.

"So . . ." Wolfe started.

Tallhya cut him off.

"Like I told Rydah, if the police show up, then I'll take the weight. I just got out the asylum and I got papers that say I'm not stable. They know I'm not working with it all."

"Really?" Wolfe looked at Tallhya with a raised eyebrow.

"I know you're mad, but I couldn't help myself. When I saw that bitch giggling and flossing on social media, fifteen feet below where we were parked, I had to react. I guess I wasn't thinking."

"That was where you went wrong," Wolfe said. "You weren't thinking. If you're going to do something that's against the law, the first rule is to always think it out first, then react."

Wolfe sat on the sofa, enjoying every moment of Tallhya's rant. She was a firecracker and he admired her heart. He secretly wished that Rydah were more like her. But then he thought again. Having two loose wires on his hands, in his home life, may be too much headache. It would grow old. Though he loved Tallhya's unpredictability, there was still something about Rydah's easygoing, peaceful spirit that tended to balance him out. She was definitely the Yin to his Yang.

"I told that bitch I'm going to beat her ass every time I lay eyes on her, and I meant it."

"Calm down," said Wolfe. "I got it from here."

Tallhya was cool with Wolfe taking care of the problem. She just had one request. "Whatever you do to her," she said, "make sure that it's done slow and painfully. The bitch deserves it."

"I said that I got it, didn't I?"

"Yes! I know you have it, but she told those guys that she wanted us to die a slow and painful death."

"Well, I got her. Let me handle her."

Rydah was still stuck on the fact that Wolfe had had them followed. "You could have told us what you were doing."

He sat down between the two ladies. Wolfe shook his head. "You back on that again?"

"Yes. I'm back on that."

"Never the one to throw anything in your face, but it was a good thing I did have you followed."

Rydah didn't want to admit it, but secretly, she was glad that he had. If JoMo hadn't intervened when he did, there was no telling how things may have turned out.

She asked Wolfe, "What did you do with Buffy?"

All he said was, "I got her."

That wasn't enough for Rydah. "Is she dead?"

Wolfe shook his head. "She's safe, just where she needs to be."

Rydah could tell when Wolfe was lying to her, and he wasn't. To ease the tension in the room, she kissed him on the cheek. "Thanks, babe, for having our back. You're always on point. That's one of the reasons why I love you so much. You're the best, and I'm glad you belong to me."

"Yeah," Tallhya said, "them dudes rolled up like the feds, moving all professional and shit."

"Yeah," Rydah joked, "but that didn't stop Tallhya from wanting to beat the life out of Buffy, though."

"I was like . . . what the hell, if the police here, I'm going down anyway."

"And she knew I was right there with her."

"Yup, pistol in her hand, wanting a bitch to move the wrong way," Tallhya said.

"Sure was. I had to have my sister's back."

"Y'all two something else. Double trouble, for real."

"So," Rydah said, ignoring the last comment, "if you didn't kill her, what did you do with her?"

Wolfe sucked in a lungful of air. "She's locked away, babe."

Tallhya said, "I want to see her. Can you take me to her? I'm still not done with her ass."

Here in this house, with Tallhya, was the only time in his life that he ever felt the need to explain himself and exercise his patience.

"Listen . . ." Wolfe addressed them both in a firm voice, letting them know he was now in charge, in case this was ever in doubt. "This girl will be handled. Trust me. I'm more pissed than you will ever know. However, you two have gotta fall back and let me handle it the way I see fit. In a way that won't come back to haunt you later. Is this understood?" He shot a look at them both.

Rydah nodded.

Tallhya was quiet.

"He'll take care of it," Rydah assured her, and there wasn't a doubt in her mind that Wolfe would handle Buffy. "Trust me. She's light work for him, sister."

"I know," Tallhya said. "Just hate making promises I can't keep."

"Sometimes you gotta pass the baton to the next runner. You did your part, and you did one hell of a job. Hell, you held it down better than a lot of the niggas I know." He gave credit where credit was due.

Tallhya appreciated the compliment. "Thank you for that." All her life, people had walked over her and never appreciated her efforts. Even her own sisters sometimes treated her like the reject fat sister. Even after they robbed multiple banks together, Simone repaid her by having her Baker Acted, leaving her in a crazy house. No one even came to visit. It felt good to finally have a sister that loved her for her and had her back. It was all she ever wanted.

Everyone was quiet.

Then Wolfe said to Tallhya, "You still haven't been out to really see the town. Since you've been here, there's only been misfortune. Time to change that. I think you sisters need to bond. Do some tourist stuff, girl stuff. Don't worry about this Buffy broad. Put that in your rearview mirror. It's in my hands now."

"And the guys?" Tallhya asked. "What about them? Mean-Mug and Flashlight?"

"Working on it."

"When you get them, can I at least come and spit in their face? For violating me."

He chuckled. "You got it, li'l sis."

"Promise?"

Wolfe reflected back to the day, when he was twelve years old, that he watched his father smack his mother because she "allowed" the dinner she'd cooked for him to get cold. He remembered the sound it had made, a cracking noise that reverberated like the whip of an angry horse jockey.

Wolfe had told his dad: *If you ever hit her again, I'll kill you.*

He told Tallhya, "I always keep my word."

Chapter 26

Legwork

The sisters agreed to lay low and let Wolfe deal with the situation. Tallhya had absolute and complete confidence that Wolfe could and would handle it, but at the same, she just couldn't leave it alone. She felt like she owed Wolfe for the $150,000 he had used to get her back. Although Wolfe said not to worry about the money, Tallhya was determined to repay him. No one had ever done anything like that for her, and the fact that Wolfe wasn't her man, that he did it because of the love he had for her sister, was real gangsta. Tallhya hoped that when she found a man of her own, he would be half the man Wolfe was. She felt like as long as she was overweight, she'd never get a man.

During her last checkup, the doctor said that at the rate at which she was healing, her body might be able to withstand the surgery she wanted in about three and a half more weeks.

No matter how hard she tried redirecting her attention to other places and things, her mind kept going back to the conversation she'd overheard between the two guys she referred to as Flashlight and Mean-Mug.

" . . . It isn't personal, just a part of the game. The American Dream . . . ." Flashlight had said.

Time to turn the tables. How? She thought. *Think. Think. Think.*

She had an idea.

When Mean-Mug and Flashlight were holding her captive, they had mentioned getting some "bum-ass wings" from The Office. Up until now, she'd forgotten about it.

She'd googled The Office, and it came back as a strip club. Not much of a lead, but it was definitely a good place to start. If her hunches told her anything, they were coming back for those "bum-ass wings."

Tallhya packed bottled waters and sandwiches in a small cooler and put the cooler in the car—a Maxima, not the BMW Rydah had rebuilt for her. She never saw the Beamer again. Wolfe told her to forget about the car. Easy for him to say. That was the nicest car Tallhya had ever had.

For two days, Tallhya used the Maxima to stake out the parking lot of The Office. On the second day, she broke luck. A burgundy Lincoln with tinted windows pulled into the lot. It was the one she called Mean-Mug.

She picked up the phone to call Wolfe, then changed her mind. Instead, Tallhya watched Mean-Mug's every move, following him for a couple of days. On the second day, Mean-Mug met up with Flashlight.

They seemed to be doing some research of their own. Tallhya surmised that they were working on the armored truck heist that they'd discussed. After she was sure, she made a trip to Best Buy to purchase one of those long-lensed, paparazzi-style cameras. She also copped spyware apps from a tech novelty store.

She used the services of a stripper to get the spyware onto their phones. It was easy. The stripper simply had to offer each of the guys her number. When they clicked on her text, the spyware would infiltrate their system. With the spy apps installed, Tallhya could see everything they saw on their jacks. Everything. Phone calls, texts, e-mails, and pictures—even Internet traffic.

Rydah and Tallhya both shared the responsibility of monitoring the devices. It was a tedious job. The boys used their phones like a couple of high-school girls.

Tallhya's phone rang. It was Simone. She put the phone on speaker.

A hyped Simone said, "Hey, girl. You with Rydah?"

Tallhya responded, "She's right here. She can hear you."

Rydah shouted, "Heyyyy!"

Simone asked, "What are y'all doing?"

Rydah and Tallhya shot a conspiratorial look at each other.

"We'll tell you later," Rydah said.

"Trust me," Tallhya added, "you don't even want to know."

Simone said, "Let me be the judge of that."

Rydah hunched her shoulders as if to say to Tallhya, "It's up to you."

Tallhya spoke on their behalf. "We been doing a lot of sightseeing and eating on the beach," she said, bending the truth. They'd been keeping Mean-Mug and Flashlight in their sights and eating sandwiches while they waited. "You know—white sand and blue water."

"Just showing her the city," Rydah said. "Enjoying each other's company."

A pause.

"Oh," Simone said.

Tallhya knew Simone like a book, and by the sound of that "Oh" Simone blew out her mouth, Tallhya knew that her sister was a wee bit jealous of the way she and Rydah were getting along. She rubbed it in.

"We're having a ball. I've never had anyone in my entire life roll out the red carpet like this. I mean Rydah, her parents, and our brother-in-law . . . I swear, they outdid themselves."

Simone asked, "For real?"

"Enough about me," Tallhya said, knowing that Simone would want to hear more. "More importantly," she said, changing the subject, "how are you?"

Simone, sounding excited, said, "I Just finished my last round of treatments a couple of weeks ago. And everything looks good."

They both screamed, "Yesssss!"

Simone said, "I'm feeling a lot better. The doctor said that I should get some sun. Relax. I'm thinking about coming to Miami for a few days."

Rydah couldn't contain her smile. "You serious?"

"As cancer," she joked.

It was one of those jokes that was only funny because the person was making fun of herself.

"Damn, sis, your timing couldn't be much better. I got something big simmering in a pot that could use your special touch. Still early, but it's definitely coming together," Tallhya said.

Simone asked, "Really?"

"If you're up to it."

Simone said, "Don't worry about me, little sis. I feel as well as I've ever felt in my life."

"I hear you."

"Then spill the tea."

"Still researching . . . but trust me, it's going to turn out something big. I just know it."

"Let us know what day you're going to get here," Rydah said to Simone.

"Whatever day my little sister says that she needs me. I could use the excitement."

"Talk to your husband, see if he will let you steal away," Tallhya suggested. "See how soon you can get here and call us back. Meanwhile, I'm still doing my homework, but it's going to come together soon."

They disconnected the phone call from Simone and when they did, Rydah asked, "Ummmm, are you going to share what you have been all closed-lipped about and where you been spending all this time?"

"I will soon, sister. Just know I'm not getting in any trouble. Just chilling, that's all. Researching some stuff."

"You sure?"

"Positive," Tallhya assured Rydah.

"I know you. . . ."

"Listen, the second I get the info I need, I promise I will share it. A few more pieces to the puzzle have to come together. Don't worry. We going to be on some damn Wonder Twins shit. I promise."

Chapter 27

A Chef Salad?

When the phone rang, Tallhya looked at the screen and thought, *What's the catch?*

It was Fonz.

If nothing else, she thought, *the man is persistent. And a helluva looker.*

Since they'd exchanged numbers three weeks ago, Fonz had made it his business to phone Tallhya at least once a day. Some days he called more than once, and he was always pleasant, polite, and so damn poised. Tallhya hadn't quite figured out what his game was yet, or why he seemed to be so interested in her.

"Hello?"

"Good afternoon, gorgeous." His voice sounded like chocolate for the ears. "How was your day thus far?" he asked. Even his bullshit small talk sounded sincere.

"Who, me?" She was on a stakeout, hunched down in the driver's seat of the Maxima with a pair of binoculars and a cooler packed with a turkey sandwich, fresh fruit, and water, watching Mean-Mug. She'd just followed him to a house in Miami Gardens. "Same ol', same ol'," she said. "Uneventful."

Fonz saw an opening and took it. "Maybe I could do something to break the monotony." Until now, he'd kept his word and only used her number to kick it on the jack. No expectations and no promises. An opportunity to get to know one another. "Let's say I take you out for dinner? To a nice restaurant."

She didn't say anything because she was focused on an older lady who came out of the house. She must have been Mean-Mug's grandmother.

Fonz took the opportunity of her silence, ran with it, and went out on a limb. "Do you like crab cakes? I know a place that makes some of the best crab cakes in the city." As soon as the faux pas came out of his mouth, he mentally kicked himself. What if she didn't like crab cakes? Or worse, if seafood made her sick? He'd given her a built-in excuse to turn down his offer. "They make lots of other great things also," he said, trying to recover from his slip.

When Tallhya opened her mouth, the truth fell out. "I just so happen to love crab cakes. It's a date," she said. Too late to take it back. Damn.

That was the fat bitch that accepted his offer, not me. She needed to get a grip on that.

"Then," with cobra-quick reflexes, Fonz said, "I'll pick you up at eight." He finished before she could change her mind. "That's good for you?"

The only thing she'd eaten all day were two apples. She said, "Eight's fine, but instead of picking me up, I'll meet you there. Just text me the info."

"Deal."

At 7:45 p.m., Fonz handed the keys to his new Rolls Royce Wraith to the valet. The three hundred thousand–dollar automobile rolled off the showroom floor with 624 horses under the hood. It was the most powerful Rolls ever produced.

Fonz cautioned the valet attendant. "Be easy with her. She has a tendency to get feisty with drivers she doesn't know."

"Sir," the attendant proudly said, "I promise to treat her like the queen she is."

"Thank you."

Fonz would've literally had a coronary if he'd witnessed the rubber the attendant left tattooed to the cement while spinning the Rolls' wheels, but his mind was occupied with his date for tonight.

Tallhya pulled up to the restaurant fifteen minutes later. The same valet attendant that had abused the Rolls, parked her car.

Inside, a six-piece jazz band performed a Miles Davis piece. Fonz met her in the lounge area, where patrons waited to be seated.

"You look amazing," Fonz complimented.

"Very nice choice," Tallhya said, admiring the ambiance of the place.

"The lighting was off when I first arrived."

"Really?" Tallhya asked with a raised eyebrow.

"That's until you arrived and lit the entire place up."

Blushing all over, she was glad that one of the hostesses, attired in a black-and-white suit, ushered them to a reserved table for two.

"Right this way." The hostess spoke with a slight accent which Tallhya didn't recognize.

"Nice table choice," Tallhya said once they were seated. They were close enough to the band to be entertained, but not too close where their conversation would be drowned out by the volume of the music. Fonz took the liberty of ordering a robust red wine, along with a light appetizer, bread, and salad.

Fonz did everything he could in order to make Tallhya feel comfortable, but none of it worked. In her mind, she looked and felt overweight. She'd worn all black too, with a waist shaper underneath her clothes to appear slimmer than she was. It was too tight, and she could barely breathe. It sucked everything in, but her fat girl tricks weren't holding up to their end of the bargain.

Fonz was good at small talk. Conversing with strangers seemed to come natural to him, as if it were something that he had to do for a living.

Just like a con artist, Tallhya thought.

The band was jamming out to a George Benson cover when the waitress returned. She asked if they were ready to order. She was looking at Tallhya as if Fonz was a regular and she already knew what he liked. In fact, Fonz seemed familiar with quite a few people in the restaurant, both staff and patrons.

Yet he remained the ultimate gentleman at all times.

"Take your time. But if you're unsure of what to try, order as many different dishes as you like." Coming from some people, the line would've sounded mean-spirited, but not from him. "We can sample them together," he said. "That's good for me, because everything is so delicious here, and my mind tends to want some of it all, but my stomach won't let me have it all."

"I'll have the chef salad."

"And what dressing would you like with that?"

"I would like to have it dressed up in a couple of crab cakes and a juicy fillet mignon." That's what she wanted to tell the skinny-ass heifer. "French dressing is fine," was what she really said.

As if he could read her mind, Fonz ordered the seafood platter with extra crab cakes. "We can share," he said. "Oh, and would you throw in a few extra prawns, please?" Fonz said as he handed the menu to the waitress.

Fonz seemed to be everything she needed and wanted in her life. He smelled good, looked good, could dress his ass off, was classy and articulate, and seemed to have his shit together. He seemed to really like her, made her feel comfortable, and had the potential to romance the hell out of her.

This nigga is just too damn good to be true. That was the exact moment that Tallhya decided that after this date, she would never see or talk to Fonz again.

Her stomached growled.

Shut the fuck up!

Chapter 28

Doggie Style

Three weeks later

Wolfe's dog kennel was 6 feet by 9 feet by 4 feet, fabricated from solid steel. On a table next to the kennel was a box of chicken and a can of dog food. Wolfe opened the can of Alpo, spooned it into a metal dog bowl, and slid it through a feeding slot.

For the first week, Buffy left the dog food untouched, but after a while, when she knew that there would be nothing else to eat, she couldn't wait to chow down on the canine cuisine. Unable to stand up in the 4-foot tall cage, Buffy crawled through her own feces and piss to reach her meal.

"Not so much fun when the rabbit got the gun," said Wolfe.

Buffy's eyes stayed glued on the bowl of dog food.

"I was taught to treat people in accordance to the way they treat me." Wolfe chomped down of a piece of fried chicken. "So," he said, "you thought it was entertaining to see my sister-in-law beat up, raped, and drugged, huh?"

Buffy continued to eat. She knew that she only had five minutes. After that, Wolfe would take the bowl from the cage—whether she was done or not.

"One question," he said. It was the same question he asked every day. "Who were the other two guys?"

Buffy answered the same way she'd answered before. She said nothing.

Wolfe's phone rang and he took the quick call. When he hung up the phone, he smiled.

"I just got two calls back to back. I got info on who your partners are. You got about an hour to decide if you wanna give them up before they throw your ass under the bus."

"They will never throw me under the bus."

Wolfe started laughing as if it were the funniest thing in the world. "We'll see, bitch!"

Chapter 29

Gotcha

Zzzzzzz . . . Zzzzzzz . . . .

Tallhya was sleeping like a baby when the spy app she had connected to Mean-Mug's phone vibrated, informing her that the phone was in use. She woke up immediately.

Mean-Mug: IHOP on Biscayne at 11

Flashlight: Cool. Riccardo is with me

Tallhya leapt out of bed, hopped into a pair of jeans, a T-shirt, and sneakers. Then she drove straight to the IHOP and waited.

Tallhya waited patiently in her car, smiling on the inside, in disbelief that her plan was finally coming together.

All of her life, she had been pushed around and given orders by family members. Now she was the one who had researched everything, and though it wasn't her plan, she was masterminding a major robbery.

Everything was falling into place. The guys were meeting with Riccardo, the driver of the armored truck, and they were putting the finishing touches on their plan.

She sat in the blue Mercedes AMG and watched as the guys arrived, ate, and listened in as they were securing their final plans.

"So Riccardo, man, if you wanna pull out, let us know right now."

"I'm all in."

"And you sure you are going to be the driver, right?"

Riccardo answered, "Been doing it for the past three years."

"Now, are you sure that the one guy is going to be a rookie?"

"Yes. It's going to be his first day out of training and his first day riding along without having his trainers with him."

"And they assigned him to your truck?"

"Yes."

"And you sure that this is going to be a day to do it?"

"Yes. We have extra money to deliver to the three major companies in that area. And on top of that, the people at auction we would've picked up. So at the point we discussed, that's where you have to take the truck down."

"Okay. We got it."

"After all is said and done, you will do the interviews with the police. You don't know anything. And once you cleared from them, at midnight that night, we will meet you with your cut."

"A'ight, cool. That's sounds about right," Riccardo said.

"So it's all set in stone, right?"

They gave each other five. "Man, this shit is going to be great. And we going to eat."

"To money, and a lot of it." Flashlight toasted with their glasses of lemonade.

They shook on their plans and Riccardo left. Meanwhile, Flashlight and Mean-Mug sat there, gloating about how things were going to be great.

"Told you it was coming sooner rather than later."

Mean-Mug nodded. "Yeah, you did." He gave his boy a hand slap.

Mean-Mug and Flashlight were as happy as a faggot with a bag of dicks. Life was about to be great for them. They sat in their booth discussing how they were about to come up and how life was about to be great for them.

They strolled out of the IHOP excited that their plan was about to come into motion.

Tallhya sat in the car and was excited that things were finally coming together for her.

Chapter 30

Ice Cream Truck

Rydah was relaxing on the couch with the TV remote, channel surfing, when Tallhya rattled her key into the lock and stormed into the house. Rydah looked up.

"Damn, girl," she beamed at her sister after seeing how happy she was. "Pass that shit over and let me inhale whatever the hell you been on."

Tallhya was smiling like an only child on Christmas morning with a room full of presents. "I got something I have to tell you."

For the past few days, she'd been keeping her movements close to the vest, but now it was time to share her plan with her sister, friend, and confidant.

Rydah perked up, tossed the remote onto the table, and gave her sister her full attention. Taking a shot at what had Tallhya so giddy, she said, "Did you finally meet up with Fonz again?"

"He did call me, but that's not it." Tallhya copped a seat.

"What did he say?"

"I mean, we talked, but right now I just don't have no time for him, though." She didn't bother explaining to her sister her way of thinking, because she didn't feel like hearing Rydah's optimism when it came to Fonz. Plus, she had bigger fish to fry right now, like this plan that she had been babysitting for quite some time now.

"Okay, okay." Rydah was done guessing. "If it's not a guy, then what is it?"

"I found a way to get a freakin' shitload of money, but I'm going to need your help to pull it off."

Joking, Rydah said, "What, bitch, you plan to rob a bank or something?"

Tallhya said, "Nope." She was thinking, *But you're close.* "I plan to rob an armored truck."

"Now I know you've been smoking something." Rydah waited for the punchline to what she thought was a joke. When the punchline took too long to come, Rydah said, "Nobody's robbing anyone's truck, girl. You aren't that hard up, and you ain't broke."

"Just hear me out," said Tallhya. "It's not as crazy as it sounds. I promise."

All types of warnings went off in Rydah's head. Up until that moment, she thought that her sister was joking. "I'll be a monkey's aunt," she said in disbelief. "You serious, aren't you?"

"Yup."

"Well, let me stop you right there, sis. We're not going to be robbing anybody's truck. Not an ice cream truck. Not a candy truck. Not a trash truck. And certainly not an armored truck. Girl, have you lost your mind?"

"If you're done," Tallhya said, "I'd like an opportunity to explain. Give me that."

There was nothing on God's green Earth that could come out of her sister's mouth that would convince her to rob an armored truck, but for shits and giggles, Rydah agreed to listen. "I'm all ears."

Tallhya told Rydah everything. The more she spoke, the better she felt. For the past couple of weeks, keeping what she was doing secret from her sister had been eating her alive.

After hearing everything, Rydah said, "Listen. You already know I got your back like a tight bra strap."

Tallhya could hear the sincerity in her sister's tone.

"But I wouldn't be much of a sister if I wasn't honest. And honestly, I don't think that this is a very good idea."

Tallhya was not perturbed. "Tell me that a million dollars don't motivate you."

"I'm not saying it do or it don't, but—"

Tallhya cut her off. "I understand. I know this type of shit isn't who you are. I still love you all the same. But this won't be my first time doing this type of thing."

Tallhya told her about the bank jobs they'd pulled back in Virginia. "And most of all," she said, "this shit is personal for me." She wanted to make Flashlight and Mean-Mug know that they'd fucked with the wrong bitch.

Rydah looked her sister dead in the eyes. "I get it," she said. "But can we find a better way to achieve that than robbing a truck? We smarter than those niggas, and there's a way that we can outsmart them. I know there's a better way."

"I don't think so."

"I disagree." Rydah shook her head. "There's always more than one way to skin a rat."

Tallhya wasn't trying to hear that. "You're always looking at the things from the righteous perspective. God and the Universe can't handle everything. Sometimes you have to trap the rat yourself. It's more satisfying that way. At least it is for me. Can you respect that, sis?"

"Of course I do, but I also know there has to be a smarter way. If we can just put the emotions aside and utilize our intellect . . . because doing life in the pen is not where we want to end up."

"Well, that's a risk we take. But if we get away with it, then look at the reward."

Rydah was operating with tunnel vision and could only see it her way. "I'ma respect your way, but you're going to have to respect mines."

Chapter 31

What's Going On?

The sound of the front door opening and closing ceased all talk about the plan to rob the armored truck. The room was thick with awkward stiffness when Wolfe entered the house.

"What's going on with y'all? The tension in this bitch is tougher than leather," he said, then planted a kiss on his boo's lips.

Rydah kissed him back. "What you talking about? We good."

"Seems like a sisterly squabble is in progress."

"We ain't got nothing but love for each other," Tallhya said defensively.

"Sometimes we gotta agree to disagree," Rydah added.

"You got that right," Tallhya quipped.

Rydah was so busy trying to hide what they were talking about from Wolfe that she hadn't noticed that he was carrying something. "What's the deal with the briefcase?" she asked, diverting the subject away from her and Tallhya's disagreement.

Wolfe plopped down on the sofa between them and set the leather briefcase on the glass coffee table. He fingered the numbered dials on the front of the case, popping the locks. He removed a large manila envelope that contained pictures.

When Wolfe began to spread the photos out onto the table, the sisters' eyes got as big as eggs.

"That's them motherfuckers right there," Tallhya said, pointing at the flicks. "That's the one I called Flashlight, and this is the one I nicknamed Mean-Mug.

"That's Abe and Prince," Wolfe informed them.

"Wow." Rydah was puzzled. Pointing at a guy in another photo, she said, "That's the dude named Tiger that I told you tried to holla at me that night at the club, the night I went out and all that stuff happened with Buffy and her leeching-ass friends." Then she looked again. "That's the guy Ken and Jake."

Wolfe drew the conclusion. "All them motherfuckers were working together that night, running the scam."

"But the dude Tiger wasn't with them. He didn't come into the picture until later."

"Right," Wolfe surmised, "because they wanted to have multiple opportunities at getting at you."

"Mean-Mug and Flashlight was after us both?" Tallhya asked, a little confused.

"You mean Abe and Prince," corrected Wolfe. "They were after Rydah. They figured that her parents were rich enough to pay any amount of ransom to get their only daughter back, hence the failed carjacking. And after they botched it, Rydah never rolled out by herself again, so they didn't get another shot. However, they somehow found out that the two of you were sisters. Saw an opportunity with you, Tallhya, and took it." Wolfe's voice was as calm as a summer breeze, but his eyes were as deadly as a tornado.

"So . . ." Rydah finally let the truth sink in. "Buffy really did have something to do with me getting carjacked?" In her heart, she already knew this, but seeing the proof was different. "Our entire friendship was bullshit." She tried to shake it off, but the thought was still disheartening for her to believe.

Wolfe was blunt. "You knew what it was off top, baby."

"I did, but to have more concrete proof . . . that shit hurts. I'm human."

Wolfe looked at her. In many ways, Rydah was very naïve and innocent. Those were a couple of the characteristics that drew Wolfe to her. That and the fact the she was the most beautiful girl Wolfe had ever met.

"Most people don't have a heart as genuine as yours, babe. Most people are sheisty and evil and solely motivated by jealousy or money," he said.

"I know, baby. I know!" Rydah said, laying her head on Wolfe's chest. He put his arms around her.

"Never change your heart, baby. In more ways than one, because your heart is so good, and we are profoundly connected. It just makes me better."

"Awwww, that's so sweet and well said."

"Real talk. A good woman is the only thing that can make a rotten nigga sweet."

"Thank you, baby."

"All that sweet shit don't mean I ain't going to deal with these niggas, though," he said.

"What now?" Rydah asked, already knowing the answer. It was written all over Wolfe's face.

"I'ma have them niggas scooped up," he told her.

"Then what? I mean, after you have them scooped up?" she asked.

Wolfe was honest. "You don't want to know," he said.

Tallhya felt no pity for them. She said to Wolfe, "Don't forget what you promised me."

Wolfe glared at her. "I gave you my word, didn't I?" He wasn't used to being questioned, and he didn't care for it. The only reason he didn't make a big deal out of it was because she was Rydah's sister. If she wasn't, he would have taught her to stay in her place.

"I know you haven't had a lot of experience dealing with real brothers, but real niggas do what they say and say what they mean."

"My bad, brother-in-law. You right. But you didn't have to put me in my place like that," she said, trying to bring light to a dark topic.

"Actually, he did," Rydah said. "You needed that."

"I did," Tallhya admitted. "So, now that we know their identities, how do you plan on going about it?"

"I'ma deal with it."

Tallhya asked, "Can I ask for a small favor?"

"I have to know the favor before I can say yes."

"Can you hold off for a couple days before you get at them them?" Rydah asked. "Please, babe, I need you to do it for me.

Tallhya looked at her sister and smiled. "Please, brother. Please?"

Wolfe thought that this was an odd request, especially coming from Tallhya. If he'd read her correctly, she was the type that wanted wrongs righted. Quickly. "Something you need to tell me?" he asked.

Tallhya was quiet, going back and forth with herself mentally, trying to determine if she wanted to share with Wolfe what she knew. On one hand, she wanted to be real with him, but on the other hand, she knew that he wouldn't let them rob the truck. And he definitely wouldn't allow Rydah to participate in her scheme.

Wolfe waited.

Tallhya asked Rydah, "What do you think?" Wolfe was her man. Let her decide whether they should keep him in the dark.

"This is the same man that had us followed. He's like Big Brother. He sees everything."

Tallhya said, "Damn." How could she be so stupid? "You already know, don't you? You're just testing me."

Wolfe said nothing.

"Well, you won't believe what I found out."

"Try me."

Chapter 32

401K

Riccardo, an 8-year employee of the Cashmore Armored Truck Company, exercised an enormous degree of patience and precision wheeling the 10-ton steel behemoth through the constipated byways and highways of South Florida. The truck didn't handle as well when it was weighed down with cash, and today, they were at the truck's limit. The company was short on help, so Riccardo and his two partners were asked to pick up the slack, pulling an additional route on top of their all ready busy regular route.

Riccardo pulled the truck into the loading area of the Hard Rock Casino. "You guys ready for this one?" The Hard Rock was hosting a popular nationally televised poker tournament. Fifteen hundred players signed up to play, each ponying up a $10,000 entry fee.

From the back of the truck, Teddy said, "Yep. Let's do this." He and Mike were the hoppers, the guys that got in and out of the truck. There were two buttons, one located in the front and the other in the back of the cab, that had to be pressed at the same time in order to release the lock on the cab's door. Riccardo and Teddy hit the buttons, disengaging the hydraulic locking system.

Teddy and Mike hopped out of the back of truck to load the money. They wore blue and black security uniforms and carried badges and guns. It took twenty minutes to load thirty bags of legal casino money onto the truck. The rest of the money was designated to be delivered to the Federal Reserve Bank for safekeeping, but before it got there, one more pickup needed to be made. It was a small bank branch on Seventh Avenue.

Riccardo maneuvered the truck into the cramped parking lot, nearly clipping the bumper off of a green Camry. Once he got the truck where it needed to be, he said to Teddy, "This is it, my friend. One last stop. You ready?"

It was Teddy's last day on the job. He'd put in his retirement papers last month after he'd paid his faithful dues to the company with not one mishap. Teddy had given Cashmore thirty years of service. It was still hard to believe that after today, it would be over.

"Yep."

They hit the buttons.

Riccardo said, "Make it epic."

"I will."

Teddy smiled as he and Mike hopped out of the vehicle, clueless how true that innocent remark would be.

Riccardo sat in the driver's sear in front of the bank thinking, *There is no turning back now*. He planned to leave the company in about two more years himself, after everything blew over. That was how long he'd decided he'd have to continue to do this job in order to not draw suspicion. He knew that the company would require him to do PTS counseling. And who knows? If he played his cards right, after the Post Traumatic Stress counseling, if he was lucky, the company may even put him on disability. But if all else failed, he'd just have to do this job for another two years or so and that was it.

He inhaled a lung full of air. *The hardest part,* thought Riccardo, *will be laying low and not spending any of the money*. When he quit, he would move back home to the Dominican Republic and live like a king.

Yup! He had it all figured out.

Life is good, he thought as he sat at the wheel of the truck, smiling, waiting patiently for show time.

Teddy made his way out of the bank. He was feeling himself, knowing that today would be his last day of having to look over his shoulder, carrying someone else's money. His mind was so gone on the plans he'd made for him and his wife once he retired that he wasn't paying attention to details—like the man dressed in black who had just crept up from the sewer Riccardo had intentionally parked next to. Teddy was three feet from the truck.

Mike, who was waiting in the back of the cab, opened the door. That's when Abe shot a heavy stream of commercial-grade pepper spray into his eyes, disarmed him, and then cuffed him with plastic flex-cuffs. As rehearsed, Prince snuck up behind Teddy and cracked him across the skull with the butt of his gun. Once Mike's limp body crumpled to the cement, Prince disarmed him.

For the sake of the cameras, they had Ken from the club, whose birthday it had been that night, put a gun to Riccardo's head. On cue, a white van rolled up with Tiger behind the wheel, and another masked guy walked up and had his gun held on the two guards who were both out cold.

Abe and Prince began to fill the van with bags of cash.

"Holy shit!" Abe said when he caught a glimpse of how full the truck was. Neither man expected there to be so many bags money, or that the bags of cash would be so heavy.

Ken, the accomplice who had the gun on Riccardo, who was also the timekeeper, announced that they only had thirty seconds. Abe and Prince picked up the pace.

Abe said, "We need more time." They were loading the van as quickly as they could.

"We don't have it," said Prince, "if we want to be able to spend any of it."

"Five seconds," said Ken, the timekeeper. "Time to wrap this shit up."

Abe and Prince, with regret, each tossed their last bag into the van. The truck was still one-third full. It almost literally made them sick that they would have to walk away without it all. There was no other choice; they would have to leave it. Ken jumped into the van.

Abe walked over to Riccardo. He had one last piece of unfinished business. He said to Riccardo, "Thanks for nothing!" and then pulled the trigger. Twice. He shot Riccardo twice in the head just for the fuck of it, since he was pissed about having to walk away with only a portion of the money.

Before any of his accomplices knew it, he ran over to Theodore and shot him in the head, and then Mike, too, never even hearing either beg for their lives.

"Fuck you do that for, man?" Prince snapped, "You gon' bring the heat!"

"Because I'm pissed the fuck off!" He spit the words out. "Fuck them dead motherfuckers! And anybody else who stand between me and this paper!"

Chapter 33

Gut Instincts

When the white van pulled off, Tallhya wasn't far behind them. She had the entire thing on video. It was their insurance policy. She texted Rydah as she followed them, already knowing their next move before they even made it.

Tallhya: Everything good on ur end?

Rydah: Mild hiccups but working it out.

Tallhya:We don't have time for no hiccups. Pls don't f' this up! We only have one shot!

HONKKKKKKKKK!
A dump truck heading down Seventh Avenue laid on the horn and smashed the brakes in order to dodge the boy running across the street.

The boy was actually Rydah in boy's clothes. She was carrying a tool box. She'd done a little work on the Suburban that Prince, Abe, and their crew planned to switch into.

The tracking device Rydah had installed on the truck gave her eyes on it. She watched from her smartphone as the fellas transferred the money from the van to the Suburban.

The crew had taken off their masks and black jumpsuits, changing back into street clothes. On the way, they'd transferred the bags of money into colorful storage totes to conceal the bags.

They were home free, or so they thought, when the engine in the Suburban suddenly died

"What the fuck?" said Abe. "Shit!"

What the fuck was right. . . .

Prince got out of the van and looked under the hood, searching for the problem. The truck was only a year old, with not even 10,000 miles on it.

Frustrated, Abe kicked the wheel. "Fuckkkk!" he screamed, frustrated.

Prince said, "It has to be something simple," reassuring his partner, who was already on edge after taking the life of two innocent security guards, having to leave a truck full of cash, and now to have his car break down with what cash they did have in it. It was turning out to a pretty fucked up day, and he knew these kinds of days usually sent Abe off his rocker.

"Our luck can't be this bad," Abe said.

Prince spotted an Advance Auto Parts store down the street. He told Tiger to take the walk. "I think it's the battery.

"Shit." Tiger was reluctant to go. "I don't trust you with the bread," Tiger said.

Prince, still keeping his cool, said, "We go back too far to start not trusting one another now. If I was going to put any shit into the game, I would've laid you down back there with Riccardo." Prince looked his friend in the eye. "Money ain't never came between us, but if we don't act soon, we ain't gon' have shit."

Tiger noticed Abe looking at him with frustration and knew he was a time bomb. He glanced at Ken, who was down for Tiger either way. He then thought about the bags of cash that he so desired, and how they had come too far to start bickering back and forth within the crew.

Tiger glared at his even-tempered friend, Prince. "The deviation of the plan got me thinking crazy. It's all good. We go back too far for this shit."

"Look," Prince said, "we need to get moving before we get made."

"You right," Tiger said. "I've never been around this much paper before. The shit got me thinking crazy."

Just then, a state trooper pulled up alongside the Suburban. "Everything all right, fellas?"

"Yeah, Officer. We just need a jump. We just drew straws for who would take the walk to the store," Prince spoke up.

"Who lost?" the trooper asked.

"Huh?"

"You said that you drew straws," the trooper said.

"Right." Abe pointed to Tiger. "He did."

On that note, Tiger started making his way down the road. The trooper smiled and tilted his hat as he drove off slowly. Everyone in the truck exhaled a sigh of relief.

Prince said, "That shit was close as fuck."

Abe was feeling himself. "Close is only good in horseshoes and grenades. We can't be stopped."

The moment they let their guards down for one second, two vans rolled up, and before they could blink, had them boxed in. Nowhere to run, they were caught slipping.

"Oh, shit!"

They were surrounded.

"Police! Don't move!" The police jumped out of the van quicker than a lightning bolt.

Tallhya watched the entire thing through binoculars from a couple blocks away. *Damn*, she thought. *They swooped in as if they'd been informed.*

Abe looked around for an escape. One of the cops said, "Don't even think about it, motherfucker," as if he could read Abe's mind.

Prince slowly put his hands up, shaking his head in disgust. "Ain't this a bitch."

"Yup! Sure is! A real pretty one!" the redneck officer said.

Prince asked, "What are the charges?"

The Caucasian cop said, "Just shut the fuck up, motherfucker!"

Innocent bystanders were gawking, looking for something to post on social media.

As the police perp-walked them to the van, Abe did a double take at the crowd of onlookers and managed to meet eye-to-eye with Tallhya. She was sitting in front of the Wing Station, eating Buffalo wings and wearing an American flag scarf tied around her head.

He thought his eyes were playing tricks on him. He squinted to make sure it was her. That's when Rydah stuck her middle finger up, flashed a huge grin, and silently made him read her lips when she moved them to say, "Yeah, motherfuckerrrr!"

But out of her peripheral vision, she saw Simone, dressed in a police uniform, jump into the Suburban and pull off.

Chapter 34

For the Love of Money

"Money . . . Money . . . Moneeeeyyyyyyyy. . . .
You wanna do things, do things, do things,
good things with it.
Talk about cash money
Talk about cash money—dollar bills, y'all."

The O'Jays' 1973 hit single "For the Love of Money" played on repeat from Rydah's Beats by Dre Pill.

Rydah, Tallhya, and Simone celebrated their victory of outsmarting the guys who had caused them all types of hurt and pain by singing, dancing, and playing in more than six million dollars in cash. Being around so much money made them euphoric. The sisters were on a rush that had them riding higher than the thirty-story condo that overlooked the city of Miami.

Tallhya lowered the volume slightly on the portable speaker. "God bless mu'fucking America," she said, worn out from doing splits and the Roger Rabbit as she took her seat at the table. Rydah and Simone followed suit. The table was overrun with money; more money than a middle-class family made in a lifetime.

"I still can't believe we really did this shit." Tallhya shook her head in disbelief. "We actually pulled this shit off."

Rydah said, "I told you that there was more than one way to skin a cat, didn't I?"

"We are waaaay smarter than those mother-fuckers, and it had to be a better way to do it than us doing it."

"You sure did." Tallhya had to admit it. "That shit was easy."

"We literally made them bozos do all our dirty work for us, and we just collected on the back end."

"Pimps up, hoes down! We pimped the hell out of them," Rydah said.

"We sure did," Tallhya said. "You should've seen that nigga's look on his face. I think he shitted a brick after he made eye contact with me."

The girls laughed.

"And the driver, that was the guy named Tiger, the guy who was trying to holla at me and I shot him down. And the other guy was Ken. The girl Charlotte that Buffy knew from church, Ken was supposed to be her boyfriend, but it was all larceny. All that shit was one big scam."

"And that's why we came up," Tallhya said with a funny face.

"And we deserve every penny of this cash," Simone said, looking at the all the cash on the table. There was still, what seemed to be countless more bags in the corner, waiting to be opened and counted. "This is it, sisters! We are set for life, and we can do what we want. But most importantly, we can live happily ever after."

In the bliss of everything, Rydah happened to look up, and she couldn't help but notice the words *Breaking News* flashing across the 80-inch flat-screen television.

"Hold on, hold on, hold on," Rydah said, grabbing the remote and turning up the volume.

"This is Lisa Sanchez from WYGH-Action News, Miami, reporting live from outside a bank on Seventh Avenue, where a murder and armored truck robbery took place early this afternoon on this hot, Miami day." The reporter was standing in front of the yellow crime scene tape in front of the bank.

"This morning, Theodore 'Teddy' Solomon kissed his wife good-bye and left for work, as he had done for the last thirty years. When he got off, he'd planned to stop and pick up a rental tux for his retirement party. The party would include his loving wife of forty years, his three biological children, and the twenty-seven foster kids he had taken into his home over the years. The retirement party was planned for tomorrow evening, celebrating his thirty years of devoted service to the Cashmore Armored Truck Company. However, those plans, along with his life, were both highjacked at the hands of what authorities believe to be four dangerous, masked men."

Lisa took a dramatic pause, looking at the notes on her phone.

"Now," she continued, "the video you are about to see is very graphic, and should not be viewed by children or anyone with a weak stomach to violence."

Lisa looked into the camera with a sympathetic face as she proceeded with the news.

"Mayhem and madness started this afternoon when Truck 651 was making its final pick up at the First National Republic Bank, when Mr. Solomon took his final walk out of the building. He was only two steps away from the truck and the rest of his life when it went down. When Michael Fuqua opened the door to let Mr. Solomon back inside, a masked man assaulted him with high-grade pepper spray. Then, the assailants shot Mr. Fuqua in the head, which then gave them full control over the truck carrying millions of dollars."

Surveillance footage from the area cameras ran across the screen, showing the masked suspects murder the guards and load a white van with the stolen money.

"If you look to the left of the screen you can see the man driving the van monitoring a stopwatch. When they reached the designated time, they stopped, leaving more than three million dollars behind. Then they shot the driver of the truck, Riccardo Santana, in the head, and drove off."

"Oh, shit!" Tallhya jumped up from the table.

Her sisters paid her no mind.

Simone fanned her quiet, while Rydah turned the volume on the television up a few more notches.

"Don't shush me!" said Tallhya

"Three honorable men are dead. An undisclosed amount of money is missing. Such a sad day for the devoted security officers and the people of Miami." The reporter lowered her eyes, shaking her head as if she herself were in mourning. "Our condolences go out to the families of these three men. Back to you, John."

The screen shot back to a camera inside the studio to the male news anchor.

"So sad, Lisa."

"Yes it is, John"

"Now, Lisa, we know that you devote your life to being the first to deliver the latest and most accurate news stories."

"I truly do, John."

Tallhya said, "You bitches better not shut me down. I think we may be in real fucking trouble."

Rydah hushed her sister. "Let's hear the entire piece before we jump to any conclusions. This is where the story gets good. This chick right here always has some shit for yo' ass. She always gets the low down on everything and takes pride in delivering the tea before anybody else."

The camera shot back to Lisa. "Now there's something," she said, "that I found quite interesting, and so did the authorities." Lisa worked the viewers as she confidently sucked the camera in with her ocean-blue eyes. "What most people don't know is that armored trucks are used to move much more than just money. Although we usually assume the trucks are carrying cash, these vehicles may be transporting anything of significant value, and this was the case here today." She used her hands to express herself, putting up one finger.

Tallhya said, "Y'all listening to this bitch when I'm trying to tell you that we are fucked. Fucked in the ass with no lube. No Vaseline. No nothing!"

Lisa Sanchez went on to say, "I happen to find it mind-boggling that this particular armored vehicle, Truck 651, was carrying highly sensitive and classified electronic files of the FBI's undercover operatives, witness protection lists, and some of the FBI's top informants' relocation addresses and pictures, along with more top secret and very sensitive, highly classified information."

Lisa looked into the camera and put up another finger to try to make her point. "Now, the fact that millions of dollars were left behind makes me think that the money wasn't the motive, but the information was. And the money was just a perk."

Then, Lisa looked into the camera, threw up her hands, and shrugged her shoulders. "This is just my own personal theory and observation, which does not reflect the views or opinions of the powers that be here at WYGH-Action News, Miami."

After the brief disclaimer she said, "I haven't been able to get the authorities or police to confirm or deny that the information was removed from the truck. However, I have a source that is absolutely positive that Truck 651's manifest did indeed indicate that such files had been picked up and were being transporting to the Federal Reserve Bank to be held overnight, and were then to be moved to the Pentagon on Monday. Again," she said, proudly breaking the news story, "it is not confirmed that this information was stolen. This is just my two cents, and as always, it's my duty to keep you abreast of all info as it becomes available.

"This is Lisa Sanchez, and do note that I'm the first and only anchor on scene here, allowed behind the yellow tape. Until next time . . ." She smiled. "Back to you, John."

Rydah was already up from the table, going through the other bags that they hadn't counted yet, looking for the jump drives that Lisa had spoken about.

"You think we have that too?" Simone asked as she got up from the table, standing nearby, anxious to see if they had it.

Tallhya came over, standing between the two sisters. "Why y'all over here searching for damn rats and shit? The same way they got that footage from outside the bank, they can get footage from one of the buildings where we jacked the Suburban."

Rydah looked up from the bags of money she was searching through. "Bitch, that's what your ass been whining and throwing a tantrum for?"

Tallhya looked at Rydah like she wanted to smack her. "For once, when I need you to be fucking serious, you all relaxed. This is the shit that can send our asses to the pen for fucking life, bitch! And usually you are the more mature one, and you are taking this shit lightly."

"That's not going to happen," Rydah said nonchalantly. "I disarmed every camera within half a mile of there."

"What?" Tallhya knew nothing about disarming no cameras. "When? And how you know to do that shit?"

"That's why I was running a few minutes behind schedule, because I was setting up a device that distorts digital cameras for up to a half mile. If a bitch was in the vicinity and wanted to make a Snapchat on her phone, she was shit out of luck. Equipment and towers were down."

Tallhya wasn't sure how something like that worked, but she was glad that it did. She said, "You the best, sis."

"Awww, hell," Simone said. "You two bitches done drove me to smoke." Her phone rang. "I'm going on the balcony to take a smoke and talk to Chase."

"Don't tell that nigga none of our business," Tallhya reminded her. "You hear me?"

Simone stopped short of the glass balcony door and looked Tallhya smack dead in the face. "Don't disrespect me like that, Tallhya. I've never told him any of our family secrets, and I never will. Ever!" She rolled her eyes. "Just have my cut right when I get done smoking." She gave Tallhya the finger before shutting the balcony door behind her.

Tallhya eyed Rydah.

"You know that bitch don't get an equal third, right?"

Rydah laughed. "You crazy."

"Nah. I'm dead-ass fucking serious." Tallhya explained why. "First, she's not the boss of this job. That would be me. She did very little, and she stole all my money last time."

Rydah got serious. "So what are you proposing?" she asked. "And are you taking into account how that is going to make Simone feel?"

"Since she's our sister, by default we going to look out for her. I love Simone. She's my blood, and I would never let her be fucked up." Tallhya thought about a number. "Three hundred thousand. That's enough for her to live off, and she will be happy with that."

Rydah asked, "Are you sure?" This was the first she'd heard about Simone stealing money from Tallhya. Curious, she asked, "What about us? How do we split the rest?"

"Down the middle," Tallhya assured her.

"What about Wolfe? We have to look out for Wolfe," Rydah said, getting straight down to business.

"I'm going to give him his hundred fifty K back, plus a healthy bonus for having our back."

Rydah thought about it. "That sounds fair."

Simone was on the balcony talking to Chase with a face covered in smiles. Rydah crossed her arms, studying Simone's body language.

She asked Tallhya, "How much you trust her?"

"I trust her," Tallhya said, "but not with my money . . . or her judgment when it comes to my mental state. I know for a fact that she would never rat on us, but still, that shit she did to me . . ." Tallhya had yet to fully forgive Simone for putting her in a crazy house and spending her money, leaving her with nothing. And she wasn't sure if she ever would. It didn't matter that Simone had a good reason for spending the money. "I love her, but I'm sorry, I just ain't over it."

Simone stubbed the cigarette out and pulled open the balcony door. "Congrats, baby. I'm so happy for you, and we're going to celebrate big time. My sister and I are going to take you out. We're all super elated for you! Love you much. And I'll see you soon."

Simone disconnected the call and walked over to Rydah's bar, fanning herself. Though she was cool as a cucumber talking to Chase, she was starting to panic.

"Vodka! Bitches, I need vodka!"

Rydah and Tallhya exchanged glances, not knowing what to think.

Tallhya said, "You're not supposed to be drinking."

"Or smoking, for that matter," Rydah added.

"It's not about what I'm 'not supposed' to do, but what I need."

"You don't *need* no drink," Tallhya said.

"Or to smoke, either," Rydah added with her arms crossed, looking at her sister. "Especially not smoking. You just beat cancer."

"Look, if you have a problem, you can talk to us about it. Drinking won't make it go away," Tallhya said.

Simone ignored her sisters nagging, continuing to scan the labels on the countless liquor bottles on and underneath the bar. "Where in the hell is the vodka? And Rydah, I thought you didn't drink like that. So how come you got every fucking top shelf liquor in the store?"

"What's going on, Simone?"

Simone inhaled and then blew out the used air. "I got both good news and bad news all in the same call."

Tallhya tried to keep it positive. "Give us the good first."

"I'm going to be able to spend more time with you. A lot more. Because Chase and I are moving to Miami."

This didn't make sense. Tallhya said, "Chase can't up and leave his job on the police force."

Simone found and poured that drink. She took a shot straight to the head and then poured another. "Chase just got a call from the Attorney General of the United States. He got a promotion. The promotion comes with a huge raise and a relocation to . . . guess where? Miami. They want him to put a task force together to solve city's top unsolved bank robberies. Starting with this armored truck heist."

Rydah poured a drink of her own. "Get the fuck outta here."

"Say that shit one more time." Tallhya couldn't believe what she just heard. "This nigga seems to be drawn to us like bees to sugar."

Simone agreed. "I know. He's boarding his flight now. They are flying him in on a military jet so that he can get started right away before any of the evidence gets cold. I'm going to meet him at the airport."

Rydah went back over to the table, sorting, stacking, and putting the money away.

"Well, we wanted to talk to you about your cut." Tallhya said.

"Whatever y'all decided to give me is cool with me. I don't expect a third of it. Plus, I know I owe you, sis," Simone said to Tallhya.

"You right. But I got you. I ain't going to do you like you did me."

"Whatever you give, I'm going to have you hold on to it for me . . . for now, please. I can't go around him or stay in the hotel with him with a duffel bag of cash," Simone said, looking off into space. "This shit feels too close for comfort. It's like history is repeating itself."

Simone reflected on how she met Chase in the first place. It was her first day working at the bank, which was the first job she'd ever had in her life. That job was at a bank that got robbed on that very day. Although she had nothing to do with the robbery, initially the police looked at her as a suspect.

Chase was the lead detective on the case, and after it was all said and done, she ended up being the leading lady in his life. After Simone, Bunny, Tallhya, and Ginger started robbing banks, he was investigating those too, and he suspected the sisters. However, in the end, he told Simone that he loved her so much that if they did have something to do with it, he would let it go. He told her to just never do it again.

Rydah sat beside her sister, comforting her. "It's not history repeating itself," she said. "Because it's nothing to investigate. And no one in this room is ever going to rob anything again. We are set for life. That's it, that's all."

"I need a Valium," Simone said. "I know one of y'all post traumatic, psychotic bitches gotta have one. Valium or Xanax—something."

"We got you," Tallhya said. "Don't worry. We Banks, right?"

"A'ight. Let me pull myself together. I'll take a shower and do my makeup. I want to look halfway decent when I get to the airport to meet Chase."

"Okay, sis. Everything will be okay," Rydah assured her sister, and Tallhya joined in for a group hug, which was interrupted by Tallhya's phone ringing.

"Hello." She paused. "This is she. How can I help you?"

Tallhya listened. "Why sure . . . yes . . . oh my goodness. Thank you so much!" Tallhya's smile could've lit up the entire North Pole.

When Tallhya got off the phone, Rydah said, "Damn, girl, do share the good news."

"Dr. Snatch's office called and said they had a cancellation. They can fit me in on Tuesday for the surgery. Bitchessssss . . ." She did a pirouette on the floor. "I'm about to be a skinny bitch."

Simone and Rydah laughed as Tallhya pranced around the house, singing.

"Tell Chase to tell them people at his job, right out the gate, that his sister-in-law needs a get-out-of-jail-free card for walking around buck naked on South Beach." Tallhya was hyped up. "I might not ever put on clothes again. My everyday outfit is going to be a skimpy bikini."

They laughed.

Their laughter was interrupted by Tallhya's phone again. "I swear, if these people are calling me to cancel, I'm going to snap and just go ballistic." But when she looked down at the phone, she saw that the call wasn't from the doctor's office.

She answered, "Hey, brother-in-law."

"Just calling to make good on my word," he said. "You still interested in having your way with these nothing-ass motherfuckers or not?"

"You already know how I feel, brother-in-law."

"Then I'm going to send you the address. Ask Rydah for the directions."

"A'ight. I will be there soon." Tallhya hung up the phone. "This day can't get any better than this."

"What now?" Simone asked.

Tallhya didn't want to tell Simone what she was about to go do, so she changed the subject. "Don't you have to get dressed and get ready to get to the airport? And you shouldn't take that Xanax and drive."

"Especially after drinking vodka and smoking. You need no Valium," Rydah added.

"Blah, blah, blah. But whatever, I hear y'all. Rydah, can you drop me off?"

Under her breath, Tallhya asked Rydah, "What's the deal with the address? Wolfe told me to ask you to explain."

"He has a code that he uses. Whenever he texts you the address, switch the first and the last numbers with one another. If the police see the address, it won't match the real one."

"Gotcha." She nodded. "That's smart."

"You know Wolfe got everything covered and will always stay a few steps ahead of the game," Rydah reminded her sister.

"A'ight, sisters. I gotta go handle my business," Tallhya said, lifting up her shirt in front of the mirror, putting on her waist shaper. She tried to rush getting all the hooks latched together.

"That contraption is going to kill you before you can even get on Dr. Snatch's table," Simone said, watching her sister squeeze and snap herself in the girdle.

"I've been telling her, but it falls on deaf ears. You know she treats that thing like it's an American Express card. She isn't going to ever leave home without it," Rydah said.

"I can honestly say that she lost a lot of weight since she been here with you, and Miami is doing her good."

"Between the eating better, diet pills, and the damn waist shaper, she be working it out," Rydah had to agree.

"I hear you bitches talking about me like I ain't here. But I'm about to be out."

Tallhya headed for the door and slipped on her shoes. Before she bounced, she said, "There's one thing that I know. We've all been through the fire. We argue. We fight. But it doesn't change the fact that when everyone is gone—Momma, Daddy, Granny, man, friends, and foes—at the end of the day all we got is each other. No matter what."

"No matter what!"

"No matter what!"

Chapter 35

Hurricane Wilma

Coral Gables

Wolfe had purchased the four-bedroom home during a down cycle of the real estate market eight years ago. It was a corner lot, built on a dead end, tree-lined street. The main thing that attracted Wolfe to the property, besides the foreclosure price, was the soundproof, semi-underground storm bunker. This was something extremely rare for Miami, but the prior owners had the 1,000-square foot, fully functional bunker built after the category 4 hurricane that pimp-smacked the coast in 2005. The natural disaster, which was labeled Hurricane Wilma, racked up $16.4 billion in damages, mostly throughout Broward and Palm Beach Counties.

Wolfe used the house as a fictitious rental property to justify a small portion of his untaxable income. He could give two fucks if anyone ever really rented the property. It was only one of thirty such spots. In fact, this particular location had intentionally never really been occupied.

The storm bunker was the perfect place to take care of business that he wanted to go undetected, such as enhanced interrogations in search of sensitive information.

Wolfe caged both Abe and Prince down alongside Buffy in the soundproof bunker, each in their own fabricated, reinforced dog kennels. He'd already killed the two other partners. Disposing of their bodies was easy. Florida is occupied by an estimated 1.25 million alligators, and Wolfe knew just where to find a family of hungry gators that appreciated good fast food delivery from time to time.

Wolfe sat at his desk, eating a piece of red velvet cake as he watched the surveillance footage, which seemed to have him quite entertained when the gators ate into the two accomplices.

"Damn, another one bites the dust," Wolfe said, making sure the destruction of his prisoners' friends were in surround sound, so that Buffy, Abe, and Prince could hear their partners in crime scream their last cries, begging for their lives.

After witnessing firsthand what Wolfe was capable of, it didn't take long for Abe to sing like a young Frankie Beverly before the rumored throat cancer. But Wolfe was taken aback by the lyrics of the song.

Wolfe took another bite of his cake and got up from the desk. He dug into an old tool bag and came out with a pair of oversized needle-nose pliers. Abe's eyes stretched to double their normal size when Wolfe reached toward his family jewels. His face was already leaking from the brutal beating Wolfe had administered with a bat.

Abe stammered, "I'm t–telling the t–truth."

Wolfe busted the pliers to bite down on Abe's left testicle. The coiled muscle ruptured under the pressure. Abe passed out from the pain.

When he recovered, Wolfe said, "There's one remaining, for now. If I find out that you're lying, you won't have any."

Sweating golf balls at the mere thought of losing another testicle, Abe said, "It was Jaffey! I swear on my son's life. Jaffey set it all up."

Wolfe, silently still holding the bloody pliers, gave Abe a hard stare as if to say, "Keep going."

Abe quickly obliged. "Jaffey paid us twenty thousand to carjack Rydah. We were supposed to hold her for ransom, and then smoke her after you paid the bread. When Rydah got away from the nigga I sent, Jaffey nearly had a heart attack. I swear."

Jaffey? That country, pimp-costume-wearing motherfucker played me for a chump, Wolfe thought. *But why?* All Wolfe had ever done for Jaffey was bankroll him the dough to stay afloat.

Then he reflected on the conversation he'd had with Rydah the other night, when he was trying to convince her that it was Buffy who'd set her up, answering his own question: *People are motivated by jealousy and money.*

The plot never changes, only the people.

Chapter 36

Surprise

Sitting in the waiting room of the doctor's office, Tallhya glanced at the dials of her new Rolex. It was 10:25. The watch was a gift from Rydah; she'd bought one for both sisters. Being that Rydah had spent very little of the money that they'd inherited from Mc-Ma, the gifts were a legitimate purchase.

But where the hell was Rydah? Tallhya wondered. She was supposed to have met her there twenty-five minutes ago. It wasn't like Rydah to not be on time. She was the most prompt person Tallhya knew. In order to keep her mind from running wild with speculation, Tallhya focused on the "Before and After" pictures that the receptionist had given her on the iPad.

The doctor was late as well.

Tallhya was getting impatient. Surprisingly, the weekend had flown by. She was at the lab at 9 a.m. sharp, getting her blood work done. Now she was waiting to see the doctor for her pre-op. If everything was okay, God willing, the doctor would schedule the tummy tuck and liposuction procedure for the next day. She prayed that all of the blood work come back correct. Tallhya wanted nothing to get in the way of her new beginning.

"Natallhya Banks." It was the receptionist.

Tallhya jumped up, quickly making her way to the open door that separated the waiting room from the main part of the clinic.

A waiting nurse flashed a smile. "My name is Kendra." Tallhya followed her down the hall to a room. Inside, the nurse took her vitals, blood pressure, and pulse. Then, after asking a few questions, Nurse Kendra informed Tallhya that Dr. Snatch was running late. "But I'm going to let you chat with Dr. McNeil to at least give you an idea of what to expect. That'll be one thing out of the way. I know firsthand you must have a lot anxiety and questions."

Tallhya thought that she sounded very professional and sympathetic. "Actually," she said, "I just want to get the whole thing over and done with, so that I can heal."

"I was the same way with my first surgery," the nurse said. "I was also filled with a mixture of anxiety and excitement all at the same time."

Tallhya gave Nurse Kendra a hard once over. She was tall and lean, with not an ounce of fat on her toned body. "If you don't mind me asking," Tallhya inquired, "how many surgeries have you had?"

"Oh, honey, let's just say that I'm an old pro at it."

She may be a pro, Tallhya thought, but nothing about Nurse Kendra seemed old. "Would you mind telling me some of the things that you've had done? I'm just curious. You look so fit."

"Let's see . . ." said Nurse Kendra. She started counting the procedures off on her fingers. "I've had the tummy tuck, lipo on my back and thighs, a butt lift, breast implants, breast lift, rhino surgery, cheek sculpture, Botox, and probably a few other things I forgot to name."

"Wow." Tallhya was amazed. "Well, you look damn good," she said. This bitch looked like she had the best body that money could buy, and her face was beautiful as well. Judging by the Florida State class ring she wore, nurse Kendra was probably somewhere in her late forties, and she looked like a retired runway model.

Tallhya asked, "Who was your doctor?"

Tallhya beamed from ear to ear when she heard nurse Kendra say, "Dr. Snatch and Dr. McNeil are the only people in the world that I would ever let do a procedure on me."

"Then I'm glad I made the choice to come here."

"Trust me, sweetie, you are in good hands. And I'm not just saying that because I work here," she assured Tallhya. "These guys are the absolute best."

"That's good to know. But my procedure's still going to be done by Dr. Snatch, right?" Dr. McNeil seemed like a good guy, but Tallhya had paid the big bucks to specifically get her body snatched by Dr. Snatch. He was the one with the long waiting list, the huge following, and did all the work on the celebrities. She hadn't come this far to be baited and switched for the sidekick.

"Yes, Doctor Snatch will be doing your work. But like I said, Doctor McNeil is just as good. Trust me. So this is how it's going to work," she said. "Doctor McNeil will be in in a second to speak with you. And in the morning when you check in, Dr. Snatch will go over the procedures again, do drawings, and show you where he will be cutting."

"All right, I guess." For the first time, Tallhya felt nervous.

Nurse Kendra sensed it. "Everything is going to work out fine. Trust me. You are going to be snatched to the gawds."

Tallhya thought that it sounded kind of tacky coming out of the mouth of a preppie and proper Caucasian chick.

"Can't wait. If my sister comes in, will you make sure they send her back? You'll recognize her. She's a skinny, already snatched version of me."

"Sure thing." Nurse Kendra shut the door behind her when she left.

Three minutes later, the door opened. When Tallhya looked up, she got the shock of her life, and so did Dr. McNeil.

"Fonz. . . ."

Both of their mouths dropped the second they locked eyes.

"Tallhya. . . ."

Not only did her name sound like a melody when it flowed off his tongue, but the smell of his cologne and his starched white coat damn near paralyzed her. She was so embarrassed. All she wanted to do was run away and disappear, but she wasn't leaving that office going anywhere until she got her pre-op and everything finalized to be on that table in the morning.

"OMG! You are a doctor?" She stopped herself from putting her clothes back on and running out of the room. "How come you didn't tell me you're a plastic surgeon?"

"You never asked. And," he said with an accusing stare, "*you* never told *me* that you were getting surgery."

"I just met you. Why would I tell you something that personal?"

"Because I'm your friend, and I would have been concerned that my friend is going into the hospital, under anesthesia, to have a major surgery."

That sounded good, but her getting plastic surgery was still none of his business. She kept her thoughts to herself.

Fonz said, "Would you be offended if I shared a personal observation?"

"It can't get any more personal than this. I don't have a shirt or bra on. And I'm under this gown."

Blushing, Fonz said, "I don't think that you need surgery. I think you are stunningly beautiful the way you are."

"If you believe that, then you must be blind," she said. "I'm like, way overweight."

"And you carry it well. I think you are gorgeous to the naked eye. However, it doesn't mean anything at all."

"What do you mean?" she asked. "You see so many beautiful women. I bet you tell them all how beautiful they are."

"Only if it's true," said Fonz. "I admit, for the past twelve years I've seen some beautiful women, and I sculpt women into nearly flawless creatures. But none of that means anything if the person isn't beautiful inside."

Tallhya wanted to call Fonz on his bullshit, but she also wanted to believe that he was really being sincere.

"Anybody's outer appearance can be transformed into what the world thinks is beautiful," said Fonz. "But what's most important is a person's heart."

When she rolled her eyes, he said, "I'm telling the truth. A person's manners, their vibes, their principles, humility, their will to love, understand, and appreciate other people, places, and things. . . . Those are the things that make a person gorgeous."

The compliments rolled off of his tongue so effortlessly, and if he said it a few more times she would have believed it. Tallhya found herself not wanting to debate with him. Her mind was asking her why had she'd ducked so many of his calls and pretended to be so busy.

Because you were out planning bank robberies and torturing niggas, bitch, she tried to convince herself, but she reminded herself what the reality was. *You are afraid of getting your heart broken again! You've got to let go of that Walter shit.*

"When I met you, I was immediately gravitated to your magnetic beauty. Even though you acted tough and gave me the run around, I would've bet that under all that posturing there was somebody who just wanted to love someone and have someone to love her."

"This is really deep, and I love the content of the conversation," Tallhya said, fronting as if Fonz wasn't saying everything she wanted to hear, "but this is like, really awkward. My friend-slash-phone-buddy turned out to be a surgeon in my doctor's office."

"You forgot to mention you dumped me after our wonderful evening at dinner."

Tallhya skipped over that conversation. "Fonz, I'm in a gown having a conversation that's making me melt. This just need to stop." She honestly didn't want to offend him. "Or continue to another time. Like, seriously."

"My apologies. It just felt so natural."

"Talking to women you barely know while they're wearing a gown is what you call natural?"

Fonz chuckled. "I don't want to ever make you feel uncomfortable. And I have a patient waiting for me. Why don't you get dressed? Afterwards, you and I can go have coffee, chat a little bit, and by the time we return, Dr. Snatch should be back, and he can finish up."

"Sounds good," Tallhya admitted.

"I sense a but. . . ."

"No buts. I'm just still a little shocked to find out that you're a doctor, that's all."

"What did you think I did for a living?"

"Honestly?"

"That's the best way to answer a question."

"I thought you were some type of scammer." They both laughed. "I'm serious," she said.

"Like a credit card scammer?" he asked

"I didn't know."

"What gave you that impression?"

"Ummm . . . ." She was getting tongue tied from all the butterflies floating around in her stomach. "It's Miami," she said, as if that would explain it.

"A credit card scammer?"

"I'm sorry. If it's any consolation, I'm glad you are not."

"Get dressed," he said, smiling.

"I'm still having my surgery," she said. "I won't let you talk me out of that."

"I know better than to even try to, but I'm going to make sure that you are safe doing it." He walked out of the room and Rydah walked in.

"Is that who I think it is?"

"Yep!"

"Well, I guess he's exactly what the doctor ordered," Rydah said.

Chapter 37

Two Things

Jaffey arrived at The Lady Lagoon strip club every morning at the same time, rain or shine. Regardless of the duties Jaffey had to perform throughout the night and into the early morning as the owner of multiple clubs, often involving beautiful women in the wee hours of the morning, his routine never deviated. Today was no different. Jaffey pranced into The Lady Lagoon draped in a one-of-a-kind tailored gold silk suit, a coffee Versace silk shirt, and a pair of two-tone brown Mauri gator tie-ups, at 11 a.m. sharp.

The A-shift manager, Mike McKinney, and his crew had been in the club since eight o'clock working to get everything in order. Girls, food, liquor, cigars, condoms, cleaning supplies, bathroom amenities . . . the list of things that needed to be done to run a successful strip club was endless. Mike was a competent manager, capable of getting the job done, and he was also married to Jaffey's sister.

Mike was restocking the bar when Jaffey walked in. He'd already diluted the top-shelf liquors by 20 percent with spring water. The added water brought in an extra $125 dollars per bottle, minimum, depending on the brand.

When Mike looked up, Jaffey waved him over.

Mike made his way to the end of the center bar where Jaffey was standing. "What up, boss?"

Jaffey hated being called boss, and that was the exact reason why his brother-in-law enjoyed doing it so often. But Jaffey ignored the dig. He had more pressing matters to deal with.

"Have you heard from Prince? He was supposed to contact me a couple of days ago."

Mike wiped his hands on a towel that was hanging from his belt. "Not a peep," he said. Mike sensed that something had Jaffey uptight. "Is there something you need me to do? You want me to reach out?"

It just doesn't make sense, thought Jaffey.

First, Prince had been secretly pulling these kinds of kidnapping and robbery jobs for Jaffey for quite some time, and he'd always brought him his share, if for no other reason than he knew that Jaffey kept the jobs rolling in for Prince. If Prince had gotten knocked, it would've been blasted all over the news. And if he wasn't in somebody's jail, then where was he? Jaffey consciously wanted to dismiss the obvious answer: Prince had run off with the money.

But Jaffey knew that not wanting something to be true doesn't make it so. Fuck. He needed his cut of the armored truck money to pay Wolfe and get him off his back. It would have been massively fucked up on so many different levels, because the whole heist had been his idea. He'd been planning this thing for over a year now, and to not get any proceeds at all from it would be fucked up.

"Just let me know if you hear anything."

Mike chose not to dig at his brother-in-law this time when he said, "Okay, Jaffey. Is there anything else that I can do?"

"Just keep doing what you're doing." Jaffey said, "You're doing a great job." He checked on a few small things before going to his office to hit the phone.

The door to Jaffey's office was solid oak, and the deadbolt lock was engaged and disengaged by a keypad mounted on the wall to the left. His privacy was worth every penny of the 3 Gs he'd doled out for the system.

The code for the lock was his mother's birthday: 06-02-34. He typed it into the keypad.

She'd passed away eight years ago. When the deadbolt disengaged, Jaffey flipped on the light switch on the side of the wall. LED track lights lit up the space like an operating room. Jaffey liked it that way. Life was shady enough as it was.

The moment he took a seat behind his desk and powered on the computer, Jaffey heard a noise. It was unmistakable.

Click-clack!

The hard plastic barrel of a Glock pressed against his freshly shaved head.

Wolfe's voice was menacing. "Who told you that Rydah had a sister?"

A shaky Jaffey said, "No one."

Wolfe reared back and cold-cocked Jaffey upside the head.

"An innocent person would have asked what I was talking about. The reason you didn't was because you already knew."

"I—I have no idea what you're talking about, Wolfe. I swear."

"Too late," said Wolfe. He smacked Jaffey with the gun again, this time harder. Blood poured from a gash on the top of Jaffey's head onto his one-of-a-kind silk suit.

"Fuck!"

"You are right! Now, shut the fuck up!"

"But I'm telling the truth."

Wolf said, "Your slimy ass wouldn't know what the truth looked like if it was fucking you in the ass without a condom."

Now Jaffey knew exactly where Prince was at. Wolfe had him. Obviously Prince had run his mouth, or Wolfe wouldn't be there with a gun to his head. Prince was probably dead.

"What do you want me to do?" Jaffey knew better than to keep lying. It would only make matters worse. "I'll do anything. Please, just don't kill me."

"Two things."

Jaffey was shaking. The temperature in his office was set to 69 degrees, but Jaffey was sweating bullets and blood. "Anything," he begged. "Anything."

Wolfe said, "You're going to sign over all three clubs to me. Then you're going to get your ass out of Florida—today—and never come back. Either that or eat a fucking bullet."

Florida was the only place that Jaffey had ever lived, and the only place he ever wanted to live. All he knew how to do was run nightclubs in South Florida. It was what he was good at. But it wasn't worth dying for.

"No problem." He was crying. "I'll do whatever you want me to do. The papers for the clubs are in the safe at my house."

Wolfe already knew where the papers were. He grabbed the laptop on the desk that Jaffey used to survey everything, and slipped Jaffey out the back door of the club in order not to draw attention.

Wolfe had driven a 1986 refurbished Impala to the club. He made Jaffey get in the driver's seat. "You drive."

It was a 20-minute car ride to Jaffey's beach house. They pulled into the built-on garage, which was connected to the kitchen. Wolfe walked Jaffey into the beach house.

"Get the papers." He shoved the gun into Jaffey's back, coaxing him toward the safe behind the oil painting in the bedroom. Jaffey spun the combination lock: 26 left, 32 right, 13 left.

"Stop right there!" Wolfe shouted. "You think I'm stupid?" Jaffey acted as if he had no idea what Wolfe was talking about. "Back away from the safe." Jaffey took two steps to the side. "You would have loved to put your hands on his gun, wouldn't you?" Wolfe removed the baby 9 millimeter from the wall safe, along with the paperwork and some chump change, about 40 grand in cash.

Jaffey said, "I'm going to need a couple of days to leave the state."

"Too bad, because you don't have it. Now sign the papers."

Jaffey did as he was told. He had to bide his time. He would leave, but it wouldn't be forever. Wolfe didn't own the state of Florida, and he didn't own him.

"Now back date them to a year ago." Wolfe stood over his shoulder.

Jaffey did exactly what he was told to do.

"And here, sign this too." Wolfe had had his attorney draw up the papers to make sure that the deal was airtight and couldn't be contested whatsoever by any of Jaffey's family.

Jaffey did so.

After Jaffey was finished signing the paperwork to Wolfe's liking, making Wolfe the sole owner of all three clubs, Wolfe shot him in the head.

Bang! Bang!

Lights out.

Chapter 38

Hoes Over Bros?

"Sister Ivy . . . Sister Ivy . . ." The faint voice seemed to get closer and closer. She was trying to hurry to her car.

Sister Jackie attempted to get her attention once more. "Sister Ivy . . . ."

Sister Ivy was trying to leave. The service had stretched out 40 minutes longer than usual. Ivy didn't have the luxury or the time to listen to Sister Jackie spill the tea on their church "friends." But she liked Sister Jackie, so she stopped.

"Yes?" Sister Ivy was in her late thirties but looked 25. She was drop-dead gorgeous, sophisticated, and had an air of sexiness about her. Dressed in all white, she turned around, flashing two full rows of pearly whites. "What's going on, Sister Jackie?"

Clutching at her heart, Sister Jackie said, "Oh, Lord." She always had to be dramatic. "Chile, you got me sweating like a Hebrew slave running down them there steps trying to catch up with you." She was breathing heavily. "You know how this girdle be, and these hot flashes," she joked. It was funny because it was true. "I just wanted to tell you how happy I am that you decided to join the Usher Board. We desperately needed some new, young blood."

Sister Ivy chuckled a little and ignored the slight that Sister Jackie had thrown at the other members. "I'm happy to be on the team," she said.

"Well, you need to know that the Ladies Auxiliary Board Number Six is going to be meeting on Wednesday at seven p.m. for a quick meeting before prayer service."

"Okay." Sister Ivy's smile exaggerated her naturally high cheekbones. "I wouldn't miss it for the world."

Sister Jackie noticed that she was headed to the car. "You not going to have dinner with us in the Fellowship Hall?"

"I have other plans." She hoped that Sister Jackie would grab hold of the hint and not hold her up too much longer with the small talk.

"Awwww. Sorry to hear that. I was looking forward to chit-chatting with you over dinner. You know Sister Donna cooks a mean piece of chicken. And that ain't the only bird she knows her way around, but you ain't heard it from me. Anyway," she added, "you know every first and third Sunday we serve dinner in the Fellowship Hall."

"I'll keep that in mind," Sister Ivy said. "We can catch up on Wednesday at the meeting." She said good-bye and kept it pushing to her car.

Once she was in her car, she carefully perused her phone for missed calls and texts. Out of twenty-four missed calls, none of the numbers were from Dade County Jail. That was a good thing. They were mostly business calls. No strange numbers, and nothing at all from Prince. Why in the world hadn't he called her?

"Help me, Jesus." Ivy made it her business to make it to church every Sunday to formally ask God to protect not only herself, but Prince, from any harm.

She thought about what the pastor had said: "Seek, and ye shall find. Ask, and the door shall be opened. Ask, and it shall be given.'

Ivy asked God to protect Prince. So she didn't worry. If she was going to worry, then there was no need to pray. And if she prayed, there was no need worry. He would be fine, she told herself. And right now, there was money to be made, ongoing bills to pay, and plenty of fabulous shit to buy.

Get your mind right, Ivy. Prince is good, she had to tell herself several times.

Once she made the thirty-minute drive home to her luxurious condo, she took a deep breath and ran into her house to change out of her church gear. When she came out, she reminded herself of what she always claimed her motto was: *Hoes before bros.*

Ivy looked in the rearview mirror to make sure her lipstick and her game face were painted on properly, and they were.

Game on, bitch.

She then started her Porsche 918 Spyder and let the engine of the best of German engineering run wild as she made the fifteen-minute drive to her other house. Ivy punched the six-digit code into the keypad, and the gate swung open. She drove the Spyder down the long, winding driveway, past about a dozen other late-model exotic automobiles. It was a collection of whips that would make the heart of a certified luxury whip aficionado skip a beat.

Pau, the bodyguard and butler, met her at the door. He was as big as a sumo wrestler—not fat, but solid as a tree trunk. She asked, "Is Molly here?"

Pau nodded. "Yeah, ma'am."

Every time she walked through the oversized French doors, she was reminded of how much she loved the place. She paid for it with cash about ten years ago, one of her proudest investments. It came equipped with all the amenities that any overprivileged girl could ever want: an infinity pool that peek-a-booed over the Atlantic Ocean, three Jacuzzis, two saunas, a game room, eight bedrooms (three of them masters), and ten full bathrooms. The house was home to a lot of history, sex, and her multimillion-dollar empire, and although she refused to call it what it was, the house was also a first-class, high-end brothel.

And Ivy was the madame!

The mansion housed at least twelve girls at all times, women from all over the world. All of her girls lived a life of luxury, courtesy of Ivy. Let Ivy tell it, she provided them with more indulgences than the richest, most privileged kept woman.

Her ladies were above the rest and sported the best of the absolute best clothes, the best shoes, drove the best cars, were seen by the best cosmetic surgeons, and had access to the best parties and the richest customers. But the ladies were constantly reminded that everybody had to pay the piper; there were no free dances. This meant that to pay for their keep, they had to please her clientele, some of the richest and most powerful men in the world.

Ivy kept them so intoxicated on living, dining, and traveling first class that many of them thought that fucking a few rich men a night, if needed, was the least they could do to pay her back. Others were happy to be a part of her stable. They already liked sex and were willing to fuck for free pre-Ivy, so why not live lavishly while doing it? The richest men were usually old, and old men didn't keep it up long, so most of the time, the work wasn't *hard*.

Ivy called out for Molly, her bottom whore to the core. They'd been together for many years. When they met, Molly was an illegal alien from Brazil who couldn't pronounce a syllable of English if she needed it to save her life. Ivy found her left for dead in the alley of a strip club in the hood. She had OD'd on pills. Ivy nursed her back to health and then helped her get her green card. Since then, Molly had not only been loyal, but helped her make a lot of money. More money than either girl had ever dreamed of seeing.

Molly was a long-legged brunette with a beautiful golden complexion and gray eyes. She now spoke three languages. She also liked to walk around the house in bathing suits that were barely large enough to cover her private parts.

Ivy asked her, "How did everything go while I was away?" She hadn't been at the house since Saturday morning.

Molly went to the safe inside her room that was camouflaged to look like a piece of furniture. "Great. I tallied everything up for you."

"No problems?" Ivy questioned.

Molly hesitated.

"Spit it out," Ivy said. "You're getting soft on me. Stop trying to protect those hoes. They don't give a fuck about us. You know these bitches. They come, they go. Only thing that stays true is you and me. Now spit it out, Moll—"

"It isn't that," Molly said. "I know they don't breed bitches like us anymore."

Ivy agreed. "You ain't never lied, Moll. That cloth we cut from, they just don't make. Now tell me what happened."

"It's Juicy."

You could almost see the anger ooze from Ivy's pores. "That bitch still fucking up, huh?"

Molly said, "The new girls are bringing in the most money right now, but they're drawn to Juicy. They can learn nothing but bad habits from her."

Ivy nodded. "What else?"

"I found out that she hasn't been forthcoming with all of her tip money."

"Is that right?"

"I'm afraid so," Molly said.

"This is good," Ivy said.

"I don't understand," said Molly.

"Don't worry about it. You will. Soon enough."

Molly searched Ivy's face for a sign as to what she had in mind. Ivy's face was a blank canvas. Molly changed the subject. "I was about to have the chef make me a salad. You want one?"

Ebony, the live-in chef, was the ex-wife of Ivy's deceased brother. Ivy looked at Ebony like a sister, but she kept her at a distance all the same. However, Ebony loved Ivy like the sister she never had.

Ebony wore many hats in the house. She was the chef, the dietician, the herbalist, the nutritionist, and the personal trainer for the ladies. Ebony was damn good at what she did. She could have gone into business for herself and made more money than Ivy was paying her . . . a whole hell of a lot more. But like Molly, Ebony was loyal to Ivy, except for a different reason. Ebony was loyal to Ivy because she'd loved Ivy's dead brother more than life itself, and she promised him she'd always have his sister's back.

Ivy took one forkful of the salad and blurted
out, "Damn, girl. I can't front. This shit is the
bomb. Oh my goodness! And just to think, a lady
from my church tried to get me to stay and eat
some greasy-ass chicken they were serving."

Ebony took pride in her cooking. "Hell to the
naw."

"Girl, I've traveled the entire world, and I ain't
never had nobody make a seafood salad as good
as this. What's in it?"

"Shrimp, lobster, and crab meat for the most
part, and some other treats."

"Lord have mercy!"

There was no greater compliment. Ebony said,
"Aw, thanks, Ivy."

Ivy helped herself to another serving. "I'm
going to start going extra hard this week with my
training," she said.

Ivy worked out harder than any woman Ebony
had ever met. She was strong as an ox but still
looked like a woman. "Girl, you look great."

Ivy gave credit where it was due. "You got
some of these bitches' abs cut up like a bag of
raw dope."

If the other girls in the house were cut up like
dope, then Ivy must have been chiseled like a
flawless diamond. Body was tight, fit, and rigid.
It was clear that missing a workout hadn't been
on her agenda in a very long time.

Ebony modestly said, "Well, I'm only doing what I signed on to do." She was cheesing, because she knew that she was damn good at what she did.

Molly had to agree. "For someone that's self-taught, you are amazing."

"Thank you, but y'all need to cut it out with the compliments. You know that shit go to a bitch's head." Ebony cleared the dishes from the table.

Ivy asked Molly, "Do we have any guests here?"

"Not yet. The Sunday pool party is set to begin in another hour or so. I scheduled a few girls to go down to Fontainebleau for their pool party also."

That's all Ivy needed to know. She rose up from the table.

"Juicccccccyyyyy!" Ivy started toward the pool.

Molly nudged Ebony in the side. "Oh, shit! This is about to get ugly."

Molly followed behind Ivy out to the pool, where Juicy was sitting with a few of the other girls around her, cackling. They were listening to Juicy tell old ho stories.

"Juicccccccyyyyy!"

Juicy got up and was on her feet fast.

"Yes!"

"Come here, bitch!"

"Coming, Madame." Juicy quickly made her way over to Ivy. "Yes?" she said with a refreshing, confident smile.

Ivy cocked back and punched her square in the face, breaking her nose. You could hear the bone crack from fifty feet away. "Get me my money, bitch!"

Juicy starting bawling alligator tears. She stammered. "I–I–I . . . ."

"*I* my ass, bitch!" Ivy smacked the stutter from her mouth. "Bitch, don't play with me."

Juicy fell to the patio like a bad hairdo. The girls that had been eating up Juicy's ho stories were petrified, looking on in shock. And that was exactly what Ivy wanted to happen. She could administer one good ass-whooping and snatch the attention of the entire house to set an example.

Once she knew all eyes were on her, Ivy kicked Juicy in the face with the toe of her high-heeled Jimmy Choos. Ivy hadn't even busted a sweat. That's what the hoes didn't know. Ivy had rumbled with some of the best men, so toe-to-toe with a bitch was featherweight work.

"Bitch, get yo' ass up before I tear into your ass for real."

Juicy pulled herself up. She had a broken nose, two black eyes, and a busted lip. She was afraid to look Ivy in the face.

"Now carry your scary ass upstairs and get my motherfucking money, bitch! Not fucking part of it! Not half of it! All of it."

Juicy took off, but she was moving too slow for Ivy's liking. Ivy couldn't care less that the girl was injured. Ivy grabbed Juicy by the hair and dragged her up the stairs.

"You hoes think these tricks care about y'all? Trust and believe they don't. They are only loyal to me. Hoes come and go, but I'm the one that consistently provides them with services and favors. Remember that shit the next time one of you decides to try and short me in any way."

Juicy handed Ivy the money she'd stolen.

"Bitch, you owe me an extra five hundred for breaking my nail while I was whipping on your larceny ass."

Juicy humbly said, "No problem."

"And mop this blood up off of my marble floors." To the rest of the girls, she looked each of them up and down then calmly said, "Now, doll babies, get back to your Sunday festivities."

Ivy made eye contact with Molly, who had always played the good cop around the house, and headed off to the room to see about Juicy.

A few minutes later, she pulled Ebony to the side.

"Have you heard from Prince?"

"Naw. I called him because he was supposed to train with me, but he ended up being a no-show, which is odd." Ebony looked up from the icepack she was putting together to take to Juicy.

"And he didn't call you back?" Ivy asked.

"As a matter of fact, he didn't." She looked off. "Which is so unlike him. You already know how that dude feel about his sexy."

"Hmmmm." Frown lines somehow managed to appear on Ivy's Botox-filled forehead. "That's odd," she said.

"A'ight," she said to Molly, who had just returned from checking on Juicy. "I gotta go make a run. Hold it down for me until I get back." She kissed her on the cheek. "I'll call you shortly."

"Okay," Molly said.

Where the fuck is Prince? was the only thing on her mind when she left the mansion.

Prince was Ivy's little brother, her only biological living family, and honestly, the only thing besides Benjamins, that Ivy actually gave one solitary fuck about. Their other brother, Lucas, was killed taking up a beef that was meant for Ivy. Actually, it was Ivy that the bullet was meant for, not Lucas. After Lucas's death, Ivy made a vow that she'd always take care of Prince.

However, it wasn't a simple promise to uphold. Prince was his own man and hated walking in the shadow of his older brother. The only thing he hated more was being referred to as Ivy's little brother. And he damn sure wasn't in the business of taking money from a woman, especially not one that shared his same DNA!

Ivy pulled up in front of the valet at The Lady Lagoon. The first person she saw was Mike. "Where in the hell is Jaffey?" she asked

"In his office, as far as I know."

"I've been calling that motherfucker and he ain't answering." Ivy was pissed. "That motherfucker got some nerve to be ignoring me, as good as I am to him."

Mike had learned long ago not to take sides when it came to Ivy and Jaffey. "Y'all two and y'all bullshit." This was normal between those two. They went back and forth all the time, fussing about pussy and money.

Ivy said, "Have you seen my brother over here?"

"I haven't seen or heard a peep from him," Mike said. "As far as I know, Jaffey hasn't either. As of two hours ago, anyway."

Ivy slipped past Mike, heading to Jaffey's office.

She banged on the oak door. "Open the fucking door."

Mike came up with a novel idea. "Maybe he's not in there," he sarcastically said.

Ivy turned to Mike. "Did you see him leave?"

"Nope. But that doesn't mean shit. Nigga be in and out all the time."

Ivy screamed, "Open the door or buzz him!" She wasn't upset with Mike, but he was the only person available right now for her to take her frustration out on.

"He's not answering," Mike said after buzzing the office.

Ivy stood with her arms folded, while Mike kept trying.

"Open up the door, Mike. This silly mother-fucker could've had a heart attack or something. You know what happened the last time he took all those Viagara and tried to fuck those three young bitches."

Mike was silent for a minute. "Turn around," he said.

"Nigga, please!"

"Turn around." Mike held his ground.

Ivy turned around slowly.

Mike punched the code into the keypad, hoping that Jaffey wasn't in there with some chick's legs on his shoulders. That's the type of shit that may get Mike fired, regardless of whether he was married to Jaffey's sister.

"Damn . . . "Mike said once he went inside. "He isn't here. His computer is gone too. He must have gone out the back door."

Ivy stood there with a raised eyebrow. "When he gets back, let him know that something is wrong with my brother. And he better not have anything to do with it, or I swear on Lucas's grave . . . and you already know how I roll. I will get to the bottom of this."

Chapter 39

All Work

Since his arrival in Miami, Chase had worked around the clock. He temporary living accommodations with Simone were a sparsely furnished two-bedroom apartment in corporate housing. He transformed the second bedroom into a makeshift workspace. Dozens of boxes, filled with reams of paperwork, lined the walls. The bed was littered with manila folders, brimming with files. Photos of crime scenes, suspects, and witnesses were either taped or thumb-tacked to nearly every square foot of two of the four walls. But every lead either came to a screeching halt before gaining any traction, or took off into a thousand different directions, like the windshield of a car shattered by a BB gun. After a while it became difficult to ascertain where one lead began and another lead ended. Witnesses looked like suspects, and suspects turned out to be witnesses.

In an attempt to break the monotony, Simone slipped into the self-imposed prison that her husband called an office. In a heavy voice, she said, "All work and no play makes Chase a dull boy."

The see-through lingerie number she wore was about an inch or two negligent of covering the area where the undercarriage of her plump caramel ass connected with her toned legs. Simone's perky breasts stood at attention like obedient solders, standing sentry above her pancake-flat stomach. She'd waxed or shaved every hair on her body besides her head.

For as far as Chase noticed, she might as well have been dressed in baggie jeans, covered in dog manure. The room reeked of old coffee and stationery. His clothes were unkempt, and puffy, dark bags loomed heavy underneath his eyes.

"I have to break that Cashmore case," he said.

Of all the cases that have been piled on him . . . she thought. *Wouldn't you know it would be the armored truck that he was obsessed with.*

Simone played it cool. At least this time he was investigating a case in which she and her sisters weren't the actual bandits. This time they'd only taken the money from the people who had really taken the money. Wasn't that different?

"Baby, you have get some rest. You can't continue to run on coffee and fumes."

"I can sleep when I die," he said. "Or once I solve the case. Whichever comes first."

Being awake for eighteen straight hours not only made him fatigued, but also caused him to be frustrated and cranky. Chase just wasn't thinking clearly—and maybe that was a good thing. Simone wasn't sure. On one hand, she loved her husband and wanted to help her man, but not if it ended with her and her sisters going to jail,

"Maybe you should get some rest, regroup, and start fresh in the morning. I promise to make the break worth your while."

Chase ignored her.

Simone pouted. Twirling a strand of hair with her fingers, she asked, "Is there anything I can do to help you? Would like for me to make you a drink, or something to eat?"

He snapped. "No. I don't want a fucking drink." The moment the outburst was out of his mouth, he wished that he could have swallowed his words. But it was too late. The stress from the job was making him crazy. He thought the promotion would enhance their lives. He'd only been in Miami for two weeks, and the job was already driving a wedge between them. The two love birds never used to argue before.

"My apologies." He begged her, "Baby, please forgive me."

"I know you're stressed, but you can't just snap on me or shut me out," she said. "Allow me to help. Can you talk about it?"

Chase didn't want to talk about it, but he didn't want to be in the doghouse with Simone in addition to the headaches at work.

"There were some electronic files that were stolen from the Cashmore heist." He sighed. "You wouldn't be able to fathom the potential shit storm it will create if in the wrong hands. Every law official in this entire country is on edge." He looked at her with complete despair in his eyes. "The name of every confidential informant ever used in the entire country is on those files. It could turn the law enforcement world on its head. So pardon me, please, if I'm being an asshole. Okay?"

"I've never seen you this way."

"I've never had literally no clue as to where to turn on a case before," he said. "It's like the perpetrators have fallen off the face of the earth. No one has a clue as to where the files are. And the fact that I was promoted with such high regards, I have to deliver the goods."

"And you will." Simone hated seeing her husband this way.

"That's easier said than done," he shot back. "You don't understand. This one case could make or break my whole career."

"And you will break it open. I know you will." Simone encouraged him, "Come on, you got this, baby! Let me put on a pot of coffee—mine black and yours with a shot of Cognac. And let's work this thing out one step at a time."

Though Chase knew better than to discuss his case with anyone, he decided to take Simone up on her offer.

Hell, he thought, *right about now, I need all the help that I can get. And at the end of the day, Simone and her sisters have masterminded bank robberies before, so maybe, just maybe, she can bring something to the table.*

Chapter 40

A Sucker-Punch

"Honey, I'm home!" Wolfe entered the house, but no one said anything, which was extremely odd, he thought, after leaving his shoes at the door.

"Babe?" He called out, and nothing. This was definitely not normal. After a long day in the jungle dealing with knuckleheads, debts owed, larceny, and bullshit, he was used to Rydah greeting him at the door, embracing him with hugs, kisses, affection, and nothing but love.

"Rydahhhh . . . baby!"

Still nothing.

Something was definitely wrong. Wolfe pulled his Desert Eagle out of his pants and crept through the house, not knowing what to expect. He was trying to shake his feelings of caring, but he just couldn't. All kinds of things ran through his head, and he hated the thought that if something happened to Rydah, it would truly have a huge effect on him. He hated that he cared for her and had vested interest in not only her, but her family too. He knew a man in his line of work shouldn't be this attached to anything or anyone.

For a split second, he thought about turning to walk out the door and out of Rydah's life forever. However, as much as his mind told him to do so, his heart wouldn't let him go anywhere.

He took the safety off, put one in the chamber, and started to assess the situation. He crept through the house one step and room at a time. He popped into the bedroom, and Rydah seemed to be in another world.

"Hey, beautiful!" Wolfe said as he entered into the bedroom. Rydah was staring off, so deep in her thoughts that she hadn't even heard him come in.

"Hey, babes." He came in closer, startling her.

Rydah snapped out of her trance and was shocked to see him with a gun in his hand. "Hey, you scared the shit out of me. I didn't even hear you come in." She was confused.

"That's not like you," he said, taking the clip out of the gun and placing it on the night table. "Where was your mind? It seemed to be on the

other side of town." Wolfe could sense something was wrong.

"Just a lot on my mind."

"Well, I'm here to listen."

"I don't know where to start, and I'm not ready
to talk about it yet. Still processing."

"Well, I'm here, and after all that we've been
through, you can trust me. And when it comes to
you, I'm definitely a good listener."

"So you remembered where I live, huh?" Rydah
said nonchalantly, referring to her not seeing
Wolfe in a few days.

"Stop that!" He came in and kissed her with
a long tongue kiss. "How could I forget? This
is where my heart lives." Wolfe hadn't been to
Rydah's house in over a week. He'd been busy
with tying up the loose ends with Abe and Prince.

She chuckled. "You are so funny. You smelling
all good," she said, getting a sniff of his Bond
No. 9 cologne. "Fresh shower *before* you come
in. That's new."

"Work, baby. Cold, callous, dirty work."

"I bet. Seems like . . . nut-busting work, if it's
the kind that calls for a fresh shower."

"Oh, that's what you think? That I've been
fucking with some bitch?" He put up his defense.

"You said it, not me. I've never known you to come in here smelling like Neutrogena body wash combined with Bond No. 9 cologne. You usually all funky, dropping your clothes at the front door. But now all of a sudden you come in here all fresh and clean. Change in behavior. I'm watching you."

"Ain't even like that. I've been dealing with them niggas. Once I was done I burned my clothes. For my own safety, I had to take a shower. I couldn't come across town like that. Funky is one thing, but DNA, blood, and bullshit is another."

"I respect that."

But now all I want is a good night's rest, spooning with my baby." He took her in his arms.

"That's fair."

"How did the surgery go?" He changed the subject, trying to lighten the mood.

"It went well. She's happy. But the guy who we met at the mall, Alphonso, he turned out to be a plastic surgeon at Dr. Snatch's office. I thought he would have talked her out of it."

"Shiiiit. You know nobody was talking her out of that. She was determined. But it went good, right?"

"Yeah, it did. Just resting, healing. Mom taking good care of her, so you know she enjoys Mom spoiling her and all that."

"I already know she sucking that in."

"Yup. She has an appointment tomorrow. All her drains will be removed, and I asked Mom to drop her over here after so I can talk to her."

"You know we about to have a beast on our hands for real."

"Yeah, don't I know it. When she's skinny, she's going to be something else."

They both laughed at the thought at how off the chain Tallhya was going to be with her new physique.

"What do you have planned tomorrow?" he asked.

"No real plans. I just have something important to talk to her and Simone about, that's all," Rydah said.

"I respect that." He nodded, not wanting to pry. "Well, we about to be in the club business." He put the manila folders and envelope on his side of the night table.

"Really?" Rydah asked. "How so?"

Wolfe yawned, not wanting to get into it tonight. "I will tell you all about it tomorrow when I wake up, okay?"

"Okay, baby." Rydah was curious, but she had much bigger things on her mind and couldn't really focus anyway, so tomorrow was better for her too.

Wolfe was so tired from being up for days that the peaceful vibe in the comfort of Rydah's home made sleep finally come down on him. He took his clothes off and jumped in the bed. "I'm tired and just want some sleep," he managed to get out. Before she could offer him something to eat, he was out like a light.

Rydah watched as the man, who never seemed to sleep without one eye open, was deep in slumber in her bed, snoring. She felt good to know that he was finally getting the rest he needed.

While Wolfe slept the night and the next morning away, Rydah couldn't get one ounce of sleep. Her mind was so heavy, and it seemed like the time until she would get to talk to her sisters turtled by.

Finally, Simone arrived and hugged her sister. Luckily, it wasn't as awkward as she thought it would be, just the two of them alone without Tallhya. During the hour they talked, Rydah learned that she and Simone were more alike than she thought.

"So how are things going with Chase being in town now?"

"I have barely even seen him. It's like I'm just here to keep his bed warm. He's working so much that we literally only sleep in the same bed. He's up and out before me, and comes in way after I'm asleep. I try to wait up for him, but most nights I end up falling asleep."

"I'm sorry."

"Don't be. It's not your fault. He keeps telling me to go out and enjoy the city. And I want to," said Simone, "but it hasn't been easy. I don't know anyone. And I don't like bothering you."

"You don't bother me at all, sis. I want us to spend more time together. I'll be glad to help with whatever you need."

"I can't even get Chase's opinion on simple things like that, because he's been so obsessed with this case and all." She shook her head, wishing that things were different.

"Is it the armored truck heist or the cold cases that mainly have him so stressed out?" Rydah asked.

"It's both, but his bosses have been applying pressure like you would not believe to try to recover that information. It's some pretty heavy shit on those missing files. Shit that has people worried about what could happen if it got in the wrong hands. A lot of folks—innocent people— could be killed."

The front door opened. They had been so engrossed in their conversation that neither sister had heard a key in the lock.

"Heyyyyy, bitches!" Tallhya barged in, loud and beaming with smiles. She walked into the sunken living room and stood in front of Simone, holding her hands out to the side. "Bammmmm, bitches! Boom-shaka-la!"

"Daaaaaamn!" Rydah was impressed

Simone gasped. "Oh my goodness!"

"You look amazing!" Rydah exclaimed. "Like a whole different person."

"And the swelling hasn't even gone done yet. My doctor said that there will be way more dramatic results in about two to three months."

"Girl, you look great. I'm so happy for you. I hope it truly makes you happy."

"She sure looks happy," said Rydah. "Happy, rested, and radiant. Shining and glowing and slim!" Rydah said.

"How does Dr. Fonz like it?" Simone asked with a raised eyebrow.

"He keeps telling me I didn't have to do it, but he comes over and checks on me."

"The doctor making house calls?" Rydah joked.

"Girl, yes! And you know Uncle Maestro all over him like the FBI, interrogating him."

"Oh, trust me I know. Better you than me. Girl, I'm glad you over there getting a taste of them," Rydah said.

"But you look great, girl, and so happy! That's why you smiling! You skinny and got a boy-friend."

"I don't have a boyfriend. But skinny? Yes, it's coming!" she said with smiles.

"We are happy for you. We truly are!" Rydah said.

The ruckus woke Wolfe from his sleep. He decided to get up and head into the living room to check out the results of Tallhya's surgery. But first he needed to brush his teeth, wash his face, and find some shorts to throw on.

"Well, thank you for having my back, but this meeting isn't about me. It's about you. You said you have something to tell us," Simone said.

Wolfe was about to slip on his shorts and wife beater but decided to ear-hustle a little longer before joining and kicking the bo-bo with the girls.

"I know," Simone said. "You sounded like it was so urgent on the phone, and since I've been here you've been kind of distant, not like your normal self."

Wolfe also wanted to know what was on his baby's mind. He wanted to be sure that her sudden funky mood didn't have anything to do with him. After all, he had just disposed of a few men and a no-good bitch. In his world, it was totally acceptable to eliminate one's enemies, but Rydah wasn't from that world. She was a lover of all things, seeing the best in everyone. One thing for sure, Wolfe thought, something very serious was going on with her, and she wasn't sharing it with him. So he'd have to find other methods to figure it out, even if it meant snooping.

"Come to think of it," Tallhya said, "you've been kind of off for a few days now. I thought I was misreading shit before."

"Are you okay?"

"Well, I want you to know that no matter what, I got you and I love you. You already know how I feel about you. So whatever it is, we can get through this shit no matter what."

Wolfe thought, *Enough of the fucking sentimental shit. Spit that shit out.* Curiosity was killing him.

Rydah looked at both her sisters. Simone took her hand, prompting Tallhya to put her hand around Rydah's waist.

"It's like . . ." Rydah couldn't quite get the words out.

Wolfe had never seen her speechless before.

"Are you pregnant?" Tallhya said, trying to guess what had Rydah so tongue-tied.

There was a brief silence.

Wolfe thought about what Tallhya had asked Rydah. How would he feel if the answer to the question was yes? He wasn't sure if he was ready for a family. It wasn't something that he'd put much thought into. For the first time in his life, he began to let his mind wander to places it had never been before. Maybe he needed to rethink the way he lived his life. Give up the streets. Focus on being a husband and the father he never had. The father that he wished he'd had. Hell, he had enough money for a few generations of his offspring to live lavish. Why not? If he was going to ever settle down and hang up boots, Rydah was the perfect woman for him. It felt weird to him, thinking of being all in with someone, but maybe the time was right.

"OMG! I'm going to be an auntie!" Simone got all excited, assuming that the answer was yes because Rydah hadn't said anything.

"I swear, I'm going to be a great role model. I'm not going to be with any crazy-ass shit. I swear, I'm going to love this child, and we are all going to give it everything we never had."

"We are. This child will have none of the dysfunctional bullshit we were subjected to growing up," Simone added. "But I think this is the gift that this family needed to bring us all together."

Wolfe began to envision pushing a little girl on a bike or tossing a baseball to a son, and he couldn't help but to think of what a magical feeling that would be for him.

Until . . .

"I'm not pregnant. Not that I know of, anyway. But who knows? We do be getting it in every chance we get."

"Then what is it?" Simone asked.

"And bitch, you will fuck up a wet dream of a nigga behind bars. Damn!" Tallhya said, shaking her head.

"That would have been good for the family," Simone added.

"Well . . . I think what I have to say is good for our family. Well, at first I did, and then I thought about it long and hard, and perhaps maybe it's not."

Wolfe was still drifting off in his own fairy tale, one he never got to live as a kid. He was ready to get the sisters out of the house so they could begin practicing conceiving.

Tallhya clapped her hand one time. "Bitch, I'm going to fight you. You blowing my high off being fine with all these tight-lipped charades. Just spill it."

"I'm trying." Rydah took a deep breath. "I just don't know where to start."

"The beginning's always good," Simone suggested.

"All ears."

"So . . ." She looked at her sisters, and they looked at her in a way to egg her on to spit out whatever was on the tip of her tongue.

"I was curious to look at the files to see if anybody in Wolfe's camp was working with the police. Though I don't know many of his friends, I wanted to make sure none of his inner circle or security were snitches. Because Wolfe has always been nothing but loyal to my family and me, I wouldn't want anything to happen to him. Especially by the law or the hands of a snitch." She shrugged her shoulders. "I don't know why. I just began to search a lot of stuff. I just felt like, why would God put this in my hands if it wasn't something I was supposed to see?"

Tallhya and Simone were both pin-drop silent, studying their sister's body language as she spoke.

"Then I became relentless, almost obsessed with trying to find something. Then I think, in a crazy way, my mind began to play tricks on me. I started to wonder about you, Simone."

"Me?" Simone questioned.

"I'm being real. Yes, you."

"Just hear her out," Tallhya said.

"I mean, I don't know much about you, and I'm still learning. Then, the fact that you are with Chase, and the events that happened in Virgina. . ." Rydah pointed out, "You can't blame me."

Simone was quiet for a split second, then reluctantly said, "No, I guess I can't."

"So I started to search Chase's case, looking for his case files of what happened in Virginia or anything on you. Just to see where he was and his thoughts on his reports as far as his job was concerned."

"And in regard to me, you came up with nothing! Right?"

"Nothing as far as you were concerned, Simone." Rydah looked at her. "Buuuut . . ."

"But what?" Tallhya defensively said. "I already know you ain't find shit on me."

"Let me finish," Rydah firmly said.

"Well, hurry the hell up, then. All that slow talking and knot-in-your-throat shit is blowing me." Tallhya looked in her sister's eyes.

"As I read all of Chase's stuff, I came across something both mind-boggling and interesting. I couldn't believe it until I got a trusted source to look further into it."

"What?" Simone said.

"And what trusted source?" Tallhya asked.

"Wolfe's investigator. He is loyal to a fault, and he finds and knows everything."

"God, Lord, you know I love my sister, and I'm grateful to her, but she is dragging this whole thing out, and I just pray, Lord, give me come patience." Tallhya looked up at the ceiling, saying a prayer.

"And it was true," Rydah said, as if she were talking in a riddle.

"Lord, just give me strength and patience. My sister is really losing her mind. Don't let this craziness be hereditary."

Simone looked at Rydah, "Okay, you are scaring me a little bit, and my mind is running crazy."

Rydah got up and poured herself a drink.

"This shit is heavy. She drinking," Tallhya said. "It's getting intense. She don't drink like that."

"Chase lied to you. He said he found Bunny dead, that she committed suicide."

"Right."

"It's true he found her in the bed at the hotel. However, she didn't blow her head off. She took some pills, but when he reached her, he saved her. He found her cell phone with her, and when he went through it, he saw that she had killed a guy in another room in the hotel. Once she came around, he convinced her to cut a deal with him to avoid murder charges."

"What?"

"Bunny is alive. He relocated her and offered her a better life. In return, she has to work as an undercover informant, to use her looks to lure some of the most dangerous criminals into dropping their guards."

"Bunny is alive?" Simone was confused.

"Yes." Rydah nodded. "The investigator got me these pictures." She went to the drawer and pulled out the photographs.

"Wait a minute. Bunny would never sign up to be a rat. She hated the police."

"I'm sorry," Rydah said, "but she did. I have concrete proof."

"Banks sisters don't do that shit."

"And Chase would never know that she was alive and not tell me," Simone added.

Rydah nodded. "I agree with you both, but I can't think of anything else that makes sense."

Simone stood up. She didn't know what to say, or what to think. "Bunny knows so much stuff that I can't say." Her mind drifted off, wondering what exactly Bunny had told Chase. Did Bunny tell Chase about her and Ginger killing Deidra and her boyfriend? And how Simone helped them cut up the body parts and get rid of it? About the banks they robbed? And the laundry list of other crimes they had committed together?

"This is just fucked up. Real fucked up. You have no idea," Simone snapped.

"I want her address. I think we should pay her a visit," Tallhya said. "And Chase? What about him? I thought you had him under the spell of your pussy. He's a threat. A threat that has to be dealt with."

"Shit is so real," Rydah said.

"You have no idea," Wolfe mumbled under his breath.

Wolfe had no idea that Rydah was in possession of the files. He wanted them all for himself, and nothing was going to stop him from obtaining them. His mind skated around the overflow of wealth and power he would have once he possessed the files.

Just that quick, Wolfe couldn't give one solitary fuck about any plastic surgery results of a fat bitch, or his dreams of having a family.

Instead, Wolfe got back in the bed, under the covers, and pretended he was asleep, as if he'd heard nothing at all. But under the high thread count sheets, all he could think about was how those classified files were going to be his in a matter of hours. He hoped that he wouldn't have to hurt anyone he cared about to get them—Rydah included. . . .